YOU REMIND ME

Linda Walters

BET Publications, LLC
http://www.bet.com
http://www.arabesquebooks.com

ARABESQUE BOOKS are published by

BET Publications, LLC
c/o BET BOOKS
One BET Plaza
1900 W Place NE
Washington, DC 20018-1211

All Kensington Titles, Imprints, and Distributed Lines are available at special quantity discounts for bulk purchases for sales promotions, premiums, fund-raising, and educational or institutional use. Special book excerpts or customized printings can also be created to fit specific needs. For details, write or phone the office of the Kensington special sales manager: Kensington Publishing Corp., 850 Third Avenue, New York, NY 10022, attn: Special Sales Department, Phone: 1-800-221-2647.

First Printing: July 2003
10 9 8 7 6 5 4 3 2 1

Printed in the United States of America

I'd like to dedicate this novel to my mother, the late Ethel Beatrice Thom, and all the women of the world who have struggled to make a place for themselves without compromise.

And to my children, Nikki, Lance and Teylor, I offer my sincerest gratitude for giving me more reasons than I can name to make you proud.

And to my three sisters, Gloria, Connie and Delores, who still inspire me to become the best that I can be.

ACKNOWLEDGMENTS

My sincere gratitude goes out to many who, sometimes without even being aware of it, helped bring me to a place which ultimately made the writing of this book possible. Thank you to Gilbert M. Rowe, the Barbados Tourism Authority, Ruder Finn, and the gracious people of Barbados for allowing me to experience a tremendously rich culture.

Thanks also to my editor, Chandra Taylor, and to the dynamic team at BET Books, especially Linda J. Gill and Kichecko Driggins.

I'd also like to extend a heartfelt thank-you to Donna Hill, Patricia Meschino, Edward Lewis and Nora Pressley, Ph.D., whose friendship, mentoring and guidance I have come to treasure.

And most of all, I'd like to thank God for giving me the passion to live each day to the fullest with His grace as my companion.

But if in your thought you must measure time
    into seasons,
let each season encircle all the other seasons,
And let today embrace the past with remem-
    brance
and the future with longing.

—Kahlil Gibran, *The Prophet*

One

Luggage from Worldwide Airlines flight 234 had been reduced to a few stray items. The Boeing 727 aircraft had been on the ground for forty-five minutes and most of its luggage had been claimed by exuberant passengers eager to begin their stay on the island of Barbados.

One extremely large box haphazardly tied with twine to reinforce its contents, an umbrella-type baby stroller, and several other pieces of orphaned luggage continued to travel an endless route. A feeling of growing panic gripped Sloan Whitaker as she continued to watch the baggage carousel circle aimlessly. Barbados would certainly present a challenge to her winter clothing since the tropical island's January temperatures reached the low eighties on most days.

Sloan felt the unmistakable signs of a headache beginning as she accepted the obvious. Neither of the two pieces of luggage she'd checked at John F. Kennedy Airport back in New York City some five hours earlier was visible, but her carry-on bag and laptop computer stood steadfastly beside her, solid proof that she had indeed made the trip. The whereabouts of her luggage continued to be a mystery as the remaining pieces on the carousel were picked up by other travelers.

Sloan quickly made her way toward the Tourism Authority representative holding a sign over her head that read JAZZ FESTIVAL PRESS. As she approached, a woman of slim build and medium height with silver-blond tresses was speaking in loud, angry tones. The range of her voice seemed totally out of context with the petite frame; her anger was quite apparent through her body language. Her hands enunciated each word, chopping the air emphatically and reaching out to no one in a show of exaggerated frustration. Sloan realized, immediately, that she was not alone in her dilemma.

"I cannot believe that they lost my bags. This is ridiculous. Who do I report this debacle in service to?" her fellow companion asked in frustration, folding her arms defiantly across her chest.

The representative apologized for the inconvenience that she had had nothing to do with and efficiently announced, for anyone who had not been able to locate luggage, that the office for filing lost baggage claims could be found at the rear of the terminal. She also calmly advised passengers to meet the remaining press party at the main entrance after exiting customs.

Sloan made her way to the claims office, managing to carefully avoid the other journalists. She felt uncomfortable with people who felt the need to create drama if there was the slightest inconvenience. And although she, too, could not figure out how the bags could have been mishandled or misplaced, she'd already come to the conclusion that she wouldn't make a big deal out of it. After all, she was on assignment in Barbados, and she had received the finalized divorce papers from Karsten only days before. Free of a husband who put the "p" in philandering for all 730 days of their two-year marriage, she would let nothing and no one upset her at this point.

The passenger list of flight 234 had consisted mainly of tourists and transplanted Bajans returning home to recharge and reacquaint their pride in heritage. Among the 121 travelers was also a considerably large presence of journalists, photographers, musicians, technicians, and other industry types who were on their way to an annual phenomenon—the Barbados Jazz Festival.

This well-respected entry in the lineup of music festivals held throughout the world had become known as one of the best. It consistently drew a remarkable level of coverage from as far away as Canada, England, Jamaica, St. Maarten, Trinidad, and Puerto Rico, as well as each of the major markets of the United States.

Sloan, armed with a background in finance, economics, and journalism, had taken on the assignments doled out by her editor, Kendall Jackson, at the *Caribbean Press,* like a magnet adhering to a pole for the past three years. The New York–based newspaper had a circulation approaching well over 150,000 and served the largest population of Caribbean readers outside of that region. But coverage of the Barbados Jazz Festival had been her idea. And after making the necessary inquiries, laying the groundwork, and connecting the dots, it had become a reality. This would be the second year she would attend the concerts, which lasted five days and nights. Press coverage would extend to conferences with both artists and promotional representatives, and she would be exposed to all the public relations events. It was a actually a lot of work; it was also a journalist's dream come true and Sloan loved it. The photography, the minute details, and, especially, the jazz were all a labor of love.

As she filled out the requisite lost baggage forms

and hoped for a miracle, she quietly thanked God and her best friend, Anita Phillips, for reminding her to pack a couple of minor pieces in her carry-on luggage.

"That way, if they lose your luggage at least you have pajamas to sleep in," Anita had said, laughing. Sloan had figured if pajamas were important, clothes were crucial and had used the empty spaces in her carry-on bag to hold several last-minute items.

Looking down at the black suede boots she wore, Sloan mentally ticked off the few items she would be able to make do with until her luggage was located. A pair of flat sandals, a one-shouldered black cotton dress, a pair of black shorts, and two stretch tops were squeezed into the sides of compartments. She breathed a sigh of relief with the realization. Toiletries, camera equipment, a handheld recorder and notebooks were also in her carry-on bag. No bathing suit, coordinated ensembles, or sheer tropical prints, but she could survive the next twenty-four hours. She completed the lost luggage claim form, silently praying that her bag would be found and returned to her quickly.

As she exited the terminal, the afternoon sun made the black jeans she wore cling hotly to her thighs. Sloan almost wished she'd worn shorts although that would have been totally impractical with the temperature in New York a crisp thirty-nine degrees when she'd jumped into the cab that morning. Her long-sleeved white blouse, opened at the neck, did nothing to facilitate airflow. Neither did the pale green angora sweater, which she had tied around her shoulders. She removed it immediately. Unbuttoning the cuffs of her blouse, she turned her sleeves up to the elbow and knotted the waist of her shirt. She then opened two additional buttons. As the light strains of the tropical breeze began to filter through, she sighed and wondered if she was indeed up to the challenge presented. After all she'd been through in the last six months, any obstacles or impediments should be lightweight by comparison. She was, in a word, a survivor. Marriage to Karsten had taught her well.

"There's nothing like traveling to the Caribbean in the dead of New York winter," her fellow traveler in distress said suddenly. They'd both completed the set of forms presented and walked the length of the corridor, which separated the administrative offices inside the terminal. "I know, especially when they lose your luggage," Sloan offered.

One other traveler, tall, dark and obviously angry, completed the requisite paperwork. And although the knapsack on his back and duffel bag at his feet contained his most valuable equipment and possessions, he was not finding any amusement in the thought of misplaced luggage. Quietly, he gauged the other two travelers while managing to remain cool and detached. He was six feet one inch tall, built more from genes than from physical exertion, and in very good shape. No consumption of red meat, limited alcohol, and never smoking anything of a tobacco nature had complemented nature's handiwork. Norwood Warren, an award-winning photographer from Chicago, was understated to say the least. He wore a gray T-shirt with Northwestern across the front, while a hooded sweatshirt lay folded on top of his black duffel bag. Camera, lenses, flash equipment and the attachments were in the bag along with one pair of swim trunks, two T-shirts and one change of underwear. The remainder of his clothing was in his checked bag, which he'd searched for, without any luck, on the carousel inside the terminal.

Having to complete the necessary paperwork was just another delay in his book. Norwood was eager to rejoin the journalists and other photographers so that he could get to his hotel. He was extremely annoyed by the delay and inexcusable inconvenience of lost luggage but he knew he would recognize the group immediately. They wouldn't resemble the average tourists, nor were they likely to be mistaken for locals returning to their native homeland. Everyone either had a briefcase or camera equipment.

Rejoining the press group, which had moved outside the terminal, Sloan smiled and reached out her hand in introduction. "Sloan Whitaker, *Caribbean Press*," she said, smiling in response to the statement her fellow lost luggage passenger had just made. "And you are so right about the transition to the tropics."

"Jodi Logan, AP. I guess we were the only two who were lucky enough to have our luggage lost," she retorted with an easy laugh. None of the anger or attitude displayed earlier was evident and Sloan marveled at the obvious change in her demeanor.

"No, I think there is another person, too, although I don't know if he was part of our group. We left him in the claims office still filling out forms. You know, I thought you were going to be pretty upset for a long time back there when you first realized your luggage was lost."

"Nah, I learned a long time ago though that with my size, I have to make a lot of noise to get noticed, so I kind of overdo it just for the record. It works too," she said, laughing.

"Okay, I'll have to remember that," Sloan said. It seemed survival of the fittest was never overrated and often used. "I only hope it doesn't take them forever to locate that stuff—it must have gone on to St. Lucia, which was the next stop on that flight," she added, as they were introduced to several other journalists by Deirdre, the tourism authority representative. Deirdre also handed each member of the group a press package containing artist information, an event calendar, a daily itinerary, and press releases highlighting Barbados, including specific places of interest and historical relevance.

Sloan noticed the man immediately. He was good-looking, self-assured, and something else—detached. She realized that he was intentionally avoiding making eye contact and registered him as a malcontent. *You never know who's going to be included in these press trips,* she thought as she attempted to assess him without being too obvious. Very often the journalists and photographers were beyond egotistical—full of themselves and just plain rude. It seemed that this latest addition to the group would fit somewhere right in the middle of that category.

"Hey," he offered to the general group.

"Hi, you must be Norwood Warren. Everyone else has already checked in," Deidre said, quickly scanning her checklist.

"Yeah, that's me—they seem to have misplaced a bag on the plane so I was filling out the forms."

"Oh, well, don't worry—the bag will probably turn up either later today or by tomorrow morning. Okay, listen up, everyone, the vans are in place so we'll be transported to your individual hotels now. Make sure you have a copy of the itinerary. You are on your own until your pickup time tonight, which is different for each hotel. Please be in the lobby at the appointed pickup time. We'll all have dinner together at the Sunbury House at eight. I should have your photo IDs by then also," she said as they were hustled into three separate vans.

The drive from the airport through the Barbados

countryside wound its way around the jewel of an island. Many homes still under construction dotted the landscape at various points and spoke of a strong economy. The driver, who introduced himself as Curtis, handled the vehicle expertly, though the English-inspired driving on the right side left his passengers wide eyed each time he approached an oncoming vehicle.

"Turning at intersections here seems so awkward," Sloan commented after a particularly hair-raising turn. "And what is that circle in the middle of the highway supposed to be?" she asked.

"That is the give-way or roundabout," he explained patiently, his accent revealing a slight trace of his British ancestry. "We know when it's our turn to go without any traffic signal," he added. The obvious pride in his voice at having mastered this particular maneuver was evident.

"Curtis, let me tell you that where we come from that would be called 'the circle of death,'" Jodi said, laughing. "Can you imagine the cabs in Manhattan not having a traffic light at Columbus Circle?" she added, shaking her head.

"No, and I wouldn't want to be the passenger in one of those cabs either," Sloan said and cracked up laughing at the mere thought. She realized then that her fellow passenger was a true New Yorker, much like herself. The other passenger did not comment. Sloan suspected that he had either been to Barbados so many times that he was unfazed by it all, or that he just didn't care.

Norwood maintained complete and total silence for the entire ride, sitting in the back, listening to the banter of his companions but really marveling at the countryside. He'd been born in Barbados, left with his parents for the States at the ripe old age of two years, and had not been back. He was filled with curiosity, wanting to know everything about where he was born, how he'd lived, and most of all, what living there would be like now. But he remained silent, wrapped in thoughts he wasn't yet ready to express.

They arrived at the hotel, which, from the outside, looked quaint and filled with exotic charm. The stucco, flanked on either side by Windsor benches, featured several varieties of Caribbean exotic foliage. The lobby entrance was filled with wicker lounge chairs and sofas accentuated by cushions covered in bold tropical prints. As they each signed the hotel registry, the sounds of calypso music could be heard.

"Where is that music coming from?" Sloan asked as the bellman looked for their luggage. "Unfortunately, some of the bags were lost so we only have our carry-on bags with us," she explained quickly.

Norwood, who was listening quietly as she'd given her spiel, added, "If any calls come in from Worldwide Airlines regarding the luggage, please notify me immediately." He felt as if he were taking charge, but knew that somebody had to. The other two journalists looked as if the only thing they'd ever handled were charge cards, shopping sprees and fashion magazines.

Sloan, listening quietly as she completed the required guest registry, didn't dignify his comment. But she wanted to. *He must think he's the head coach of some kind of team,* she thought. She instinctively resented his authoritative air and his presumptuous attitude. He'd made it a point not to exchange more than ten words with any of the group and his lack of friendliness added to the feeling of unease created by the whole lost luggage experience.

Jodi, in the meantime, had wandered over the small bridge connecting the pool and lobby. A bar, which spanned at least seven feet, led to the restaurant located just a few yards from the pool area and was the site of several couples gyrating and pulsing to the provocative Caribbean beat. A four-piece band with two male singers was the source of inspiration.

"Looks like we've struck the mother lode; they're doing one hell of a 'Dollar Song,'" Jodi said excitedly as Sloan caught up to her.

"You are funny. I take it you like Caribbean music."

"Like it—it's my livelihood. I'm the music specialist for calypso, soca, reggae, dancehall—anything out of the Caribbean. I truly love it," she ended earnestly.

"Wow, I don't think I realized until just now how popular those types of music had become and I never realized one could specialize in it. I mean, I like some of it but it's definitely the jazz that I'm here to cover."

"As are most of the journalists. But they've got a great lineup of local talent as well, not to mention headline artists like Beres Hammond and Monty Alexander, both of whom are from Jamaica."

"That's right—I do remember hearing that they're scheduled to perform," Sloan said. "I'm looking forward to Boney James, Nancy Wilson and Al Jarreau."

"So am I. I actually like all kinds of music. Monte Alexander, one of the finest piano players of all time, should be something to see. By the way, what time are we being picked up tonight?" Jodi asked, reaching into her bag.

"Well, seven, which means we have exactly one hour and twenty-five minutes to unpack and be ready for the night's festivities. I say unpack with the utmost respect for the time it'll take for either of us to make ourselves presentable," Sloan added, laughing.

Jodi, impressed by the house band's treatment of several calypso hits, having covered dozens of concerts and attended Trinidad's Carnival as well as

Cropover in Barbados many times over, was visibly excited.

"I say, let's go to our rooms, drop this stuff off, and come back down to hear some more of this great calypso music. We deserve a drink after all we've been through today. Then, we can try and figure out how we can work a miracle with whatever clothes we have."

"You know, that's the most sensible thing I've heard all day. Unfortunately, I have a headache so I think I'll just cool out until our pickup time. Sorry to be such a drag but I think the flight, the lost luggage, the whole thing just got to me in the last twenty minutes or so," Sloan explained.

"Don't worry about it. If you need something to take, let me know—I think I have half of Rite Aid in my bag," Jodi said, laughing.

"No, but thanks. I came well prepared for almost any medical emergency, too. I'll see you down in the lobby around seven."

The hotel faced the ocean, its exteriors beautifully done in white Spanish stucco. The rooms were decorated with the exotic colors of Caribbean spices. Vibrant touches of persimmon, avocado, lemon yellow, and lime green adorned the bedspreads and draperies. Chairs covered in Haitian cotton fabric with a large floral pattern sat in one corner and at a desk. A huge mahogany trimmed mirror occupied one entire wall, creating an illusion of additional space and relaxed elegance.

Each room overlooked the ocean with a balcony outfitted with a white wicker table and armchairs. It created an inviting atmosphere for the visiting guests and many took advantage of it either in the early morning or late at night. The view offered the ocean's blue depths shading gradually as the offshore waters heated by the sun turned from turquoise to emerald green. Sloan, eager to commit the beauty of the scene to film, immediately unpacked her Nikon F70 and fired off several shots with the wide-angle lens. She knew that the photos would capture the late afternoon sunlight beautifully, including the two small boats docked off the shoreline. And although her story's focus centered on jazz, the artists, and their performances, location shots were always an interesting way to round out the assignment. She couldn't resist.

With the early morning flight, the travel, and all the coordination in the days prior to her departure, she hadn't had any time to digest or reflect on something which had been of monumental importance—her newfound freedom. She suddenly realized with an increasing calmness that there was something else that she hadn't felt in a long time. Serenity. She didn't have to worry that Karsten would come bursting through the door any minute to begin a new chapter of whatever argument they'd left off on that morning—or the evening before for that matter. His overnight disappearances, thinly veiled alibis, and demoralizing remarks were over at last. "Knight Rider," as she'd begun to think of him, was no longer an issue in her life, no longer an element in her future.

Sloan looked into the bathroom mirror as she quickly washed her face and then brushed her teeth. Her hair, which she'd pulled back into a ponytail for the flight, hung heavily down her back. Its auburn highlights would shade a more vibrant tone with the strong rays of the sun in the next few days. Her five-foot seven-inch frame was trimmer than when she'd been here last. She attributed it to the stress of the divorce and to the fact that most nights when she returned to the apartment, she couldn't bring herself to prepare anything even remotely akin to a proper dinner. Miraculously, she'd actually lost the weight in all the right places, having trimmed down from a comfortable 160 pounds to a little over 135. By no means was she a featherweight, yet on her midrange frame, her weight looked trim and slim. Remarkably clear skin had always been her forte and, as she stared into the bathroom mirror now, she marveled at her reflection.

"Well, I don't exactly look like I've been through hell," she said out loud. She laughed then and began removing the few items of clothing contained in her carry-on bag. She also removed the remaining camera equipment, checked the lenses, counted batteries, and sorted through the writing pads, tape recorder, and other equipment she would be using in the days ahead. Separating her film by speed, Sloan noted which rolls she would use at daytime events as opposed to those to be used for night photography. In the coming days, organization would be key in getting both her story and the accompanying photographs.

After taking two Advils, she lay across the bed and closed her eyes.

"Well, they're prompt around here, that's for sure," Jodi remarked as the bus pulled into the hotel's entry way. It was 7:02 P.M.

"Yeah, that's because we're probably first on the pickup list for tonight. Wait until we're closer to last. Then they'll be late because they almost always have to wait for somebody who's running late at one of the other hotels," Sloan explained matter-of-factly.

Norwood was in conversation with one of the hotel

staff members as they entered the lobby. He noticed both Sloan and Jodi as they walked across the tiny bridge which spanned the pool and turned away.

His reaction to Sloan, who'd changed into a dress and done something to her hair, was immediate. He felt as if all the wind had been knocked out of him; it was not a good feeling. The reaction was not welcome, so he chose to ignore it and her. He continued his conversation, as they reached the lobby's front and noted the arrival of their transportation.

All three boarded the tour bus, which had a comfortable seating capacity of forty-one passengers. Air-conditioned and equipped with a state-of-the-art sound system including public address functions, it would transport members of the press housed on the eastern and northern sides of the island. A separate bus was assigned to pick up those journalists being housed on the south coast to save time.

The windows, which were large and tinted, did not allow for visibility from the outside. A PRESS sign was perched in the front windshield and would gain the vehicle entry into the secured areas of each concert location.

Sloan had showered and changed into the black one-shouldered dress. It fit her trim figure snugly and reached just above her knees. The sandals she wore were very low and not really meant for a dress, but she realized they were a far better choice than the suede boots. Recharging her batteries with a short nap always worked. She felt renewed. The natural humidity in the tropical climate had caused her hair to revert to a natural curl. She looked like a rock star with a major ax to grind. Light makeup, lip gloss, and mascara completed the transformation, which was, under the circumstances, almost miraculous.

Jodi, who had changed from the T-shirt she wore on the plane, wore a red-stripe halter top. Thong sandals, normally reserved for the beach and pedicures, adorned her feet. They would have to do because her only other shoes were loafers. She had pulled her blond hair back into a high ponytail and she looked all of about twenty years old. Both women agreed that if their luggage was not found in the next twenty-four hours, someone would have hell to pay.

Norwood was accustomed to traveling and its innate challenges but he hated to lose control of anything. He'd showered and put on a black sport shirt with gray piping around the collar. His black jeans and loafers would have to do because all of his other clothing was now unavailable. His frustration evident, he looked incredibly irritated, unapproachable, and not at all friendly. Despite it all, he was still drop-dead gorgeous.

As the bus made its way through Christ Church and into the parish of St. Lawrence, several other journalists, photographers, and members of the press were picked up. Some had arrived earlier in the week and were staying at various hotels dotting the coastline.

Two writers from England, Trevor Martin and Glenn Denby, were picked up at the Accra Beach Hotel. Newly refurbished and gorgeous, the beachfront property had a majestic lobby that opened out onto the busy street. Everyone introduced themselves and were engaged in conversation as the bus sped along, intent on keeping its deadline of 8:00 P.M.

At the next hotel, the Southern Palms, a party of two joined the bus: Lorenzo Smith, a photographer and Web site developer from Los Angeles, and Johnson Dade, a jazz radio personality from Atlanta.

Once again, introductions were made and conversation ensued.

Lorenzo sat directly across from Jodi. After learning of her affiliation with Associated Press International, he was full of questions about her travels and the extent of additional coverage she'd been exposed to during her tenure with them.

"I had no idea they were into Caribbean music festivals though. I've always thought of AP coverage as staid and counterculture," he admitted.

"Not at all—lots of stuff is being done now because the Caribbean is such a huge and important marketplace in terms of tourism. That spells dollar signs for the rest of the world economy, so there is an increased awareness and renewed interest," Jodi explained.

Johnson Dade, who now sat across the aisle from Sloan, reminded her of an obnoxious know-it-all. It was his attitude. He was built, having pumped iron all through college and into early adulthood. Now, standing at an even six feet and weighing 201, he looked solid and something else. Determined. His hair, dark and wavy, seemed never out of place. His complexion was smooth and brown. But his eyes gave him away. He never quite made complete eye contact, always seeming to focus on something just out of range. It created uncertainty. And unknown to her, he'd earned a long-standing reputation of never-ending female companionship. Most of the time, he waited for them to approach him. That made it easier when he was ready to let them down. His voice, rich and deep, was his greatest asset and he knew it. Nightly broadcasted over 1,200 megawatts in the eight to midnight time slot, his radio show had become a hit in a little over six months. The popular Atlanta station known for playing everything from classic to contemporary and urban jazz had declared him "the

Velvet Knight." WATL had created its own midnight phenomenon with smooth jazz as its hook. With an ego to match both the size and depth of the Mississippi River, Johnson Dade commanded and received pretty much anything he wanted. And what he wanted right now was to dominate the deliciously enchanting creature sitting across from him.

Sloan sensed almost all of this immediately and, though she was polite, even friendly to him, he felt her reserve.

"So, is this your first trip to Barbados?" she found herself asking even though she didn't really care. She'd promised herself that when and if she ever got out of her marriage, she wouldn't let it change her perception of life or the people she encountered. She'd be open to new experiences. What she hadn't prepared herself for was encountering the same old thing. And that's exactly what he represented.

"Yes, it is and so far, it's been really interesting," he admitted, glad to be in conversation with any attractive woman. He'd noticed her immediately as he entered the bus but hadn't wanted to stare. She had the most amazing skin he'd ever seen. Flawless, smooth, and the color of creamy milk chocolate, her skin looked as if she lived on berries and fruits, its moisture apparent. And her hair looked untamed, exciting, and sensual all at once. He figured she was probably married. Women that looked like her usually were. That would make it even more interesting and less messy to end. She represented everything he was challenged by—beauty, brains, and accomplishment.

"What exactly do you do?" he asked to keep the conversation flowing, recognizing that the effort put forth now could pay off handsomely in the days ahead if executed with just the right touch of finesse.

"I'm a photojournalist for the *Caribbean Press*, a

newspaper out of New York City," she explained. "Actually, this is my second time here. Last year was fantastic but the lineup this year is even better."

"Well, Atlanta may have an awful lot going for it but this place is awesome. So far, I like what I see. I'm really looking forward to the concerts, too," Johnson laughed, mentally assessing how long it would take him to break the ice with the beauty queen. He figured once she realized his status as a radio personality, she'd fall in line like the rest of them. But he also knew he had several days to unravel his charming web. He'd take his time.

Meanwhile, Norwood Warren had taken a seat toward the back of the bus and remained quiet and alone. Tall and slim, with closely cropped salt-and-pepper hair, he had a mustache that did little to hide an engagingly sensuous mouth. Smooth, clear skin the color of pecans left in the sun too long adorned his six-foot two-inch frame. But it was his eyes that were always a surprise to anyone who dared look into them. Deep pools of rich, chocolate brown that drew you in, made you hesitate, and then, more often than not, caused you to back down.

He'd overheard each and every conversation but was having none of it. He lived in a world of his own making and intended to keep it that way. His only way of reaching out was through the images projected by his photography. He'd won several prestigious awards and contests and had even come extremely close to winning a Pulitzer back in 1998. His assignment was simple and direct. Obtain several "cover quality" photographs of each headline artist to be used in conjunction with a coffee table book; it would be published by Avigo Publishing sometime in the coming twelve months.

He'd been offered this assignment because he was

the best. And he would deliver it because he knew he could. But on his terms.

Avigo Publishing knew he was the man for the job as soon as the concept had been greenlighted. They'd contacted him immediately knowing he could conceivably be booked already. They then made him an offer which he couldn't refuse. A six-figure up-front fee, all access passes to each artist's performances, and final approval on the selection of photographs to be used in the book. And even then, Norwood almost refused.

The deal breaker had been that he'd be out of town for at least a week and a half. He figured he could use the time away from familiar surroundings to get his head together. Although he and Kassandra had not spoken now for close to a year, he'd been unable to get the memory of all that they'd shared out of his head, or the images of that fateful afternoon out of his mind. Maybe a change in environment would enable him to finally put that chapter of his life to rest. He needed something to make him forget that a woman he had actually considered making his wife had betrayed him so cruelly.

The concert lineup offered Boney James, a master on the saxophone, Monty Alexander, who hailed from Jamaica but who had since gained international recognition, and several other noteworthy masters. Marcus Miller, a guitar wunderkind from the East Coast now living on the West Coast in Los Angeles, was the icing on the cake for him. He'd even recently put together all the music for the movie *Two Can Play That Game*, which had starred Viveca A. Fox and Morris Chestnut. Miller was one of the hottest young musical scribes on the scene and Norwood was looking forward to capturing some of that genius on film. Rounding out the jazz would be the legendary Chaka

Linda Walters

Khan, Al Jarreau, and Earth, Wind & Fire. It was a powerhouse lineup.

He was aware of and inspired by each artist's ability to record, produce, and write some of the best classic, contemporary, and fusion jazz recorded recently. He also knew that it was no small feat that he had been chosen to capture what it was all about.

Legends of jazz had enticed him to come out of his cave which, like it or not, had been his residence for the past year. Hopefully, he'd be able to keep to himself, get his photos, and not step on anyone's toes in the days ahead—no interaction, no conversation, no pleasant exchanges of small talk, or any other distractions. That was his intention, his modus operandi, his mantra. If he had his way, he'd keep it like that the entire trip.

Despite his indifference, he'd noticed the "New York" journalist. In his mind, Sloan seemed overpriced, underdressed, and overrated. He dismissed her with the others, knowing that he intended to avoid the entire lot of them for his stay on the island.

He couldn't help remembering the way her dress had clung to her and briefly wondered if she was any good at writing or taking pictures. With a body like that, she probably couldn't even focus the damn camera properly, he thought. He wasn't sure why it annoyed him to think of her, but knew that it did, and he wanted it to stay that way.

Norwood sat back, put his feet across the remaining seats in the aisle, and closed his eyes, allowing nothing of the sounds around him to filter through. He could control that and much more, but he could not control the ache that followed him day and night. The ache failed to disappear although he refused to acknowledge it; that ache was Kassandra.

Two

Chicago

Lake Shore Drive's five o'clock traffic upheld its reputation in congestion, delays, and overall mayhem. Norwood had no choice in routes if he wanted to get back into downtown Chicago in time. He'd taken the winding roadway knowing that although it would most certainly be heavily trafficked, any alternative would put him even farther from his destination. It would only add time to the moments necessary for him to pick up two additional lenses, his tripod, and other necessary lighting equipment for the night's shoot.

His studio, which was located in an office building off Rush Street in what was commonly known as "Greektown," had taken the call and transmitted it to him across town.

"Are you sure that they said Randy Weston?" he'd asked when he'd finally been contacted. It would not be the first time there had been a mistake made in transmitting someone's name or contact number.

Kallie, his receptionist, was unimpressed. "Yeah, they'll be here at six o'clock and I definitely have to leave at five fifty-nine, so please get back before that, okay?" she'd stated flatly as Norwood had mentally calculated the cross-town drive during rush-hour traffic.

He'd transported some of his equipment home only days before, thinking that he might make use of it over the course of a weekend, equipment that he now realized he would definitely need for the evening's assignment. His telephoto lens that also had the ability to scan for infrared light, his umbrella flash that he always used with portrait shots, along with several polarizers he'd need to use were all now at his house in the second bedroom which also doubled as a small studio.

Using his cellular phone, Norwood called the condo. The high-rise building, situated on the shoreline below Lake Shore Drive, offered a breathtaking view of Lake Michigan, Navy Pier, and the Adler Planetarium. There was no answer. "Damn," he muttered under his breath. Kassandra's booking must have been extended or she would have been home by now. Or she was out shopping "magnificent mile," the upscale shopping district that ran along Lake Shore Drive. Looking at his watch, he noted the time. "Three forty-seven P.M.," he said to no one in particular. That would leave him approximately two hours to cut across downtown Chicago, pick up his equipment, and then make his way through rush-hour traffic back into the downtown business district.

As he made his way in the heat of midday traffic toward the apartment he shared with his fiancée, Kassandra Algernon, Norwood contemplated that he was a fortunate man.

Images Inc., which he'd started only four years before, had become a thriving photo gallery, complete with video assignments, still shots, and portfolio work for artists and models alike. His bank accounts, both business and personal, reflected the success he'd achieved. And although his personal life was going smoothly, too, sometimes he acknowledged that there was something lacking in the relationship he shared with Kass. He couldn't put his finger on exactly what that was though. They'd lived together for the past eighteen months, but he'd come to realize that something was different recently. He also realized that he wouldn't be able to ignore it much longer. He knew how he felt about her, knew he loved her and wanted, at some point, for them to formalize their union. He'd even bought her a one and one-half carat, perfect, round-cut diamond engagement ring. But they'd never discussed a date.

Norwood knew that Kassandra wanted to see her career take off and that she was really committed to making that happen. Maybe they'd pull it together as soon as some of the work slowed down. He was busy, she was busy. It was a normal hectic, frantically paced relationship between two young up-and-coming professionals. That was what he comforted himself with on good days. And on bad days, he tried not to think of it at all.

Kassandra had come into his life just as he was breaking into the business. An aspiring model and actress intent on obtaining a portfolio that would catapult her into instant success, she had been hell-bent on becoming a successful model in New York City. His name had been given to her by another model—one whose portfolio spelled hot, hot property. Each realized that the chemistry between them would probably produce a fantastic book, but by the time they'd negotiated the deal and completed the required photo sessions necessary to develop her portfolio, the issue of New York had become a moot point. She'd moved into Norwood's loft, begun going on "go sees" designed to fill catalog work and assignments local to the Chicago textile industry, and apparently forgotten about the beckoning lights of the eastern seaboard.

Five feet nine inches of bronze molded to
perfection was a good description of Kass. With
shoulder-length, coal-black hair and legs that
reached from the floor to the ceiling, she was a
knockout. But Norwood's camera-ready eye saw
through to more than that. And just as he'd known
that she wasn't really ready for New York, he also
knew that lately she'd become more restless and dis-
satisfied with the catalog work she was now regularly
assigned. It had taken two years but the thing that
had drawn them together was now unraveling of its
own accord.

He meant to talk to her about it but every time he
even got close to any heartfelt discussion, she pulled
away and closed herself off from him. *Wait until she
hears that I'm shooting "Randy Weston" tonight, she'll be impressed—maybe that'll get her to open up,* he thought as he
pulled into his parking space. Oftentimes, in the early
stages of their relationship, they would talk way into
the early morning hours about their dreams, hopes,
and desires. They could both become almost giddy if
the prospect of a particularly hot group or designer
was possibly within the realm of access. He remembered those days well and with a great deal of
fondness. He also acknowledged, regrettably, that
things had somehow changed. It concerned him that
he couldn't for the life of him actually remember
when or how the change had occurred.

As he turned the key in the lock of the apartment
door, some sixth sense told him to turn around and
walk away. He actually shook his head as he entered
the apartment.

Voices could be heard murmuring in the bedroom
and he instantly reacted, the adrenaline flowing to assist him in his next move. As he approached the door,
he recognized Kassandra's laugh and relief flooded

his entire being. *She's probably here with one of her girl-friends trying on clothing from a shoot or something,* he thought.

He knocked at the door, softly calling her name. "Kass, honey, are you decent?" he asked. Silence was his only answer. Puzzled at the lack of response, Norwood slowly pushed the door inward. He would never forget the image that greeted him. It seemed magnified, almost as if he were looking through one of his telephoto lenses, fully zoomed in with a cloud polarizer in place to enhance the dreamlike quality. They were still entangled in each other's arms, though frozen in place by his unexpected entrance. No one spoke. Breathing was suspended. The silence hung in the air heavily and seemed to extend time. Kassandra moved first then, dismounting from her lover's body gracefully, even under such awkward circumstances.

At that moment, Norwood's stomach churned acid. His heart beat painfully, a dull ache spreading quickly throughout his chest. He felt as if he were having a heart attack but fate denied him that luxury. No, he'd have to live through this one, this pain, this humiliation. He turned around, walked into the storage room, got his equipment, and blindly drove to the studio. It was only after he'd begun shooting the quintet which featured Doc Powell, Randy Weston, and two equally talented musicians on bass and percussion that he'd begun to unclench his jaw, uncoil his anger, and unleash his fury.

But he'd used the medium that was his passion to do it and it showed brilliantly in the finished product. Sharply focused with raw emotion captured on each of the musician's faces almost as if recorded note by note, that night's work was some of the finest he'd ever produced. The photographs, originally slated to accompany an article inside the issue, also made the cover of the following month's edition of *Jazz Report*, an industry magazine known for its in-depth coverage of jazz's greatest musicians.

They'd never discussed his walking in on her and Jordan Campbell. In reality, it was just another catalog model she'd met through assignments and work. But in the real scheme of things, it was as good an excuse as any to throw in the towel on a relationship that had obviously run its course. When she'd announced two weeks later that she was moving to New York, Norwood had not questioned her. He knew it was time. They both did.

His equipment became his constant companion, his whole world. Lenses, camera body, flashes, were all his mistresses. After all, they gave you what you wanted with no questions asked. They were fairly complicated but once you learned how to use them, manipulate them, gauge them and their ability, you were home free. No more guess work. No disappointments. No surprises. At least not ones that ripped your heart out.

Photography itself was filled with many uncertainties. And there were often distinctly unknown qualities. You never knew if the f-stops you set were going to give you the exact lens opening you needed, or how the light was going to reflect off its source and onto your subject. So there were often unexpected and unanticipated moments. But Norwood could handle those events. As close as he was to his work, he maintained the ability to remain objective when necessary. That's what made him one of the greats behind the camera. It's what set him apart. And now that he was recognized for that skill, he vowed to keep it in place, work it, and never again let his guard down. Not for anyone or anything.

Beautiful women surrounded him every day at the studio. He turned himself off to them and concentrated solely on the work at hand. And if, every so often, he felt lonely or tempted to make an exception, the image of Kassandra poised above the body of her lover effectively strangled that notion. He kept himself extremely busy not allowing any unfulfilled blocks of time to occur which would even allow him to think or feel anything related to his current social status. He'd found the perfect formula for distancing himself from the world. Photography was his life, his love, his armor.

It was impenetrable and he wore it well.

Three

Barbados

The Sunbury House Plantation, a historic site set in the hills above St. Philip, was beautifully hypnotic in the evening light. Standing brick sections of the original buildings created the perfect elements for lighting and cast an impressive glow on the now revered grounds. Originally the site of a massive and prolific sugar-producing plantation, many of the now archaic tools used to harvest crop still lined the remnants of stalls offering a view into the past. Portions of wagons, crude tools which had been used for cutting and harvesting sugarcane, as well as several other items of antiquated equipment, were there to be displayed, discussed, and filtered into today's high-tech consciousness.

Classic Bajan cuisine, which included flying fish, fried marlin, and kingfish, breadfruit, jerked chicken, rice and peas, macaroni pie, coleslaw, green banana, fried plantain, cucumber salad, and beef stew served buffet style, had been prepared by two local restaurants.

Drinks ranging from rum punch, piña coladas, Cockspur, and other local rums were served throughout the evening. The Barbados Tourism Authority, responsible for creating the itinerary for the journalists during their entire stay on the island, had spared no detail in making sure everyone there had a good time. A small local band played throughout the evening as the guests were introduced to several key members of the Tourism Authority including the president and vice president.

Sloan and Jodi were attempting to achieve a quick resolution to their lost baggage problems. Deirdre, the BTA press coordinator, listened to their suggestions patiently.

"I will call the airport tomorrow morning and send a car for the bags if they're in—otherwise, we are authorized to offer you girls vouchers for at least one outfit," Deirdre explained. She knew from past experience that the bags would most probably turn up at the airport by midday.

"Honestly, I just really want my own clothes. There's a couple of new outfits in that suitcase. I was really looking forward to one in particular," Sloan commented.

Johnson Dade, overhearing the conversation, interrupted at that point. "You girls should just relax. You look fine in whatever you wear anyway. Have you tried any of the kingfish? It's delicious," he announced in an attempt to share with Sloan, Jodi, or anyone else for that matter.

"No, thanks, Johnson. I've had enough," Sloan responded. "Although I will have another drink because I should be celebrating," she added, more to herself than to anyone else.

"Please, call me Dade, everyone else does," he said as she stood to leave the table.

"Sure, no problem." With no further explanation, she made her way toward the bar. Set up under a palm tree on the outside deck, it was manned by a staff representative offering a full selection of spirits and tropical drinks, including beer and sodas.

Sloan felt an overwhelming sense of freedom. She was on a tropical island with an assignment that encompassed the three things she loved most—journalism, photography, and music. The fact that she was now free of a marriage that had failed miserably only added to her feeling of exhilaration. Karsten was quickly becoming only a memory—albeit a bad one.

As she approached the bar area, Dade caught up to her, eagerly matching her stride for stride. Before she could even think of reacting, he was halfway into ordering another drink for her.

"What is that you're drinking?" he asked, eager to be of absolutely any assistance.

"Actually, it's only Diet Coke. I save the really exotic stuff for much later in the trip," she offered, glad that she could throw some cold water on his obviously burning embers.

He laughed, not at all dissuaded. "I guess I'll be looking forward to that occasion. Promise you'll have a real drink with me then?" he asked, winking as if they were sharing in some well-calculated conspiracy.

"I'm sure by that time you'll have found someone else to order a drink for," she responded candidly. His demeanor, attitude, and overall approach reminded her so much of Karsten that she could hardly contain herself. What she really wanted to do was to tell him to buzz off and leave her alone. Instead, she held up her glass in a mock salute and graciously moved away, smiling all the while.

"In the meantime, I'll have another rum and Coke," Dade announced to the bartender.

Norwood walked the bar to get another beer, his second of the night. His mind was crystal clear. And although he had absolutely no interest in throwing his hat into the ring, it was pretty clear that the cool-cat radio DJ from Atlanta had been shot down by the beauty from New York. She stood by the bar, calmly sipping her drink, as though she had successfully defended the fort against one last stand. He liked that.

Norwood walked up and placed his order. Turning to reach for a napkin, he was surprised to hear a soft voice with a distinct New York lilt. "Why me?" she asked no one in particular. Her laughter was like a warm and gentle introduction to her personality.

"Is that a rhetorical question?" Norwood responded immediately, realizing that he was breaking every rule he'd established less than six hours ago.

"Most definitely—I don't think the answer is ever forthcoming," she said easily.

Sloan was determined not to allow the self-absorbed, overconfident Johnson Dade to get to her. She knew that he was watching her from across the room and sensed any actions displayed now would hopefully discourage him from becoming a real problem for her. He'd already offered her a drink, and half the food on his plate. He'd made it quite clear that he was very interested in more than just idle chatter about publicity, press releases, and photography. Perhaps being friendly to everyone else would make it clear to him that she was not at all interested in him and was just being cordial to all the journalists in the group.

"So, what do you think of Barbados?"

"Actually I was born here but haven't been back since I was a toddler. I'm kind of looking forward to maybe finding my 'roots" so to speak. Let me have another beer," Norwood responded as he stood alongside the bar. "I don't think we've met—my name is Norwood Warren," he said, extending his hand.

"Sloan Whitaker." She noticed the darkness of his eyes and the intensity of his stare almost immediately. Their hands met at that moment and Sloan was struck by the warmth and firmness of his grasp. A jolt, much like an electric current, ran through her. She immediately drew her hand back.

"I'm sorry. I think you shocked me or something," she said, examining her hand quickly.

"I know—that happens sometimes. I can't even wear a watch on my right hand," he said in explanation. She noticed that he indeed wore his watch on the left forearm.

"Wow, that's really weird. Have you ever had that checked by a doctor?" Sloan asked, genuinely intrigued. She had definitely felt something when their hands touched but she wasn't sure what it was. She had been too caught up in his eyes.

"No, up until now it hasn't presented a problem. But that's the first time it has actually shocked another person. I'm sorry. I hope I didn't hurt you or anything," he said, genuinely concerned.

"No, not at all. It just felt a little weird," she replied, suddenly feeling very exposed and vulnerable to a total stranger.

"So, where are you from—oh, wait, I think I heard it when we were on the bus. New York, right?" he asked, now smiling again.

"That's right—the *Caribbean Press,*" she added. "How about you?"

"Chicago—I'm a photographer," he responded as they each sipped their drinks. "I was a sergeant with the U.S. Army," he added. He couldn't stop himself from looking at the curve of one shoulder which was exposed from the dress. Her skin shimmered in the moonlight, and he suddenly wanted to press his lips against the indentation of her clavicle. The thought caught him off guard and he cleared his throat to bring his attention back to what she was saying.

"Really, now I'm impressed. All that discipline and creativity, too. Are you currently on staff somewhere or do you freelance?" Sloan asked. Inwardly, her response to this tall, dark stranger was far different from that of Johnson Dade. She found herself wanting to know what kind of pictures he took, what kind of equipment he used, what his definition of form was, and so on. And, if truth be told, in the back of her mind, the thought of him in uniform was compelling. She'd always been drawn to men in uniform of any kind, military, law enforcement, emergency response, whatever. Any kind of uniform, thanks to her favorite uncle who'd served in the U.S. Navy for more than a decade.

"Actually, I have my own studio, Images Inc. We are so busy currently that the assignments are lined up, at this point, until well into 2003," he added, smiling, which surprised him because he realized that he was actually enjoying the conversation.

"Wow, that's great. I can't imagine making a living just by taking photographs. I'm a journalist but I'm just now starting to develop a comfort level behind the camera. My strong suit has always been writing but my editor kept asking for pictures to accompany each story. I bought my first Nikon and took some classes about two years ago," she explained, feeling like a novice in the midst of such photographic accomplishment.

Norwood, who hadn't planned on mingling with anyone during the entire trip, suddenly found it comfortable to be conversing and fraternizing with this one member of the group. He couldn't explain it, didn't even want to examine it too closely, because he was unsure of his reasons.

He'd promised himself anonymity through the entire trip but he realized that the woman standing before him was exquisite. That was the only word he could think of to describe her. Her skin, her smile, her hair were all done without effort but the final result was stunning. And she was bright. She wore intelligence much the way some women wore their makeup—close to the surface and without pretense.

Tall and extremely well put together, she reminded him of a 1970s lava lamp which looked stable from the outside, but continually moved and changed form inside its chamber. One curve melded into another, ever changing, ever melding and reforming. Her body, compact yet softly voluptuous, spoke volumes through the one-shouldered dress she wore. Although she wore relatively flat sandals, she was still tall, probably around five feet eight inches, he guessed. She looked into his eyes without effort, without fear. He realized that she had only intended to be cordial and that had been enough for him. Until she'd touched his hand. That innocent gesture of civility had sent a pulsing sensation all the way through his palm and into his spine. It caught him off guard and he realized that he was quite possibly entering uncharted waters.

They moved wordlessly toward the railing overlooking the hilltop. Filled with lights from the nearby homes, it was beautiful, serene, and intimate. They felt it but were individually compelled to maintain a very comfortable silence. That silence was suddenly interrupted by a nervous laugh.

"Well, what are you two discussing—world peace?" Dade asked intrusively as he cleared his throat. Working on his third rum and Coke, he was feeling absolutely no pain.

"Actually, we weren't discussing anything at this particular moment," Norwood offered honestly.

"We were silently admiring the beauty, the serenity of our surroundings," Sloan explained patiently. The two years she'd tolerated Karsten's infidelities had taught her a few things. Patience was, indeed, a virtue; however, it had its limitations.

"Well, isn't this cozy?" he offered, obviously feeling compelled to interrupt whatever connection had been established between the two. Norwood's military training and instinct immediately kicked in. In the face of the enemy, the policy was to "dig in" and he did just that.

"Sloan was just telling me that she was ready to go back and join her table, so if you'll excuse us," he offered as he led her away. Dade, too embarrassed to speak, was fuming. *Where had the geek come from? He'd played Mr. Antisocial all evening only to come alive at the twelfth hour. Now he's trying to damn near walk away with the prize. I'll fix his ass,* he thought to himself as he prepared to join the others who were now finding their way to the buses.

"Thank you so much," Sloan said as they approached her table and she began gathering her belongings. Jodi had already joined the group on the bus. There were still a few journalists who hadn't gotten onboard yet and were standing around engaged in conversation.

"You don't have to thank me, it was fun. I actually got a kick out of seeing his face. Obviously the guy doesn't hear the word 'no' often enough," he added, laughing.

"I think you're probably right. Maybe it's a lot easier for him in Atlanta. He should try that stuff in New York—he'd get clobbered. Women do not play in my neck of the woods," she said, laughing now, too.

"Yeah, I get that impression. So, how come you're cutting me so much slack?" he asked, a little surprised at the words coming from his own mouth. He realized, at that exact moment, that he was flirting. And enjoying himself doing so.

"Actually, I was just being sociable. Don't take it as an invitation to move into my room," Sloan retorted sarcastically.

She'd managed to discourage the other barracuda and now seemed to find herself in the clutches of "Jaws" himself. What was it with men? Were they all inclined to be interested in only one thing, no matter what you said or did? She was becoming extremely annoyed. If the answer was to only consort with the females of the group, so be it. She hated to limit herself like that but it seemed the only solution to an obvious problem. Men were jerks and she obviously attracted the cream of the crop.

"Look, I didn't mean anything by it. I just thought that you and I seemed to hit it off back there," he said in explanation. The last thing he wanted or needed was for her to feel that he was harassing her.

"Well, let's just keep it simple. You take photos, I take photos. Perhaps we can compare negatives sometime," she said, convinced that she had almost jumped from the frying pan into the fire, but also convinced that she could extinguish it effectively if necessary.

"Fine. Fine. Look, let's draw a truce. I think you're okay. It's no more complicated than that. And I certainly don't want you to feel that I'm some sort of super creep like that other dude," he said as they walked toward the bus.

"Okay, maybe I was a little quick to judge things. Forgive me, but I've had a rough couple of months. Let's just forget it. Look, I think I'm going to find the rest room before I board the bus," she said and turned to walk away.

She needed to clear her head. The path leading toward the rest room area was dimly lit but fully illuminated by the moonlight night. The natural tropical greenery created a forest-like effect, which was beautiful and tranquil. Sloan entered the ladies' room feeling both angry and somewhat confused. "Men," she mumbled to herself as she proceeded to reapply her lip gloss and run her fingers through her hair.

She realized the bus was probably ready to depart soon, so she hurried outside. She ran blindly into Johnson Dade, who had obviously also felt the necessity to visit the rest room. He seemed to be having difficulty focusing for a moment and then broke out into a wide grin of recognition.

"Hey, it's my friend from New York," he said with an exaggerated drawl as he attempted to quickly grab her arm. He'd moved forward quickly, catching her off guard.

Sloan moved out of his grasp easily and simply kept moving in the direction of the parking lot. Dade followed, his footsteps suddenly gaining in both speed and steadiness.

"Hey, wait up—they won't leave us," he offered as he actually managed to reach her side. "Look, let's start over again, I only want to be your friend," he offered.

"Friends—sure," Sloan remarked and was startled when he not only flung one arm around her shoulders, but managed to pull her to him in a clumsy embrace.

"Oh, will you just let it rest?" she managed to eke out while solidly pushing him away. At that moment, Norwood suddenly appeared out of nowhere and spun Dade around bodily. The anger in his voice was apparent in his stance and demeanor. He appeared capable of defending himself and anything else in the immediate area, including Sloan's honor.

"Man, what exactly is your problem? Don't they teach you brothers in the South not to manhandle the women?" Norwood asked, his legs spread wide, arms tense, apparently more than willing to engage in defensive tactics if necessary.

With the pungent smell of rum coming from the hard-breathing Johnson Dade, Norwood realized that the man was not only arrogant, he was apparently drunk.

"Who the hell are you supposed to be anyway, rescue nine-one-one?" Johnson asked with a definite slur. "The lady and I were just talking. We don't need you to interfere," he added, flailing his arms to try and reestablish his balance.

Sloan, who hadn't uttered one word since Norwood walked up, laughed more from tension than the absurdity of the situation.

"You know, this is so ridiculous. Johnson, you had better get yourself together because we have nothing to talk about. Absolutely nothing," she added, as she broke through the invisibly drawn lines of both men and headed quickly toward the bus.

Norwood, unable to believe that she had actually laughed when she was so obviously in real danger, caught up to her easily and stepped in front of her.

"Is this some kind of sick game you play with men—tease them, lead them on, and then claim offense when they grab for the bait? Granted that fool is drunk, but you're obviously in possession of all your faculties," he spat out angrily. His dark eyes bored into her, taking in every pore, every curve, noticing her every breath. That simple yet necessary action accentuated the outline of her breasts against the clinging fabric of her dress. That a function that was necessary to sustain life made her even more appealing seemed ridiculous and annoyed him immensely.

"You don't know what you're talking about, 'Chicago.' I did no more to lead that jerk on than I'm leading you on now." Overcome with indignation, Sloan's eyes flashed defiantly, challenging him. He was so close to her and looked so threatening that she felt compelled to raise one arm in a reflex action. She had no real intention to strike him, just to let him know and acknowledge that she could, indeed, defend herself if necessary.

Norwood's military training in hand-to-hand combat, classic martial arts, and good old-fashioned street defense caused him to react before he knew it. He reached out and found himself grasping her slender wrist in a dead-bolt lock. At the same time, he took a small step forward, closing the gap between them. But instead of defending himself, he found himself suddenly lowering his mouth to hers. The contact caught Sloan off guard and she struggled to break the connection, but he still held her in a viselike grip. His lips were at once demanding and questing. Sloan struggled to be free, but it was useless.

Then in a fleeting moment, everything changed as a liquid warmth seemed to spread from her stomach to the inner core of her being. His lips softened and became less demanding as she acquiesced. Sloan found herself pressing forward to continue the contact. His hand freed her only to find its way around her waist. Pulling her closely to him, he breathed in her fragrance and was aroused even more. They engaged in a struggle of wills, each unwilling to relinquish the vanquished territory. Their lips continued the breach, their tongues questing and demanding. Finally, breathing heavily, he lifted his lips from hers, a look of total conquest on his face even in the darkened moonlight.

"You know, you should be more careful. I don't think you're as tough as you pretend to be—even if you are from New York," he murmured against her temple. Her scent was distinctive yet alluring and he wanted to kiss her again but was afraid he wouldn't be able to stop this time. His lips lightly brushed hers. Then he freed her and walked away.

Sloan remained motionless for what seemed like an eternity. She was trembling with anger, rage, confusion, and passion all pulsing through her body. She wanted to scream, wanted to slap his face, wanted to be in his arms again, all at once. She had never felt so at odds with herself, never so confused yet so aroused, in her entire life. She struggled to regain her composure, uncertain as to her next move, unsure of her emotions. Slowly, she headed toward the bus.

The men's rest room was empty and Norwood took his time, washing his hands and allowing his breathing to return to normal. He couldn't explain nor defend what had just taken place but he knew that she had been equally caught off guard.

Moments later, Norward entered the bus. Sloan had taken her seat and sat looking out of the window seemingly mesmerized by the darkness. He boldly took the seat beside her, knowing he was breaking all the rules. She looked calm, although he realized that the little scene just played out had to have unnerved her. He knew that guys like Dade, with the added octane of three rum and Cokes in their tanks, could be more than a handful. But he also realized that she had utilized her most basic instincts—disarm the opposition with an appearance of calm resolution—then flee, if at all possible. The fact that she had also resorted to the use of humor told him that she was a survivor of the highest caliber. He both admired and respected that. But he also wanted her to realize that he was not part of the enemy camp. And that the kiss they'd shared had meant more to him than he'd initially been willing to admit.

"Look, if that guy gives you any more trouble, let me know. I don't think he meant anything by it. I think his rum was talking for him," he added with a serious look on his face. He instinctively knew that he had to make some kind of peace with this woman. No matter what took place after tonight, a foundation was being laid in the fleeting darkness offered by the bus's interior.

"Thank you for what you did back there. I am definitely not interested in anyone or anything at this point," she said, determination apparent in her voice. What she wanted to add was that the ink on her divorce papers was still wet and that she wasn't ready to entertain the thought of another romantic entanglement for years to come. She hoped that he'd get the hint that she was not in the least interested in him, even if he had succeeded in kissing her just moments before. "I don't know what I did to turn him on," she added.

Norwood swallowed his first response. "Have you looked into a mirror lately? Not to mention the guy's two partners, rum and Coke," he said. They both laughed then, unable to stop themselves for several minutes.

"Friends?" he asked, reaching out into the darkness to take her hand.

"Sure—and thanks again for the rescue," she responded, her hand sliding easily into his. Once again, their touch was accentuated by an almost electric current. It permeated the tropical atmosphere, overshadowed the words on their lips and transcended explanation.

Sloan could still feel the warmth of his hand as the bus began its journey back to the hotels. Silently peering out of the window, she was extremely aware of Norwood's presence and could smell his cologne, some kind of tropical spice mixture. She could also feel her heart beating . . . faster than it had in a very long time.

Norwood sat back in his seat, grateful for the darkness which surrounded them. Each one of his senses stood at full alert, his body ready to engage in the most consequential battle of all. He wanted to make love to Sloan.

He knew she would probably slap his face if she was aware of the vivid and very carnal thoughts which occupied his mind at that very moment. Knew that she would be shocked if she could see the unmistakable evidence of his body's response to her which, thankfully, was shrouded by the darkness of the bus's interior. He momentarily chastised himself, thinking that he was possibly no better than the rum-swilling Casanova he'd rescued her from just moments before.

No, that was definitely not the case. His feelings, his reaction, his intentions were not based on any alcoholic influence for one thing. Pure lust was honest enough for him although he recognized that she would probably offer as much resistance to that line of reasoning as she had to Johnson's approach. But he also acknowledged that the weeklong assignment ahead would offer him the opportunity to initiate the necessary strategic maneuvers. Military strategy was nothing new to him, only this time, the tour of duty and assignment would encompass a self-fulfilling objective. It would last seven short days and six long nights. It would be an interesting battle to play out, the intricate nuances still to be developed. He smiled in the darkness. It seemed he was back in action. Miss Whitaker, Miss New York, Miss Uninterested, or whatever she wanted to call herself, did not have a chance.

Four

Kassandra heard it, but continued to lather her hair, the suds dripping down her back in a cascade of thick foam. She ignored the persistence of the phone; the machine would pick up by the sixth ring. Her apartment, a studio in a brownstone on the Upper West Side of Manhattan, was small, but extremely cute. She'd painted all the walls double-bright white, stenciling one wall of the kitchen with a bold diagonal stripe of red that extended from floor to ceiling. Parquet floors, which had recently been stripped and polished, shone brilliantly from the high-gloss varnish. And although the sunlight which filtered into the living room area came from a single large window, the overall effect was bright and sunny. Kassandra had maximized the available light by hanging chrome vertical blinds. They not only reflected brilliantly, but also drew the eye to that side of the room. A lush, three-foot palm tree entirely occupied one corner. Wall hangings housing boldly colored solid squares of fabric within chrome frames, hung in sets of two on either side of the window. Each frame offered a representation of one of the primary colors. Brightly colored pillows covered in red, blue, yellow, and green velvet lined the pullout sofa which doubled as her bed and repeated the theme of stark white accentuated by bold contrasts.

Kitchen utensils in egg-yolk yellow and sun-striped dishes she'd brought with her from Chicago reinforced the vibrancy of the diagonal red stripe on the kitchen wall. It was cheerful and bright, yet antiseptic.

The bathroom, home of the only other window in the tiny apartment, was also painted stark white. Blue and yellow towels hung alternately on a vertical towel rack and pale yellow carpeting covered most of the floor. A large, oval-shaped mirror hung above the pedestal sink. Originally it had been covered with several layers of paint resulting in a hybrid of color but Kassandra had removed it from the wall, painstakingly covered the glass, primed it, and then painted the oval frame a brilliant shade of cornflower blue. It served as the core piece in the room. Each time she looked into the mirror, she realized that the move she'd made halfway across the country had, indeed, been the right one. Decorating the apartment had been a labor of love and a means of expression. In all the time she'd spent with Norwood, she'd never been as content as now, living alone in a city of some nine million people. And although she'd come to the realization that she had, in fact, loved him—it hadn't been enough. There was something else to be done and New York was the only city where it could possibly take place.

Rinsing for the final time, Kassandra realized that she was almost out of conditioner and mentally calculated the pickup at the Duane Reade drugstore on Avenue of the Americas. She stepped out of the shower at exactly 6:05 A.M. realizing that she'd have to hurry to be on time with midtown traffic and rush-hour mayhem.

The move to New York had not been easy. It had taken nearly six months before she'd started receiving bookings and legitimate photography assignments.

Fortunately, the steady work she'd done in Chicago had enabled her to create a "survival" fund. She'd used it to finance that first six months of New York living, including the apartment, her pullout sofa bed, a white wrought-iron bistro set dining area she'd created, and the other odds and ends which she'd painstakingly purchased to pull the tiny apartment together.

VISIONS Agency Inc., a temporary employment agency which focused primarily on placing extremely attractive women and men into highly visibly positions within the fashion, television, and film industries, had offered her assignments immediately. Some were better paying than others, but Kassandra quickly learned how to decide which ones to take on and which ones to decline. Long-term assignments generally spelled more stability and sometimes even offered a higher hourly rate with specific industries also holding more appeal than others.

One assignment at the headquarters of cosmetics giant Revlon, located on Park Avenue at Sixty-eighth Street, had been a gem. Her position as receptionist had not only afforded her the luxury of many complimentary samples of cosmetics, it had actually exposed her to a world of corporate contracts and business alliances.

Kassandra made friends easily. That trait paid off handsomely when one of the public relations managers suggested she call Agency Models Inc. and use his name. She agreed to have dinner with him two weeks later. But she had drawn the line when he had insisted on coming up to her apartment. She was no whore and politely told him so.

Now, as she blow-dried her hair, with a huge yellow body sheet wrapped around her slender body, she realized that in the eight months since she'd left Chicago and Norwood's bed, she hadn't been intimate with anyone. Hadn't had the inclination to nor allowed herself to indulge in the vague opportunities that had come her way. Most of the models she came into contact with on the sets were not in the least bit interested in her. And although she'd kept in contact with Jordan Campbell when she'd first arrived in New York, they hadn't spoken for the last couple of months. It seemed there was a multitude of catalog assignments to be had on the West Coast, not to mention the opportunity for work in television. Jordan had relocated only months after their brief encounter.

The fact that a relationship had developed between them at all had actually been unexpected on both their parts. Kassandra had missed all the signs and had actually been caught off guard. They'd had lunch twice and talked while setting up for different shoots over the course of the monthlong assignment they'd both been booked for. The client, D'arcy MacManus, was known for expecting perfection and the photographer was also known for not letting the client down. That had meant long days, work that lasted well into the night, with overtime not ever being a relevant issue. Perfection in mind, body, and spirit, Kassandra found working with the other professional easy and without compromise.

Kassandra was clearly very different from the gaunt figures of the average model. Although she was tall and slender, there was a voluptuousness about her that was uncharacteristic of most models. An ample bust filled her clothing to dangerous proportions. Her skin was an exotic shade of bronze which only accentuated the long, thick, coal-black mane that hung to her shoulders. It only served to accentuate her keen features. The camera loved her and so did a wide range of clients. The product they would be advertising in the shoot, a popular skin moisturizer, called for the two specimens to represent the picture of healthy, sun-kissed skin. In the final photographs chosen, they relaxed against each other, Kassandra and Jordan back to back, their faces toward the sunlight. The advertisement represented youth, vitality, and sex—the epitome of contemporary American culture—and would sell millions of dollars of face cream to a market that hardly needed it.

Throughout the posing, postulating, and photographing, neither had been willing to acknowledge the growing attraction. Kassandra had never kept it a secret that she shared her life with someone. But one evening, in the innocence of a shared cab ride across town, and the surprise revelation of several mutual acquaintances, they realized that the shoot had somehow sparked a friendship. Neither had foreseen the raw sexual tension that would somehow lead to their ending up in bed together that afternoon. It was only supposed to be a celebration of "wrapping" the photography session. But it had blossomed into that and more and then Norwood walked in. His entrance had seemed surreal at first—then embarrassing.

Kassandra made no attempt to apologize. Nothing could be said to effectively substantiate her behavior and she realized that. Two weeks later, after making the necessary arrangements, she'd boarded a flight to New York City. She left the ring Norwood had given her as a symbol of their impending union on the nightstand with a note simply inscribed "Kass." She didn't have the words to say anything more.

She and Norwood never discussed what had gone wrong in their relationship. And she realized, belatedly, that Jordan had simply been a symptom in the growing rift which existed between them.

Kassandra pushed the play button on the answering machine, continuing to moisturize her body now that her hair had been blown dry. It hung in precision cut fineness about her shoulders, straight, thick, and black, casting an Egyptianlike naturalness about her.

"Hey—this is your sister Anita just checking in to find out what's going on. I hope you're not sitting there listening to this. I figured if I called early enough I could catch you. Listen, I know we're supposed to have dinner this evening but I may be stuck here at the station. We're working on several breaking stories at this very moment and if developments go like I think they may, I'll have to cancel tonight. I'll page you later with an update but wanted to let you know my situation. Anyway, girl, I was looking forward to shooting the breeze with you—I'll talk to you later. Bye."

Kassandra knew from past experience that Anita's position with WNEK Channel 12 News oftentimes called for never-ending dedication and a commitment to getting the job done. She also knew that she would be late if she stopped now to call her. Making a mental note to call the station at the first break in the shoot, Kassandra walked to the closet which lined one wall of the living/bedroom.

After selecting a matching pair of black Jockey for Her underwear, Kassandra stepped into a pair of black jeans and a black turtleneck sweater. Black boots and a black suede jacket completed her attire. A pair of large gold hoop earrings were her only jewelry and no makeup adorned her exotically beautiful face. The makeup artists on a shoot demanded a natural canvas in the same way an artist would, so she never wore makeup to the set. She grabbed her Versace satchel and headed for the door.

Today's shoot would be for Doyle Dane Bernbach, whose client, Dewars Scotch, needed additional shots for its new advertising campaign. Full-page, all-color advertisements would be placed in several nationally distributed fashion magazines which reached the highest circulation in the country. It was a multimillion-dollar contract and DDB was taking no chances in its representation. They'd given final green light on the photographer and the makeup artist, as well as the models. The concept was simple: casual elegance personified by a chic businesswoman having drinks with a male counterpart. The power lunch shortened to a few quick drinks of one particular brand of scotch whiskey spelled success. The readership demographics included the twenty-nine through fifty-five age group—the highest earning group per capita in the continental United States, and the client had spared no expense at the agency's suggestion. The photography shoot was being held in an upscale restaurant on the West Side. Its art deco interior only added to the ambience of the intended look and feel. Exposed brick walls, high ceilings with spot lighting, and huge red leather club chairs completed the formula-for-success environment. Each model would be attired in a business suit from the Armani line, with accessories in jewelry supplied by Bulgari. Classic chic, elegant form, and corporate dynamics all rolled into one full-page advertisement would constitute millions of dollars in revenue for both the client and the industry in general.

Kassandra finished dressing and hailed a cab at 7:07. She had exactly twenty-three minutes to get across town. She managed to make it in nineteen.

It was 6:30 when Cordell Johnson, an extremely well-known and talented New York photographer hired to produce the final product, began shutting down the set, positive that he'd acquired all the shots necessary for a clean page. Kassandra, slightly fatigued but happy to be at the day's end, removed her makeup, changed into her own clothing, and headed crosstown.

She had spoken to Anita and they'd agreed to meet at Fiorello's on Broadway and Sixty-eighth Street across from Lincoln Center for dinner. It was one of her favorite Italian restaurants, offering some of the finest cuisine on the West Side of Manhattan.

Anita, who could always be counted on to be late, did not disappoint. By the time she walked into the bar area, squinting as her eyes adjusted to the dimly lit interior, Kassandra was finishing the glass of zinfandel she'd ordered.

"Girl, you look fantastic—when did you have your hair cut into that blunt style?" Anita asked. They air kissed each other, yet managed to offer a sincere embrace in greeting.

"My stylist came up with it about a month ago. I think he suggested it so that he could get to keep the ends cut really sharp. Now each time I go in for a wash, he absolutely has to do some kind of maintenance work," she answered, making room for Anita alongside her. The seats which lined the length of the crowded bar area had long been occupied by other patrons who were also meeting friends, coworkers, and dinner partners at the popular eating establishment. Some had arrived well before four-thirty, beating the mass exodus from the office buildings surrounding the Lincoln Center area.

"You look pretty cute yourself with that short haircut. It frames your face precisely and brings out your eyes," Kassandra offered sincerely.

"Well, thanks. You know I fought for years against cutting my hair but now that I have, I actually love it. It's so easy to work with and I just wash it every day in the shower, moisturize it, and then put some gel into it to keep it in place."

"Well, it looks great. Remember when we were kids and Mom put those kiddie kit perms in our hair?

Mine didn't take or something went wrong and my hair rebelled. Yours was fine though," Kassandra laughed. The image of her thick mane of hair, rebelling against the mildness of the solution their mother had attempted to use on her unruly locks, sent both women into spasms of laughter.

"Yeah, and then I walked around for the next month thinking I was the cat's pajamas 'cause you still had to keep yours in braids. This was some unruly stuff in those days," Anita said, shaking her head.

"It's only through the advances of technology and the professionalism of some really good stylists that this stuff is tamed, even now," Kassandra admitted. "I asked for a table in the back so that we could really get comfortable. Name your poison so that we can get the ball rolling on our 'girls' night out,'" she added, laughing.

"I'll have whatever you're having. It seems to have put you into a pretty good mood from what I can tell," Anita offered, laughing now, too.

"Bartender, please bring us another round of white zinfandel," she said, just as the maître d' approached to tell them their table for dinner was now ready.

The bartender signaled that he would have the drinks brought directly to their table and they proceeded toward the booths lining each side of the dining area.

"So, tell me, girl, what the heck has been going on with you lately? Thanks again for all the help you and Marc gave me in the move. I have to bring you up to date on everything 'cause when I start to tell my tale of the past year, you won't be able to get a word in edgewise," Kassandra cautioned.

The waiter brought their drinks to the table, placed menus in front of them along with water and bread. The restaurant was well known for its phenomenally delicious "peasant bread." Accompanied by extra virgin olive oil and freshly chopped tomatoes, it was thickly sliced, toasted brown, and covered with a light sprinkling of garlic and cilantro.

"Okay, well, first let me apologize for being late which you know is my normal status anyway. It's just that we're working on several stories and needed the copy for tonight's eleven o'clock news before I left. There's a fire burning in Washington Heights that's been dubbed suspicious, so there's a contingency of police present at the scene conducting an ongoing investigation. Our news team that was on site couldn't get close enough for the cable feed so there was a problem with that. Then, the weather center is tracking a developing storm. It looks to be headed toward some of the Caribbean islands. Girl, it never stops. And as long as news is coming off those Associated Press wires, we have to address any of the stories the general manager feels are most relevant. It's called 'developing news.'"

"Wow, that stuff sounds so exciting. I'll bet you're never bored doing your job," Kassandra said, impressed and proud of her younger sister's solid career path. Sometimes she wondered if she'd chosen the right career, and her description of the unfolding events in her day seemed suddenly dull.

"No, but sometimes it can feel as if you're on the verge of a meltdown. I mean there are some stories that really get to you and if you have one too many of those in a row, it affects how you relate when you leave the station. That's why every now and then, I need a mental health moment. So, let's drink to mental health," Anita laughed, lifting her glass in tribute.

"Most definitely—I'll also add to that. I'd also like to drink to getting out of town before sundown, which is what I did in Chicago. It was definitely sundown on my relationship with Norwood. If I had stayed any longer, the 'relationship sheriff' would have been looking to run me out of town 'cause I did some bad things," she said, her voice slowing and deepening to imply the harshness of her behavior. They both laughed then at the absurdity of the concept.

"So, I guess it's over with Norwood then?" Anita asked. She had known of Norwood only via telephone, but had come to develop a fondness for her sister's obviously talented boyfriend. Some of the photographs he'd taken had even been featured in a coffee table book featuring young up-and-coming photographers. She and Marc had taken pride in what they hoped would soon be another family member. When Kass had called and told them of the split, they'd both been deeply saddened, feeling as though they had lost someone they both admired. But Kass was her sister, her friend, her blood. And since her return to New York, she'd done everything in her power to give her the support she knew she needed. Although Anita was happily married to her childhood sweetheart, she had always been intrigued by Kassandra's exotic lifestyle. It seemed fast paced and exciting, included photographers, agents, actors, and oftentimes was hectic. At least, that was the outward appearance. But Anita was also practical, and she wanted happiness for her sister in the final analysis.

"Yeah, it's definitely over. The last time I spoke with him was almost one year ago. I left his ring with a note that, I am sorry to say, didn't even include an apology. It was almost as if I wanted to destroy any feelings he'd had for me. I honestly think I blew it and for the life of me I cannot tell you why I was so cold." Her voice sounded like a whisper as she uttered the last words.

"Maybe you didn't really love Norwood," Anita said quietly, hoping that she was wrong.

"No, I think I did, but you know I really think I was

scared. Scared of the commitment he was asking me to make and scared that I would have had to give up my dream of becoming a success in the 'industry,'" she added quickly.

"Wow, I sincerely hope you are not having second thoughts on any of this. After what you just told me, it doesn't sound like it's something you'd be able to go back on after all this time. Girl, as fine as Norwood is, he's probably deep into something else by now." The photograph he'd sent, of him and Kassandra standing in front of Chicago's Navy Pier, had done them both justice. Anita remembered he had one of the most masculine, yet handsome faces she'd seen in a long time. Even Marc, whom she loved deeply, paled somewhat in comparison.

"You're probably right and I'm not even trying to play a game of looking over my shoulder. But I will tell you this, in all the months that I've been here in New York, I haven't come across anyone who can hold a candle to Norwood. Nor have I gone out on a date with anyone even remotely as exciting or attractive. I haven't slept with anybody in the past nine months," she revealed, a note of defiance apparent in her voice.

In the silence that followed, Kassandra picked up her menu and scanned it. She needed that time to reflect on all that she had revealed to both Anita and to herself.

It only took a few moments for her to decide on the veal marsala, polenta, and broccoli rabe. As she placed the menu on the table and looked up, she realized that Anita was staring at her, mouth open in exaggerated shock, her statement still lingering heavily in the air.

"Are you serious?" she asked. "I mean, I know you haven't had much extra time with pulling the apartment together, going on job interviews, and making the rounds to modeling agencies and all. I thought that you were at least dating casually though," she added. "Kass, with your looks, it doesn't seem possible that you wouldn't be out every Friday and Saturday night," Anita ended.

"That is such a crock," Kassandra countered. "Look, let's order dinner 'cause I'm starving. Then we can get really discuss the grim details of single life in a big city and how us 'beautiful people' have to cope with loneliness, separation, and the pitfalls of living in a society that does not encourage interaction."

Anita laughed as she scanned the menu. "I guess I shouldn't complain when Marc leaves his dirty clothes on the bathroom floor, or doesn't run the dishwasher as often as I'd like."

"No, don't complain, girl. 'Cause the one thing I'm learning day by day is that men come with a price tag—and it's usually marked 'may need assembly and great care.' That's where we come in. We have to put them together and then hope that they will continue to operate efficiently, smoothly, and function at optimum levels. And then, sometimes, it's us that need to be tagged," she ended.

Anita laughed. "You're very funny and probably right. I think I'll have the eggplant rollatini and a Caesar salad with anchovies. Marc won't allow me to have anchovies with him around so I'd better take advantage of his absence. He says they make me feisty."

"I've never heard that one before," Kassandra laughed, also placing her order.

"Neither had I, but he swears it's true. We'll see tonight when I get home," Anita said, then winked one eye.

"I'm glad we decided to get together for dinner. I needed to be able to have some 'open mike time' and you're the best audience ever," Kassandra stated, genuine fondness in her voice.

"So am I, although between the fires raging in the Bronx and the storms brewing in the Caribbean, it's any wonder I was able to leave the studio."

"Well, let's have another drink to that—fire, water, and earth—or is it Earth, Wind and Fire?"

"Great idea—only let's change that order to ginger ale for the next round," Anita said. She was thinking ahead. The long subway and bus ride ahead of her to the Queens neighborhood she and Marc called home would not be bearable if she was half tanked. Thank God it was Thursday. Fridays were always a challenge because they had to ready the schedule for the weekend news as well.

"Fine, it's probably less calories, too," Kassandra added.

Anita smiled then, knowing that nutrition and calorie counting were never far from Kassandra's mind. She also realized that she hadn't altogether put the day's events out of her mind. The news room and the information from the Associated Press news wires, which had been relayed just before she left, were still fresh in her mind. She hoped that by the next morning when she returned to her desk as assistant producer, the fire would be out; hopefully without the loss of life, and with relative ease. However, the tropical depression developing in the Caribbean had been upgraded to a storm warning in the short span of nine hours. Anita knew that it held the potential for far greater damage thereby posing a major threat to the region. Only time would tell how that story would play out. Time and the days ahead.

She turned her attention back to Kassandra just in time to hear her say "What does a girl have to do to get some action in this town?" and laughed.

"Tell me, Kass, just how desperate are you?" she whispered, the teasing in her voice accompanied by a raised eyebrow.

"Anita, don't even go there. Desperate is not part of my vocabulary but things are getting a little tight if you know what I mean."

"You know, seriously, there is someone at the station who was going through a divorce but he's reportedly a big dog, girl. You don't want to mess with this dude 'cause he's got a reputation for being a serious playa." She figured forewarned was forearmed, though she was pretty sure that Kassandra could take care of herself in almost any arena.

"Listen, I am a big girl, as they say. If he's fine, got a good career, and got his stuff together, you know he's gotta be a playa. That's only 'cause there's so much for him to handle that he probably has to juggle. Give me the benefit of the doubt. I ain't no slouch, girl," she added, taking a sip of her ginger ale.

"Well, let me do a little research first and then I'll get back to you. If what I'm thinking is correct, you may have to thank me for many years to come, girl," Anita said, shaking her head slowly. "'Cause this brother is fine as they come. He could make a sister think about leaving home," she added, laughing.

"Oh, no, you did not go there. Anita, you know darn well that you ain't going nowhere without Marc. That man is your sun, your moon, your stars, your destiny. I've seen the way you two look at each other. Actually it's downright nauseating sometimes the amount of feel-good vibes that flow between you two," Kassandra responded, shaking her head in feigned disbelief.

Anita laughed, acknowledging that she did in fact love her husband very much. Their marriage of three years was solidly intact. But there was no denying that

WNEK's main cameraman, who was rumored to be newly divorced, caused many of the females in Studio 1A to salivate each time they encountered him on the set, in the corridor, in an elevator, or in the company cafeteria.

He would most certainly be a challenge if even half the rumors were accurate. If it was anyone other than Kassandra, she'd say forget it. But with her beauty, and a successful modeling career poised to take off, Kassandra Algernon was a force to be reckoned with. Perhaps she'd be just the challenge that he'd be willing to rise to. Rumor had it that he was on the brink of breaking into music videos.

Now, all she had to do was think of a way to bring Kassandra to the attention of Karsten Battle.

Five

Barbados

The rhythmic sounds of waves lapping at the shore-line woke Sloan from a deep and restful slumber. She stretched her body lazily, reaching one arm up and then the other before she came to full wakefulness. The realization of her whereabouts slowly filtered through her consciousness and she smiled, swinging her legs to the floor.

Glancing at the clock radio on the night table, she realized it was only 7:30 in the morning. She and Jodi had agreed to meet at the hotel's outdoor restaurant for breakfast at 8:00.

Sloan quickly showered and pulled on the one pair of shorts contained in her bag along with a striped yellow top and the black sandals she'd worn the night before. After washing her hair in the shower, she combed a leave-in conditioner through it, tying it into a single braid which hung heavily down her back. She knew that the sun would only enhance the conditioning properties. Her camera case was slung haphazardly over one shoulder as she exited the room. Sloan was eager to capture the early morning sunlight in photographs of the coastline, the pearl-colored beach, and the multicolored shades of blue coming off the bay.

* * *

Jodi, polishing off a cup of coffee, turned her face up to catch each one of the sun's early morning rays and delighted in its warmth. She felt like a kitten sunning itself in its favorite spot, which for her was the Caribbean.

"Hey, I see you survived last evening's entertainment after all," she said as Sloan joined her. Jodi laughed then, remembering the look on Johnson Dade's face as he'd come back to the table after a short conversation with Sloan and Norwood King.

"Just barely. I think this trip is going to be a little more interesting than I'd have predicted," Sloan answered, shaking her head in amazement. The waitress brought orange juice and coffee. She began filling their cups.

"Yeah, I know what you mean. Lorenzo is pretty interesting. Did you ever notice that West Coast men seem to be more laid-back than those from the East?" Jodi asked. The question hung in the air as both women compared notes.

"Well, between Johnson Dade and the other guy from Chicago, Norwood, or whatever his name is, I don't know which one is more intense. Actually, that Dade character reminds me a little too much of my ex—he's off the hook," she said.

"I know what you mean. He seems to be on some kind of quest and I don't mean to find the most unique angle to the story or the photograph which best captured the spirit of the entire festival. What the heck happened before the bus left Sunbury Plantation? Johnson Dade got on looking like he'd just been insulted and you and Chicago looked like two cats who'd just swallowed a very large canary," Jodi said.

Jodi seemed on the verge of discovering a huge

secret, but Sloan knew that she could confide in her—to a certain extent.

"Girl, things were about to get very ugly and then Norwood ended up doing some kind of macho thing like he was coming to my rescue. I guess Johnson had had one too many rum and Cokes and was feeling his oats. Anyway, I was really glad to just get on the bus and not have to deal with either of them," she said. "No comingling is my motto," Sloan offered. She couldn't bring herself to acknowledge that Norwood had actually kissed her. Nor could she accept the fact that she'd responded.

"Look, I think ninety percent of the industry is genuinely interested in getting the job done. There is a small percentage, though, that would just as soon also entertain some kind of 'hookup' while they're off on these exotic locations. You know how men are," Jodi stated flatly.

"Yeah, I think I saw a little of that last night—I guess I've been a little naïve," Sloan countered. "But I'll tell you one thing, they're both barking up the wrong tree 'cause marriage to my ex taught me the ropes. Those guys are grade A amateurs compared to him." Her resolution to totally forget the events of the past night were even more solidly reinforced in her mind as she spoke. It had all been a huge mistake. She was resolved to treat it as though it hadn't happened at all.

Jodi laughed. "I kind of figured you could take care of yourself so I wasn't really worried—at least not when that Johnson character started laying tracks anyway. But I have to tell you that the guy from Chicago, Norwood, or whatever his name is, is really fine. He has one of the tightest rear ends I've seen in a long time. Not to mention legs that seem to go on forever and the added bonus of being just a little bowlegged. Very sexy," she added, her head immersed in the breakfast menu.

"I hadn't noticed all that. He seems to be a decent photographer though and said he has his own studio. Anyone who can earn a living in photography has my respect," Sloan said and signaled the waitress. She carefully avoided mentioning the kiss. She wasn't sure if her reaction had been a result of his timely rescue, a form of gratitude, or if it had been pure lust. She did know that she planned to avoid him for the remainder of the trip. She would do everything in her power to stay out of his way.

After breakfast, the beach beckoned and they both headed toward the shoreline. The sand reflected the sunlight brilliantly and they walked slowly, familiarizing themselves with their surroundings. Sloan shot an entire roll of film capturing sailboats, jet-skiers, and parasailers, while she marveled at many of the additional hotel properties which stretched out along the beach. The Caribbean was a frequent destination for travelers from England, Canada, and Germany, and many were filled to capacity with tourists from Europe who had decided to escape the harsh reality of winter.

"Since our pickup time is not until a little after eleven A.M., why don't we go in for a while?" Jodi asked, nodding toward the water. "I'm willing to roll up my jeans and let loose," she added.

"You go ahead. I'm going to check with the front desk about the luggage. Maybe they have heard something by now," Sloan answered as she repacked her camera case.

"Yeah, you're right. I guess I'm so eager to have some fun and relaxation that I'm willing to sacrifice the more practical points."

"I understand though. I guess I'm so used to being in charge of things that I don't allow myself to relax until everything is in place," Sloan responded, almost apologetically.

"Well, that's a good trait actually. Good looking out, as they say," Jodi laughed and joined her as they both walked to the hotel's reception desk.

They were relieved to learn that, although it was only 10:15, someone had already called from the airport and reported the wayward luggage as having been found.

"Should we try and get a ride to the airport to pick it up?" Sloan asked, hoping that there was some way that this could be arranged.

"No, that won't be necessary. We instructed them to send all three bags here. We understand they should arrive sometime this afternoon," the clerk stated, his crisp British tone apparent though softened by the Barbadian accent. He was more than accustomed to the day-to-day matters of hotel management and in reassuring its guests.

"Great, then we just have to make do until later today." Sloan was already rummaging through her large shoulder bag for her copy of the agenda. "Oh, it's a trip to the oldest church on the island and then a tour around the island and lunch, so I guess whatever we have on will have to do."

"I am so glad that they found the luggage. I was having nightmares thinking that it might not ever be found and we'd have to get through the next several days with the threads on our backs," Jodi laughed.

"Thank God. We were definitely lucky 'cause sometimes they really can't find the bags. Then you have to file a report and it takes months to be compensated. Well, I guess we can go up and get whatever we need for today's trip. I'm going to get some more film and stuff."

"Okay, I'll meet you back down here at eleven-fifteen. You know, I think I have a little blue tube top which I remember grabbing out of the dryer at the last minute. Thank goodness I stuffed that into my pocketbook. Otherwise, I'd still be wearing that red-striped halter that I had on last night. And these jeans are hot but I refuse to cut them off because when I get back to New York, I'll need them."

"Yeah, tell me about it. Luckily, I had this pair of shorts and one other top stuck into my carry-on bag. Otherwise, I'd be wearing the jeans I had on yesterday, too. All right, see you in about forty-five minutes." She wondered if the third wheel of their party would be on time, noting that he'd not been seen during breakfast or their brief walk on the beach. *Well, I'm not his keeper, that's for sure,* she thought, as she prepared for the day's activities.

Sloan washed the conditioner out of her hair, and brushed it back into one long braid. Large oval hoop earrings were her only jewelry except a watch and one gold bangle which adorned the same wrist. She then applied sunscreen to her arms and legs. Mascara, tinted sunscreen, and lip gloss were her only makeup. She proceeded to repack her camera case, including two rolls of 200 speed film, a UV polarizer to screen out the sun's ultraviolet rays, and a pack of double AA batteries, just in case.

Oversize black sunglasses hid much of her face as she made her way to the lobby. Checking her watch, she realized it was 11:15 exactly. Jodi was nowhere in sight. The afternoon sun, already high in the sky, was beginning to send the temperature well into the upper eighties. Sloan could feel the tropical heat seeping into her pores and was glad that she'd spritzed on the Victoria's Secret Pear Glacee before leaving her room. It made her feel cooler. She'd also packed a small atomizer into her bag for a refreshing blast any time during the course of the day. Vivid memories of the heat-filled afternoons here on the island were fresh in her mind and she knew that the midmorning temperature was a mild precursor of what was to come. Evenings were a delightfully cool but comfortable range of seventy-five degrees and above.

At 11:30, Sloan called Jodi's room. The line was busy. The bus was nowhere in sight. Sloan, feeling the need to do something, pulled out the Nikon manual which had accompanied her camera's purchase and flipped through the pages.

She was firmly engrossed in a chapter outlining depth of field and its nuances in capturing quality photos when Norwood strode into the lobby.

"Good morning."

"Hi, where's the girl from AP?" he asked formally.

"She's getting ready. The bus is late." Sloan wanted to avoid conversation with him, feeling that it would somehow align her in some way. She also wanted to avoid looking at him but found her eyes drawn to his jeans and gray T-shirt, noting the way they fit his athletically trim body.

"Hey, sorry I'm late, or am I?" Jodi asked, bounding into the lobby looking around for a sign of their transportation as she looked at her watch. It read 11:36.

"I was on the phone with my editor in New York and forgot about the time. But I'm glad I'm not late. I guess last night's on-time schedule had me fooled," she offered, sitting down on the bench next to Sloan. She wore a light blue tank top and her black jeans. She'd rolled them up to ankle length in an effort to try and avoid the midday heat.

"I told you they'd be late from time to time. It all depends on what the other pickups are doing. Sometimes the schedule gets thrown off completely just because one person is extremely late. It only serves to back up the pickup of each of the other journalists staying at the other hotels," Sloan explained. As she finished, the roar of the bus's engines could be heard and both stood up, ready to get the day's events under way.

They entered the coolness of the air-conditioned bus and were extremely grateful for the respite from the afternoon heat. Due to the location of the afternoon's destination, the pickup times had been reversed and most of the other journalists were already on board.

Jodi, Sloan, and Norwood each walked toward the back of the bus but Jodi stopped to talk to Lorenzo.

"I hope you're up for the sight-seeing afternoon of a lifetime," he said and she laughed. "Our guide says we're going to tour the entire island." Jodi then sat in the window seat of the aisle opposite him and they lapsed into easy conversation.

Sloan continued onward and slipped into the next empty window seat she came to, while Norwood continued on to the farthest row in the back of the vehicle. She still wore her sunglasses and her vision had not adjusted to the dimness inside the bus. Johnson Dade sat directly behind her. He was delighted that she'd chosen a seat which gave him an excellent vantage point for conversation.

"So, how did you sleep?" he whispered softly into her ear as she sat back into the cushioned seat. Recognizing his voice immediately, Sloan almost got up and moved but she didn't want to appear to be rattled by his presence. She decided to remain seated.

"Fine, and yourself?" she managed to grind out without turning around.

"Okay—I had a couple of interesting dreams though," he offered, and Sloan knew that she had only to seem even remotely intrigued and he'd elaborate. She changed the subject quickly.

"It's a lovely day, clear blue skies without a hint of

clouds," she offered, hoping that weather would be a safe enough subject.

"Yeah, it is," he responded, clearly disappointed that she hadn't responded to his obvious insinuation about her in his dream. He had a headache and his mouth was dry. He wanted a drink of water or anything cold and wet in the worst way. More than that, he wanted to fix the major pain in his butt, the Chicago arm wrestler.

Meanwhile, Norwood sat in the rear of the bus. He'd chosen the seat for observation. Intent on somehow managing his objective, he'd come to the conclusion that by observation, he could better gauge his subject. He would then gather the information he needed to fully assess, approach, and overcome the target. Strategic planning had always been his forte.

St. Nicholas Abbey was the site of the oldest church on the island. Built in late 1789, its oak interior was replete with a pipe organ and the design of that century throughout. Behind it stood a cemetery which still bore the remains of many of the island's earliest settlers with headstones marked by surnames like Curry, Rowe, Maycock, Babbington, and Drew. Set high among the hills, the marvelous precipice offered a breathtaking view of the southern coast of the island.

The journalists and photographers had a field day taking photos of the coastal scenes, as well as the impressive structure of the chapel with its formal arch-constructed steeple.

Norwood found himself shooting scenes that he knew he would have no use for in the context of his assignment, but he recognized the beauty of the location as well as its importance to the history of the island itself. He found the grave sites fascinating and was shooting his second roll of film when he noticed that

Sloan had begun shooting scenes of the coastline some fifteen hundred feet below with a telephoto lens. He watched with mild curiosity as she handled her camera much the same way he did—as an extension of herself. He realized that she was probably extremely good at what she did. His mind shifted back to the kiss they'd shared the night before and he smiled inwardly, chastising himself for his roguish thoughts.

He continued to shoot the gravestones, fascinated with the condition and preservation of the area, as well as the artistry evident on each headstone.

Immersed in capturing as much of the island's beauty and culture as possible, Sloan was focused on the unique trees inhabiting much of the cemetery area. They appeared to be almost petrified, were without leaves, and shone ash white against the blue skies and the sunlight. Their starkness contrasted beautifully with the dark shadows cast by the gravestones and she alternated her shots, carefully adjusting her camera's f-stops to allow for the change in available light. So intent was she on getting it right that she wasn't aware of her fellow photographer.

Norwood came up behind her and spoke very quietly. "Make sure that you're controlling the aperture on those shots of the trees. There is an extensive amount of sunlight coming in," he advised calmly.

Sloan looked up then, her concentration broken, genuine surprise written on her face.

"Thanks, I've been closing it down by an eighth each time I take a shot. They are so beautifully stark that I couldn't pass them up. I think they'll make great fill photos to accompany my piece," she said quickly. She avoided making eye contact with him although they stood only a shoulder's width apart.

He realized then that she was a little unsure of his motivations and that made him smile.

Even white teeth showing, with a shadow of a dimple on one side of his mustache, he was even more handsome in the daylight. Sloan realized that although he seemed to take his work seriously, his approach to her was definitely flirtatious.

"Look, thanks for the interest and everything, but I'm fine. I've had quite a few photographs published in the past couple of years. I think I know what I'm doing."

"I'm sure you do. It was just a suggestion. Don't be so touchy. I wasn't criticizing your work. Everybody can use a little help sometimes," he added then. What he really wanted to say was, "Don't be afraid of me, I won't bite," but he knew that was not altogether true—especially when he realized his true intentions.

"Yeah. Thanks again for the suggestion," she said as she prepared to return to the front of the church where the bus was waiting. They made their way slowly toward their fellow journalists who were still admiring the historic site as well as browsing the local vendors who'd set up shop with everything from jewelry and seashells to T-shirts and locally crafted items.

They entered the bus some minutes later, eager to reach their next destination. Lunch would be served at a seaside restaurant overlooking the breathtaking view of the southern coast's shoreline. The buffet meal consisted of large aluminum serving tins filled with oxtail stew, rice and peas, green salad, green banana, brown stew chicken, steamed cabbage and carrots, and steamed fish. Cold beer, soft drinks, and rum punch were also served at the bar inside the restaurant.

Long picnic-like tables and benches were set up both inside and out offering either the spectacular view or the solitude of the restaurant's interior. Most of the members of the press chose the indoor benches, saving the sun, the view, and the outdoors for after the meal.

Sloan and Jodi found themselves at a table which encompassed most of the other passengers on their bus, as well as some newly arrived journalists.

Johnson Dade had chosen to sit outside, soaking up as much sun as his reddish brown complexion could absorb. He felt right at home within any group and had struck up an easy comraderie with several of the Canadian journalists. He kept a wary eye on "Chicago" and was surprised to see that the babe from New York was having nothing to do with him either. He'd already come to the conclusion that she was an uptight, stuck-up, parsnickety yuppie. But getting into her pants would be a coup—over her and that creep from Chicago, or the Midwest, or wherever he was from. He'd have to address that issue much later because inside his head was a drone of thumping sounds; the pain reliever he'd consumed earlier was obviously ineffective against this level of discomfort. He decided to grab a Heineken from the refreshments stacked up at the counter, making his way past the other journalists seated inside. He avoided making eye contact with any of them.

Norwood and Lorenzo sat on the opposite sides at the end of the table and were both engaged in consuming lunch with a vengeance when Sloan and Jodi sat down. They looked up, smiled, and continued their conversation without pausing or changing the subject.

"Man, I'm telling you, in L.A., it's incredibly different. The people resort to cosmetic surgery at the drop of a hat. And anybody who is not in 'the business' is just not even on the planet in their minds. It's unbelievably plastic," Lorenzo stated flatly.

"Well, Chicago does not have that problem at all. It's ironic how comfortable I am there 'cause my parents were actually born here, somewhere in Christ

Church. I promised to try and get someone to take me there while I'm here so I can take a few photos. The family has all disbursed to the States now, mainly large cities like Chicago and New York. Have you ever given any thought to going East?" Norwood asked then. His plate had already been reduced in volume by at least half, but it still held a good amount of food. Little by little, he was putting a sizable dent in it. His lean physique was the product of two things—a rapid metabolism and good genes. His high energy and lean stance had served him all throughout his years of military service.

"Not really. Los Angeles is all I know, man, but I sure get tired of the superficial element. I think New York would be like a breath of fresh, arctic air at this point. I've been there twice and definitely liked what I saw. The energy was off the hook," he added.

Sloan, engaged in conversation with both Jodi and two other journalists from England, Trevor and Garry, found that she was having a difficult time following their conversation. Her concentration would drift in and out, hone in on the topic under discussion, and allow her to offer an appropriate if not thought-provoking comment, then her focus would drift away again. All of her resolve, all of her control was devoted to not making any eye contact with the other end of the table.

Norwood, who was casually sipping a beer, watched her discreetly. And he realized although she did everything she could to avoid making eye contact with him, that she was still very much aware of him. He knew he had his work cut out for him but he also knew that he would proceed carefully. Very carefully. Stealth had been the mandate of his unit when he'd been stationed in Europe. The 716th Unit of B Battery, Seventh Artillery of the 169th Brigade prided itself on maneuverability under fire. Quick, quiet, and effective. Stealth consistently proved a highly effective methodology.

Norwood knew that, in this case, it would prove invaluable. He realized that the target was not only sensitive, she was wary. Those two qualities made for a more complex maneuver. But she was damn well worth it. And although the nagging reminder of his failed relationship with Kassandra lingered within his psyche, he rationalized that he was not out for a lifetime commitment, just a little island romance.

The kiss they'd shared had been unexpected. He'd done it almost as a warning to her on how not to behave because he'd felt she was leading Johnson Dade on. But it had held surprise for him also. Not only had she attempted to coldcock him, but then she'd actually turned the tables around and darn near rocked his world. She'd unexpectedly responded to him, fitting into his arms as if she belonged there. And though he didn't want to admit or acknowledge it, he'd reluctantly ended the contact because he hadn't wanted her to know just how much she'd affected him. More than he wanted to admit.

At the very least, she was a paradox. At best, she was a hellcat. Either way, it confirmed that the Barbados Jazz Festival, held in the place of his birth, was promising to be an interesting assignment in more ways than one.

Six

The segment producer glanced quickly at his watch, gave the signal to begin taping and held his breath. All eyes in the production booth were on the show's host, who began delivering the opening monologue. Camera one reined in for a tight one-on-one shot.

Karsten Battle carefully refocused, pulling out slightly as he brought the image in to its sharpest point. The producer held up two fingers, the signal used to open up to a two-shot which would then include the show's morning guest, the Reverend Al Sharpton. Precision timing, nerves of steel and hands that instinctively knew the location of each feature on the CCD, or charge-coupled-device, state-of-the-art videotape equipment, were a must. He carefully continued to make sure that the images being broadcast through his camera lens to the stations picking up WNEK Channel 12's signal were crystal clear, sharp, and in focus. That was the easy part and the part that came naturally.

Karsten Battle had fine-tuned those qualities early on and actually was at the point where he stood ready to entertain the next level in his career plan—music videos. The few loose ends he was just now pulling together would make it a goal within reach. He was determined to make it a reality—a goal attained. And at that time, he would be positioned to take advantage of and bring to fruition all that he'd dreamed of. Along the way, he'd made some mistakes and it had cost him, but he'd grown from the experiences. And learned a great deal. He smiled now in spite of the complex feelings he was experiencing. His newfound happiness was being challenged, as usual, by his internal turmoil.

Duality was no stranger to him. Karsten had always lived on the edge of two worlds. Born of mixed parentage, he had his Brooklyn-born mother's combination of bone-deep convictions, deep sensuality, and full-strength vinegar, ultimately wrapped in a coating of rich chocolate brown. Her beauty both exotic and ethereal at the same time, Ethelyn Battle's teenage love affair with an Italian shoemaker's son from Bay Ridge should have culminated in a product marked "Made in Italy"; instead it produced a chasm within a second-generation Italian family and confusion in a Bedford Stuyvesant home. Tightly knit soft curls the color of deep auburn tinged with golden brown highlights offset a complexion that was even and warm, and covered every square inch of Karsten's body. His physique took on the proportions of a Greek Adonis when he was about fifteen, causing some to speculate about how often he worked out in a gym or health club. But it all came naturally. He enhanced it by lifting a set of barbells daily and running whenever he got the chance.

His eyes, the unusual color of caramel burned just a tad darker, were fringed by lashes that were the envy of anyone who dared get close enough to measure and did nothing to hide the intensity of his stare.

He spent a good portion of his teen years under the hood of a beat-up 1963 Rambler. The slant fin engine had been a breeze to repair, especially after he'd finished the second year of Introduction to Mechanics–Level IV during his sophomore year at Automotive Technical High School. And when he turned seventeen and finally got the engine to turn over for the first time, he slowly and methodically taught himself to drive behind the track at Midwood High School.

His Italian grandfather's love of fast cars and fine women, as well as an appreciation of fine Italian suits and leather goods, was ingrained in his genes. But the blueprint for an inherited trait of no-nonsense had been passed down from the sensibilities of his African American mother's family. Voted "Most Likely to Succeed at Anything" in his senior year of high school, he was the hero of the black kids and the envy of the whites. Cool was never a façade where Karsten was concerned—it was natural. Inborn. And he couldn't have explained it if he'd tried. But that had never become necessary.

The fact that there weren't any girls enrolled at his school was actually a plus; he'd been identified as a chick-magnet from the time he was only six months old. It was then that his mother had declared somewhat defiantly, "Some mother's daughter is sure gonna suffer," as she held her son up toward the ceiling, looked up at his smiling, toothless grin, and fell in love with him for the first time. It had taken Ethelyn one hundred and eighty days to forgive his father, accept herself, and include her son into her heart, her soul, her life. She instinctively knew that it would happen that way over and over again for him throughout the years; despite his good looks, love would not come easily to him or for him.

She prayed that it wouldn't cause as much pain as her love for his father had caused her to endure. His looks and personality ensured that his life would unfold as only those who are both exceedingly charming and attractive can—with great privilege and favor. His only detraction would be a psychological stance that had been unavoidably tempered by early childhood experiences. That was the bad news. The good news was that no entitlement issues would ever bog him down with unfulfilled dreams. He'd make his way of his own accord, with talent, perseverance, and sheer conviction. Photography had come as a God-given gift.

Karsten's love of photography developed rapidly and unexpectedly when his mother gave him a Yashica A box camera as an eighteenth birthday present. She'd purchased the portrait camera from a pawn shop on Fulton Street for eleven dollars, the shop owner guaranteeing her that it should have cost at least double that. Included in the deal had been its original brown leather case and flash "fan." The oddly shaped camera was often the cause of conversation; Polaroid instant cameras were the current rage and this didn't come close. But the photos it produced far outclassed its competition and he'd gotten it to work by reading and rereading its manual much the same way he'd managed to figure out auto mechanics—one step at a time with thorough concentration and application.

Karsten mastered its operation that summer, realized that he was fascinated by the unexpected results of the camera's function, and enrolled at Pratt Institute for the coming fall semester. The realization that automotive engineering, as they'd elected to dub it, might not be what he wanted to do with his life came to him spontaneously. He'd taken to photography much the same way that he'd taken on auto mechanics but with one very distinct difference. The promise of a future.

With mechanics, he'd never envisioned a lucrative future—the automobile shop was an environment which included grease and dirt on a daily basis. In photography, the finished product was clean, clear and communicative, which was what had drawn him to the craft. With the intrinsic power held by the medium of television, it was a natural draw. In terms of a media type, it was the ultimate in creativity as well as having the ability to provide an extensive reach to any viewing audience. He enrolled at Pratt Institute in the fall of 1973 to master his craft.

The thing he could not seem to master, and had never understood, was the whole "one woman/one man" theory. Granted, his mother's example in life had not been a fairy-tale romance to be passed down from mother to son. In fact, his father's family had not wanted anything to do with him, had never officially acknowledged him. But he'd known of them and that had been enough. He'd promised himself that he would never treat family the way they'd treated him during the years he was growing up. The overlooked occasions, the missed birthdays, the countless denials. He was more than painfully aware of the fact that he was somehow part of some shameful secret—that the product of his mother and father's ill-fated union was somehow an unacceptable reality. And because of that, he vowed never to put any child of his through that same ordeal.

The Brooklyn undergraduate school for the arts, located downtown in the center of a neighborhood on the cutting edge of gentrification, proved to be an excellent training ground for his increasing interest in and respect for photography. Drawing students from across the continental United States based on its history of exceptional training and its ability to churn out some of the best in architecture, design, and film as well as other creative arts, Pratt Institute proved to be a formidable training ground for the innate talent Karsten possessed.

Four and a half years and one degree in the arts later, he found himself behind the main cameras at the studios of WNEK Channel 12 News.

Karsten felt right at home almost immediately, especially after word had gotten around that he was single, eligible, and straight. He'd never bothered to explain to anyone that he was in fact very much married to a fellow photographer who happened to be a brilliant writer for one of the city's most widely circulated newspapers.

He'd managed to keep those details to himself for one reason and one reason only—he'd never believed it would last. In fact, they'd only married after Sloan had become pregnant several months before graduation. It pained him to think of his unborn child coming into the world under circumstances that matched and equaled his own birth and childhood. So he badgered her until she finally gave in, although she, too, questioned the validity of a marriage borne not of love but of circumstance.

They'd met in photography class although neither could remember when the friendship changed to more than that. But they both remembered a weekend stay at her apartment off campus that blossomed into his returning night after night over the course of the next several months. They also both realized with some disappointment that it was probably doomed from the start.

But it had never really been about the emotional tie between them; they'd relied on each other more as fellow photography buffs allowing for the convenience of sharing the same space. And it came apart just as quickly as they both realized that neither had the maturity nor the self-discipline required to foster such a union. By then, Sloan was six weeks pregnant. She miscarried at the end of her first trimester and only two weeks after they'd gone through the hastily performed ceremony at City Hall in lower Manhattan.

Karsten, for the most part, was the first to breach the sanctity of the marriage. In fact, almost immediately after Sloan had miscarried, he realized that his commitment was not to her, but in fact to an unborn fetus that would not now or ever reach maturity. In the very same way the relationship had never had the chance to grow and expand, so had their unborn child never progressed to a survivable stage. So he chalked the whole thing up to the laws of nature and decided to move on with his life.

Karsten bailed both emotionally as well as physically and Sloan paid the price in the next year for something that no one should ever have to pay for—idealism.

It was almost as if Karsten had come to the conclusion that a failed marriage was also a license to foster as many encounters with available women as possible. He behaved more roguishly than the average single man, knowing that he could not offer any level of real commitment with the women he became involved with so long as the certificate of marriage between him and Sloan still existed.

Unfortunately, the women he attracted had no qualms about their attempts to establish a "priority" status in his life and, on many occasions, left arbitrary pieces of evidence of their liaisons in the most obvious places. They were unaware of his "lame duck" marriage; it wouldn't have made much of a difference anyway.

Although he never actually revealed that he was in fact "married," a dog usually knows when it's trespassing on another's turf. In the same way, many of

Karsten's hastily chosen lovers seemed hell-bent on making sure that whoever else he was involved with was also aware of their presence in his life. Thus the unexplained hang-ups on the telephone during the middle of the night, the intimate pieces of apparel left behind, and the seemingly innocent looks delivered with malice aforethought from neighbors, all added up.

Never one to throw in the towel in defeat, Sloan realized with some regret that the marriage had no future. And she'd be damned if she'd allow a mistake in birth control to cause her to be humiliated for the rest of her life. She actually believed that, at some point, perhaps they'd both come to their senses and realize that it was quite possible that they were the best thing either of them had going. But it never happened. And as time went on, it became increasingly apparent that it never would.

The late night phone calls with hang-ups and the resulting interrupted sleep, the unmistakable attachment to a young woman who'd just moved into the building, and the unexplainable appearance of a pair of panty hose in Karsten's camera bag one Sunday morning when he'd gone into it at the breakfast table were more than she was willing to tolerate.

Sloan filed for divorce and demanded that Karsten move out, which he did. But New York divorce laws constitute at least one year of separation with the involved parties living under separate quarters, so they both had to wait for the final papers. Meanwhile, life went on.

Karsten's dreams had expanded from his work as a cameraman for network television to include directing and video production. His love of music, which came naturally to him through the music his mother had played throughout his childhood, now challenged and inspired his creativity. Marvin Gaye, Buddy Miles, Ramsey Lewis, Nina Simone had all played a part in his childhood. They were part of the core of his existence because they had been part of the repertoire of music he'd been exposed to from the time he was able to recognize that music was a constant backdrop to their daily lives. Ethelyn Battle had loved anything with strong musicianship as part of its background and the seventies had a lot of that to offer. Karsten had managed to soak up the richness, the melodies, and the strikingly complex beat of some of the most talented and innovative artists on the music scene at that time.

His dedication to his craft, along with recognition and a sincere appreciation of music, melded to create an angst which led him to the cutting edge of creativity. Music videos were his next level of challenge and he'd recently put the word out that he was more than ready for a commitment on that level.

A new group titled New Deal had contacted him after word had gotten around that his photography credentials and music orientation would probably make for good video production. And his newness to the industry would probably result in a price tag that was within reason. They'd discussed the nuances of what was at stake, negotiated the terms, and contracted for two videos from their newly recorded first album. The second single, "Faithful," released just three weeks prior, was already climbing the charts and on its way to double platinum status. And their first single, "Destiny Knows No Doubt," had already gone platinum three times over.

Karsten would function as producer, director, and photographer in the venture, the first of its kind for him. His excitement was palpable, his dream finally within reach.

He should have been ecstatic, but he felt empty instead. And although he recognized that it wasn't Sloan or any of the others that he missed, he also realized that he needed someone to share this newfound success with. It wouldn't feel real until he'd shared it, described it, allowing the enthusiasm to be heard in his voice and reciprocated by acknowledgment.

He dialed Ethelyn. The phone rang twelve times without an answer.

Karsten knew that she was probably still at the evening service of Brooklyn Tabernacle. He also knew that the one thing which could possibly trip him up, the one thing that he'd never been able to control and get a handle on, was still there ready to somehow negate the full measure of his overall success and accomplishment.

And so, on a day in which he felt overwhelming achievement, far-reaching happiness, and unparalleled accomplishment, he also acknowledged a void in his life for which there seemed no fulfillment. Duality had come full circle for him, once again.

Seven

Barbados

"What do you mean we have to claim our bags back at the airport? I thought they were being delivered here to the hotel." Norwood's voice, raised considerably in anger, could be heard for some distance as Sloan and Jodi approached the lobby. They soon realized he was up in arms for a concerted cause.

The day clerk was explaining, without much success, why their bags were still being detained at Grantley Adams Airport and apparently would not be available for another day or so.

"There must have been some mix-up of the identification made when you filled out your forms. Otherwise, they would release them and a representative from the hotel could courier them back for you. This is rather unusual and I do apologize for any inconvenience," he added. Norwood had become silent and the departure from his earlier stance was chilling.

Sloan, accustomed to acting as mediator and peacemaker in her job as a journalist wherein she often had to bridge the gap between a reluctant source and her editor, immediately decided to try her hand. "Look, would it make things any simpler if we all just went out to the airport and claimed the pieces that belong to us? I mean, we need the things in those bags like yesterday. To have to wait another day for them will be added torture," she explained calmly.

Norwood remained silent but Sloan could tell by an almost indiscernable tic in his jaw that he was steaming; she couldn't remember when she'd witnessed such control or felt such magnetism. He stood only inches from her, his profile one of stoic tolerance, infinite patience, and superbly managed rage.

"Let me see what I can do. If I can arrange a car to take you to the airport, it'll have to be within the next ten minutes because my shift is over and the night clerk won't do it," he added.

Jodi, who had made herself comfortable on one of the rattan love seats, rummaged through her straw bag, and looked up suddenly. "I just remembered that my editor is supposed to call me at five-thirty. I need to take that call because she's making arrangements for a connecting flight to Trinidad at the end of the week. You guys go on ahead and sign for my luggage. I have to stay here. Okay?"

"Sure, that's no problem. I just want my luggage at this point—no more delays, no red tape, no hitches," Sloan said. Frustration was evident in her voice, her manner, and her expression. She just wanted the whole luggage episode to be over with and over with fast.

Norwood listened to them, continued his campaign of disassociation and waited for the clerk to return. In his mind there was only one thing worse than inconvenience—incompetence. Someone, something, somehow had caused the bags to be mistakenly forwarded beyond their intended destination. Now he was being told that because of administrative constraints, he would have to go on a treasure hunt to secure his own belongings. He was not at all amused.

"Okay, Rodney can take you guys back to the airport

in about fifteen minutes, compliments of the hotel," the clerk concluded as he hung up the phone.

Norwood's silence was broken then with a hearty laugh. "Well, I would certainly hope so," he added. Sloan shot him a look that spoke volumes. She'd tolerated his smug superiority back at the church when they were both shooting location shots. She'd even declined to comment when he'd made several vaguely rude suggestions as the bus transported all the journalists back to their respective hotels. And although she agreed with him for the most part, she would not allow that to be the grounds to forge an allegiance.

"Look, can we just try and make the best of a really uncomfortable situation? It's not been any fun having to make do for the past day and a half, knowing that all my stuff should be within reaching distance," she said then, looking directly at Norwood, almost willing him to challenge her.

He wanted to accept the challenge. But he wanted to feel her body pressed tightly against his even more. Wanted to feel the warmth of her lips against his again and the pulsing of blood which had coursed through his veins as he'd held her in his arms. He turned away and walked toward the van as it pulled up. He'd be damned if he'd give her the satisfaction of knowing any of his innermost thoughts or feelings. Not yet anyway.

"Do me a favor, will you? Just keep this for me until later. I don't feel like lugging extra stuff with me on this search and rescue mission." Sloan's cynicism was not lost on Jodi, who was also fairly disgusted with the inconveniences they'd experienced in the past thirty-six hours. She handed Jodi the camera bag with exaggerated finality.

"No problem. I'll bring it down if you like when we leave for the concert tonight. What's the pickup time?" she asked while rummaging through the straw bag on her shoulder.

"Seven sharp. And keep your fingers crossed that we're able to find all of the bags because I think our buddy from Chicago is going to blow it if that's not the case."

"I think you're right. I would not want to be on the other side of it—he looks like he has a really volatile temper," Jodi offered. "I wonder what's really bothering him?" she added.

"I don't know and don't care to find out. Just as long as he doesn't try and give me a hard time. I'll stay on my side of the van, thank you," Sloan added, laughing as she walked toward the waiting vehicle.

Norwood, who watched her as she approached, wasn't really as angry as he appeared. His military training had brought him to a place where anything less than accuracy was unacceptable. He held himself and everyone around him to the same high standard. In his mind, lost luggage was not an acceptable reality, especially if it was based on human error.

Sloan entered the van, sat on the opposite side from Norwood, and looked out the window as the driver took off. Silence ensued for the entire ride to Grantley Adams Airport, neither passenger willing to unravel the cloak of tension that permeated the air.

They entered the reclaim area of the baggage check separately, with Norwood hanging back to allow Sloan to precede him. The clerk, a young Bajan woman, was on the telephone giving directions to whoever was on the other end of the line.

Sloan, deciding that rudeness would not gain her any advantage, waited patiently until the young woman hung up and addressed her in her soft English-inspired accent.

"Yes, may I help you?"

"I really hope so. Our bags were lost in transit yesterday. We arrived on Worldwide Airlines flight
two-three-four out of JFK in New York. Unfortunately,
it seems our bags remained on the aircraft and continued on to St. Lucia. We received a call at our hotel
today that they'd been returned." Sloan pulled out
her claim form and handed it to the clerk hoping that
this would be the last of the ordeal.

"And you, sir, do you also have your claim form, or
are you two married?" she asked as she looked at the
two forms Sloan had handed her. Before she could explain that the second was for another journalist who
was not present, Norwood stepped up to the counter,
cleared his throat, and said very slowly, "No, we are
not married. But obviously that doesn't matter because my bags were lost, too." His voice seemed to
come from far away and its timbre sent shivers up
Sloan's spine which lodged somewhere around her
throat. She was sure that he'd said it with annoyance
just to see what her response would be—to test her
and get her goat all at the same time. But she'd not
give in to the temptation to lash out at him, not give
him the satisfaction of knowing that he'd affected her
in the least. Instead, she remained silent, intent only
on retrieving her luggage and Jodi's. The tension in
the air was palpable and the clerk wasn't sure if it was
totally directed at the lost luggage or some other element. She only knew that it would be in the best
interests of all involved for her to straighten out the
mix-up and allow the two "Yankees" standing before
her to return to their destinations.

The clerk fled, mumbling something about "checking inventory," and disappeared through a set of
double doors. Sloan and Norwood avoided looking at
one another and retreated to lounge chairs set up in

a small waiting room. Ten minutes passed, but they felt more like twenty before she returned carrying two red suitcases in tow, one more banged up than the other, with part of the handle dangling off the larger of the two. "Is this your luggage?" she asked softly, directing her question to both Sloan and Norwood.

Norwood looked at Sloan, who in turn looked back, and they both burst out laughing, the ridiculousness of the situation settling upon them simultaneously.

"No, not at all," Sloan responded first.

"I am afraid it's not mine either," Norwood offered, wondering how in the world this strange mix-up had occurred and if he would ever see his bags again. "Look, my bag is black with gray accents on it. It has my luggage tag on it marked Images Inc. Studio Photos. Why don't you take another look. It has to be back there," he added. The laughter had obviously taken the edge off both his anger and his attitude. Sloan watched the clerk return to the outer office and shook her head.

"If this wasn't so sad, it'd be hysterically funny, but I honestly am concerned that we may never get our bags," she said, acknowledging her greatest fear.

"I know just what you mean. And the thing is by the time we get this straightened out, it'll be time to leave the island. It's a good thing that I didn't pack any of my photography equipment in my checked luggage. That would be the kiss-off. I might as well have not come in that case," he acknowledged.

"Right—like my editor really wants to hear that I flew all the way to Barbados and left my ability to capture any part of the story in my checked luggage. He'd have a fit and I know it. As it is, I was lucky to have a change of clothes in my carry-on luggage, but after today, I am all out of everything—shorts, tops, you name it. It's all in a bag that's somewhere between

New York, Barbados, St. Lucia, and the next neighboring island."

"Well, maybe it's made its way to Martinique, because that's the closest island after St. Lucia. *Parlez vous Français?*" he asked then, the phrase coming to him suddenly. And though he doubted that she spoke French fluently, he smiled as she struggled with her response.

"*Oui, je suis tout.*" It came out awkward and stilted, her uncertainty obvious. "I only remember a few phrases from high school but I do remember liking the sound of the language. It seemed so sophisticated at the time," Sloan said as the memory came back to her.

Norwood watched her face, its expression changing as the memory filtered through. He realized that he wanted her to like him. The thought had never occurred to him before that moment and it both surprised and unnerved him.

"You must have been something else in high school," he offered, his mind already imagining her as a tomboy with an attitude.

"Actually, I was quite the serious student—straight A's of course—but with a serious jones for sports, too. I played varsity volleyball and was on the swim team also. I ran track for a while, until my knees gave me a problem. I used to run the forty-yard dash—and win most of the time," she said, smiling at the memory. "What about you?"

"Well, I ran track, too. I played a lot of basketball and actually went to college on a scholarship because of it. But the love of photography came early on. I separated my collarbone one summer playing ball at the local park—guys from the South Side of Chicago always play rough. Anyway, I was laid up for the entire summer and an older cousin had just gotten a Yashica

A camera for his birthday. He couldn't use it, didn't want it, and just gave it to me one day. I studied the manual, took the time to make sure I understood the mechanics, and the rest is history," he said. He stopped then, surprised that he'd opened up to her, wondering why he had. He also marveled at her genuine interest in his minor revelation.

"That's funny—you never know what a kid will take to, do you? I'll bet they all wanted you to be the next Michael Jordan—with you coming out of Chicago and all," Sloan said.

She was glad that he'd shared the story with her. It made her feel as if he was treating her as a colleague—one of the boys, not just a ditzy female.

"Yeah, you're right—it took me at least a couple of years to realize that my true talents did not necessarily lie in running, jumping, and shooting hoops. When I opened my store in Lincoln Park, my mother was proud as a peacock that her son had made it out without using a basketball. I'd promised her that if she'd allow me to continue with the photography as well as play ball within reasonable time frames, I'd never let her down. That studio was my commitment to her that I was serious about making something out of myself using photography as I'd promised. She was beaming," he said, smiling now at the memory of his mother's face and the happiness she'd exhibited.

The clerk returned then, with two suitcases in tow and another being held by an additional employee. The look on Sloan's face as she finally recognized her bag was pure joy. "That's it, that's mine that he's holding," she said excitedly, waving her hands and almost clapping with joy.

"And that one you have is mine—thank God," Norwood said, relief clearly evident in his voice.

"Let's just hope that this one is Jodi's—can you check the ticket against this form please?" Sloan asked, handing over the paper that Jodi had given her earlier.

"Yes, this matches—you'll have to sign for them both," the clerk instructed her. The bags were released and they returned to the van triumphant. Rodney was in conversation with two other van drivers awaiting passengers to be transported to neighboring hotels and Sloan and Norwood loaded their bags into the back of the vehicle.

They entered the van then, finding seats across from each other, the earlier tension somewhat eased by the resolution of their ordeal over missing luggage.

Sloan looked at Norwood wondering how he'd receive her next words, then plunged forward awkwardly. "You know I was still pretty angry with you over your behavior last night. I sort of felt you had taken advantage of a situation that was already pretty over the top." Somehow, she'd reached a place wherein she felt her honest feelings could be revealed. Unsure as to his reaction, she held her breath, eagerly awaiting his response but dreading it at the same time.

"Really—well, I wasn't. And you didn't act like you were all that angry when I kissed you. I got the distinct impression you liked it—liked it a lot, in fact," he said ruthlessly. His words hung in the air like daggers he'd aimed at her heart, the silence between the two creating a barrier which neither wanted to cross.

If she thought that just because they'd been able to exchange some civilities as they retrieved their long-lost luggage she could now start up with her "Miss Innocence" act, she had another think coming, he reasoned.

"You know, if you weren't such a hardheaded, moralistic, egotistical . . ." Sloan sputtered as Rodney entered the van, effectively halting her tirade of diabolical adjectives.

Norwood, stunned at her sudden change in character, laughed then. She was beautiful, stubborn, quick tempered, and a pain in the neck. But he had to admit that he liked her. Liked her more and more each time she offered him a glimpse into who the real Sloan Whitaker was.

Now, all he had to do was get her to like him, too. And he had all of seven days and six nights to do it.

Eight

New York City

"Look, if we can't shoot it from the preferred angle, then let's set up with the camera slowly focusing in on each member of the group with the girl approaching from the right," Karsten advised. "That'll mean alternating rows, with a distance of at least six feet of space between each subject." White shirt rolled up to the elbows, well-worn jeans, and Timberland boots supported the appearance of an artist whose focus was clearly on his craft. And although he'd recently taken to wearing a baseball cap turned backward, adorned with the video's title stitched across the front, his direction still carried the weight of a master.

His technical advisor, Alton Driggs, whom he'd worked with in the past as an understudy and more recently as backup photographer, instinctively realized he was dead-on and began to redesign the set. Karsten's instructions also sent the key grip and three other technicians scurrying to rearrange several pieces of equipment as well as props. The set, which was located in a cavernous studio warehouse on the West Side of Manhattan, had been converted into a sound stage resembling a college study hall. All four members of the nation's hottest singing group, New Deal, had been strategically placed in various seats and were patiently, if not anxiously, awaiting their cues. The video would have each of them in a separate camera shot as they sang the title track, "Faithful," from their recent hit album, *Destiny Knows No Doubt.* Somewhere into the first chorus, a new student would enter the room, all eyes would focus on her, and the camera would zoom in also. With her face bathed in light, the camera would dignify her beauty thereby reinforcing her power in the male-dominated environment she'd just entered. They'd searched for just the right model/actress for more than six weeks, finally choosing from over three hundred applicants. A relative unknown in the video world, her face would soon be viewed via satellite on internationally telecast networks including BET and MTV. More than one billion homes in the next months would receive that imagery, creating instant recognition for the lucky ingenue. Video often created immediate celebrity status.

The imagery would then contain separate shots of the "beauty" in various scenes of interaction with each individual group member—then reality would set in and the camera would bring the viewers back to the college study hall, focusing on the remaining lines of the song.

"Okay, look, can someone call down to hair and makeup and tell them that it's okay to send up the model—we're just about ready to roll tape here," Karsten advised as the set director okayed the new position of several props. Checking and double-checking the camera lens, as well as the lighting which would be needed, Karsten's back was to the door.

Kassandra, nervous and uncertain in a medium that was altogether new to her, entered the set area with her head held high despite her inner turmoil. The pleated skirt, knee socks, and shirt with an ascot almost made her want to laugh. In her estimation, wardrobe had overdone it. Nobody dressed that way anymore, let alone anyone in college. Her hair, done in one long braid down her back, only made the pronounced cheekbones of her face stand out even more prominently. And with the minimal use of makeup they'd chosen, she did indeed look all of about nineteen.

The agency had contacted her one month earlier, told her it was a possible recurring role, and never once mentioned "music video." She had gone on the "go see," auditioned by walking onstage and reading two lines of dialogue, and then been called back. They'd asked her to stand next to a "stand-in," instructed her to flirt with him without any specific prompting, and she'd done her best to comply. It felt slightly uncomfortable, but she'd remembered other times on shoots when she'd visualized different scenarios to put herself into the mood, and done just that. Thoughts of Norwood, then Jordan Campbell, had come to mind. She'd instantly transferred them to the group member who stood before her. Smiling seductively, she tilted her head coyly, moistened her lips and gave him her best come-on smile. Leaning in even closer, she'd almost touched him breast to breast, careful not to close the half inch of distance between them. Someone yelled "Okay" and she'd mumbled "Great" as the group member had said something like "Sure." Neither felt sure of the outcome but Kassandra knew that the second call back was usually the clincher and felt she'd done her best. She also realized that the pay scale was phenomenal. If things turned out well, there was an endless list of possibilities with the sheer numbers involved in video.

She received her answer only two weeks later when her agent of only two months, Yvonne Silver, called her with the news.

"Kass (which she'd taken to calling her from the

very first), you got it. The shoot starts in exactly one week and I am so damned proud of you I could kiss you," she practically screamed into the receiver.

"Are you serious—I almost have to pinch myself to believe this. . . . This is so great. I have to call Anita and tell her that her meddling finally paid off. If it hadn't been for her needling me, I might not have answered the open call for this one."

"Don't remind me—you really have to have more faith in yourself and in me. That's why you hired me—remember? That audition came into my office on the same day I called you. It was only fate that your sister knew some of the crew members," Yvonne reminded her.

"I realize that, Yvonne, and again I want to thank you for your hard work. I know it wasn't easy to get my name put on the list. I think I'd still be there waiting to be seen otherwise. At least six hundred models, actresses, and wanna-bes turned up at that open call. It was through your perseverance that I was seen on that first day."

"Yeah, probably, but truth be told, it was definitely you that got the call back and the final selection. So, we'll have to celebrate sometime soon. Call me when you can."

"I will, and thanks again." That had been over two weeks ago, with a slight delay ensuing between the suggested filming date and the actual start date. Now, as Kassandra waited patiently for the crew, extras, and entire set to begin shooting, her nervousness waned somewhat and she realized that she was in a familiar environment. The differences between still photography and video were tremendous but in the end, the same results were still warranted. And the lighting was probably the most crucial element.

"Okay, are we ready to roll?" Karsten asked, turning

from his conversation with Alton and another technician. Although he'd masterminded the entire concept, design, and delivery of the project, he'd allowed his assistant to pick the girl for the video, trusting his judgment totally. They had history together, had worked together on previous assignments, and Karsten knew that Alton would know exactly what to look for—poise, proportion, and most of all, sensuality. Those three proponents translated through the camera like no other attributes. And although this was for a music video, there would be no dancing so that ability was not a necessity.

Karsten looked over at the young woman who was standing just inside the realm of his camera's angle and squinted. She appeared to be no more than a mere teenager, yet his practiced eye immediately discerned the ripened body of a distinctly more mature adult. Picture-perfect skin, hair tied back into one long braid, and huge doe eyes stared right back at him, causing him to blink, then readjust both the camera and himself. "Damn, she looks like a baby— but what a baby," he muttered under his breath, realizing that he'd changed the camera angle ever so slightly as he watched her walk across the set.

"Okay, let's everyone take their places—everyone take their marks," Karsten instructed, annoyance in his voice. He wasn't used to being rattled by anyone or anything, and certainly not by a model dressed in high school garb. "Come on, let's go, we don't want this to take all day," he added, knowing that each hour they remained past 8:00 P.M. would cost an additional $10,000 in fees.

The hastily held two-hour rehearsal had taken the edge off the newness of the medium for Kassandra, but she was still nervous. Carefully reviewing the instructions as she waited for her cue, she focused solely on what she had been told. Enter the room, take the fourth seat from the right in the second row, and as she walked past each member, the camera would record their reaction to an extremely attractive female student. Subsequent shots would document each member's interaction with the temptress, yet each would remain faithful to a significant other at the end of the video as suggested by the title song.

Someone yelled "Action" and music from the title track could be heard playing in the background. Kassandra carefully waited for her cue and then stepped onstage. She slowly walked toward the seat which had been carefully marked by a tiny X within a white circle; her only outward sign of nervousness was the slight hesitation in her step. But it actually played into the photographer's shot; he needed the slowed momentum to highlight the shot of her face.

Even at a side angle, she was beautiful and Karsten again exercised professional control to contain his reaction. This was not the time to let his newfound bachelorhood get the best of him and he'd be damned if he'd let some newly minted "video chick" rein in on his state of mind. He rolled footage for two twenty-minute segments, then repositioned his subjects and rolled another two tapes. Secure in his knowledge of the finished product, Karsten realized he was getting it down just from gut instinct. It had always been that way with him.

The day went quickly with progress being made on all fronts. "All the major interior shots are in the can with this being done," Karsten confirmed to the crew as each member went about cataloging equipment before restoring it to protective cases and carryalls. "The next couple of days will be on location in and around the city—get a copy of the schedule and touch base with Alton to confirm. I think we shoot at a park in Roslyn,

Long Island, on Saturday morning," he confirmed as he looked at the schedule quickly, then stuffed it into his back pocket.

The group members had left the set, along with the model, only moments before and Karsten was wrapped up in breaking down his video equipment. Key grips continued to dismantle the lighting, removing the key lights, back lights, and barn doors, which blocked out glare, from several pieces before storing them in protective cases for transport.

"Hey, man, good work today—especially in light of the disadvantage of working with a somewhat inexperienced entity. I think we did okay though, considering."

"Yeah, well, the finished product will be determined by the edits—you know that. And I feel really strongly about the location shots meant to highlight each member's interaction with the model," Karsten added. His focus included all of the components of the video and the realized version, including the theme and the ending as well. And although this was his first contracted music video, he was solid in his belief that he was right on target with his approach.

"Yeah, speaking of interaction with the model, did you check her? I mean, I doubt if she was really jail bait, but damn, she sure made the concept believable. And with a body and a face like that, I'm sure there are lots of cats out there that would surely be willing to do the time," Alton said. Suppressed laughter was just underneath his breath, and Karsten smiled knowingly. His comments were all the more hilarious because Karsten suspected he was a card-carrying gay, but that didn't seem to deter or detract from his ability to gauge an attractive woman.

"Listen to you—I didn't think you noticed things like that. Here I am behind camera one, figuring I'm the only one noticing how Shorty is filling out the blouse, killing that skirt with those legs, and doing serious battle with my heart."

"No, man—I saw it, too, but it didn't affect me in the same way. I just registered 'danger—hot spot up ahead' and got on with my shoot thing. You know she's new to the game, too, so the fact that she didn't let nerves or inexperience get in the way was a real plus. I'd give Shorty an A plus for today's shoot—definitely. And with those long legs, Shorty is just the right term for her 'cause it's a polar opposite," Alton confirmed. Both he and Karsten laughed, knowing that their subject would probably be livid and extremely unimpressed by their exchange.

"Well, don't give her a final grade just yet. We still have a couple of days of location shots left. I'm keeping my fingers crossed that all our cast members live up to today's indoor shoot. Location shots can be a lot more challenging—we have the weather, the set, the uncontrollable issues to deal with. The park setting should be beautiful but can possibly pose problems if the weather doesn't cooperate, or if the general public in the area wants to be intrusive. You know the possibilities," Karsten added. He wasn't half as worried about the cast members' performances as he was about the overall environment on a location shoot.

"Yeah, once again, my man, you are so, so right. Well, we'll just have to see what happens on the subsequent shooting days. I'm putting my money on a successful conclusion. This just feels right and I have to thank you once again for giving me the opportunity to work with you. I realize it's your first jam for Centex Records. I can't tell you what it means to me to be assistant cameraman on this gig. You know what I'm trying to say don't you . . ."

"Yeah, don't even go there. Your work speaks for itself and I didn't select you because I thought I would be doing you a favor, or that you would botch any aspect of this assignment. You're a good, solid photographer, one who knows his craft and then some. I was lucky you were available, so stop trippin'. . . ."

Karsten's sincerity was apparent and that made Alton even more pleased. It also made him slightly uncomfortable. He knew Karsten was straight and that he'd just recently been divorced. Rumor had it he was a lady killer with a capital "K," but they were colleagues and his feelings of admiration, respect, and genuine appreciation of his talent were totally legitimate.

"Okay, enough said. I'm going to give the signal for the transportation to be brought around back so we can load up. I'll see you on Saturday morning—seven A.M. at the set."

"See you there, man—thanks for a great day of shooting," Karsten added, readjusting his cap and turning it to the front. It signaled to both him and the world at large that he had indeed completed a day's work.

Crossing Eleventh Avenue, Karsten headed toward the garage where his car was parked. The black Range Rover had been his companion now for the past two years—he'd bought it when he and Sloan first married thinking it would be the perfect vehicle for transporting their offspring around town. Months later, when he'd realized there would be no need for infant car seats, strollers, or other paraphernalia, he realized he'd already fallen in love with the sheer size and dimension of the vehicle. The unencumbered view of the roadway it offered was another bonus and it made driving the vehicle an advantage of great proportion. He recognized that he'd come to love the height, the size, the imposing stature of the English truck as he pressed the remote entry and saw the automatic response as the vehicle unlocked.

At that same moment, he recognized the model from the shoot as she walked hurriedly along Fifty-fourth Street, headed toward Eleventh Avenue. She wore a navy blue velour sweat suit with yellow piping along the sides, and blue and white sneakers. Her braided ponytail swung as she walked and a yellow backpack straddled her shoulders. She looked all of about eighteen, even younger than she'd appeared earlier, and Karsten hesitated. He started the truck, paid his bill, and pulled alongside of her slowly. Lowering the tinted window on the passenger side, he realized she was ignoring him intentionally, probably accustomed to being propositioned often and with great intensity.

"Excuse me, Miss, but I thought you might like a lift—that backpack looks a bit heavy," he said quickly. With his cap turned to the front, he gave a totally different appearance. Kassandra did not recognize him at all.

"No, thanks—I can make it," was all she uttered and then continued to walk, even speeding up her pace somewhat. *Men, what a joke* was what she was thinking to herself, knowing that the area was known for bold street walkers, risque characters, and homeless vagrants who would hustle for money in any way possible.

"I'm sorry—we didn't formally meet on the set, but I am Karsten Battle, the photographer from the video you were just filming."

Kassandra's head shot up then, her reaction immediate. "Oh, I am so sorry, but you know this area isn't the best. I thought you were just trying to hassle me," she added as she moved closer to the vehicle.

"I know. My offer still stands. I can drop you at the nearest train or whatever," he added, knowing that it sounded like a pickup line although he was only trying to do the right thing. Hell, it was to his advantage also. He couldn't leave a cast member in a question-able area while he just idly passed her on the street. But he also knew he was breaking all of his own rules by his offer.

"No, I think I'll just walk. It's only another couple blocks over to Eighth Avenue and I can get the sub-way uptown there," she offered with a quick smile. Kassandra didn't want to appear ungrateful, but she really wanted nothing to do with him. If all that she'd heard was correct, he was the thing she most feared in the world—an exact replica of herself only in male form. And she wasn't about to put herself into any sit-uation to be able to determine how accurate that description might or might not be. Not now or ever.

"Well, if you insist—why would you want to walk two more deserted blocks in this area?" he asked, becoming both alarmed and challenged by her de-termined gait. Close up, she looked all of about sixteen, in his assessment, the kind of sixteen-year-old that perverts and lechers loved to accost on lonely, uninhabited streets. Although it was only 8:30, the sun had long since been driven from the sky and the increasingly long shadows being cast by the towering buildings created an atmosphere that was far from encouraging.

"Look, if you're worried about me, or about the ap-pearance of getting into my vehicle, let me assure you that I have only honorable intentions at heart." Karsten smiled then because she looked over at him to assess his sincerity and he knew he'd guessed right. She was definitely wary of men, and quite possibly of people in general. He'd have to remember that.

"Okay, okay—I guess I should be grateful that some-one even cared enough to stop and give me the option of a lift. Thank you, honestly, it's just that I've only been here for a few months and everyone says to never trust strangers. I don't even recognize you from the shoot. Didn't you have a hat on or something?" she asked, not recognizing the cap now that it was secured firmly but turned facing front.

"Yeah, this hat but it was like this," he said as he flipped the cap around.

"Oh, okay. I guess the lights were in my eyes somewhat, too," she explained quickly. She felt a little foolish making such a big deal out of riding with him for all of two blocks after she'd been on the same set with him all afternoon.

"Not a problem. Actually, I find it commendable that you're being so careful. New York is a big city with a lot of people in it—both good and bad. You were right to stand your ground back there." What he really wanted to say was that he felt like he already knew her after having her in his viewfinder for most of the day. He could describe every angle of her face, each plane of her cheekbones, and would love the chance to measure the length of each one of her long, shapely legs.

"How far uptown are you going?" he asked then, realizing that he wanted to talk with her, find out where she'd come from, and where she was going, in the real sense.

"I'm at Ninety-sixth Street and Columbus. If you drop me at the Seventh Avenue line, it would be perfect."

"Right, Seventh Avenue and Fifty-seventh Street it is," he responded, inserting a CD into the dashboard.

"I wanted to thank you today for making it so easy for me. I was really nervous and I know I probably screwed up a couple of times. This was my first music video," she said, suddenly feeling that she could at least be honest with him.

"Actually, the day's take was fine. And you didn't

screw up at all. If anything, I may have to edit some of the reaction of the group members to you. Remember, the name of the song is 'Faithful.' We chose you to represent all the temptations a young man has to face when he has made the ultimate commitment to be true to his love. Some of the takes show a little too much interest on the part of the group's members. But I can handle that in the editing room. You did a great job though. We were talking about it as we wrapped up." He neglected to add that their assessment of her extended beyond the day's professionalism, knowing she would probably demand he stop the vehicle if she were really aware of his reaction to her.

"Wow, I was so nervous and sure I had screwed up at some point. Have you been shooting music videos for a long time?"

"Actually, this is my first music video. I'm a cameraman with one of the networks. That's my day job which is why it has to be shot on weekends, evenings, and holidays."

"I see. Well, you and the entire crew are definitely professional, even somewhat intense. I am actually looking forward to the location shoots."

"Look, I don't mind dropping you uptown—it gives me an opportunity to unwind as I drive. I'm also enjoying our conversation," he added quickly, hoping that it wouldn't be a deal breaker.

"You don't have to do that—I mean, I appreciate it, I really do, but it's out of your way and I—"

"Listen, it's not a big deal. . . . Truthfully, I don't get the opportunity often enough to enjoy driving the thing. Working in the heart of midtown Manhattan, the subway is the preferred and most sensible mode of transport during the weekdays, especially with all of the restrictions after September eleven. I never drive in so it just sits in my garage collecting dust until the weekends. And now that I'm shooting video every weekend, I really don't have the time to fit in any long-distance or out-of-range driving. You'd be doing me a tremendous favor by letting me drive a mere forty blocks out of my way, Kassandra."

Kassandra's guard, which had immediately gone up when he'd stopped, was still in place. But as they continued to talk and she realized he was far from a serial killer or some other form of sociopath, she began to relax. Aside from the fact that he was drop-dead gorgeous, he seemed to be charming and intent on taking the ride.

"Okay, you have me convinced that I'd be doing you a favor, though I'm not at all sure that it makes any sense. And, please call me Kass," she added quickly.

"Kass—I like that. It sounds classy but very casual. Is that with a C or a K?"

"K. My mom got it from a book she read when she was a teenager—her favorite author was James Baldwin, but I think she changed the spelling. I love it because you rarely find another person with it."

Karsten headed toward the West Side Highway then, which would put them closer to Columbus Avenue. The trendy neighborhood, with gourmet shops and streets lined with fabulously maintained brownstone town houses, had always been a favorite of his. New York had lots of great neighborhoods and the Upper West Side mirrored Brooklyn's Park Slope in many ways.

By the time they arrived at Kassandra's, they'd discussed his Brooklyn upbringing, her Chicago roots, and their current neighborhoods. Three thirty-six West Ninety-fifth Street was a four-story brownstone with huge windows, high ceilings, and four single-bedroom apartments.

"I cannot begin to thank you for the lift. Can I offer

you something before you turn around and trek all the way to Brooklyn? I can't believe that you went this far out of your way and I feel so guilty. You must let me offer you a cup of coffee, soda, a glass of wine, or at least a beer?"

"No, nothing, thank you. I'll take a rain check on it though. If you're really sincere, you'll allow me to take you up on that invitation sometime soon," he added, smiling as she climbed out of the vehicle.

"All right—you have yourself a deal. I owe you one for your gentlemanly hospitality and chivalry. And they say that knights with horses don't exist anymore . . ." she said, laughing as she waved to him.

"Yeah, and nobody believes the concept of a damsel in distress either—but I found one right on Fifty-sixth Street and Eleventh Avenue," he laughed. She turned and waved. Grinning broadly, he turned his cap backward again, and almost said, "See you tomorrow."

As Karsten watched her enter the building, he wondered what the hell had come over him.

Nine

Barbados

Sir Garfield Sobers Gynmasium, named after the Bajan cricketeer who literally changed the history of the game, had a capacity of at least three thousand occupants. It was almost full with a mere scattering of empty seats toward the balcony. The two-story amphitheater had been outfitted with state-of-the-art acoustics, comfortable seating, and lighting mechanisms that rivaled any comparable opera house or stage setting.

Loyal Jarreau fans, looking forward to an evening filled with jazz, be bop, rhythm and blues, and, most of all, Al Jarreau's inestimable style, with his signature delivery, jammed the parking lot and entrance to the amphitheater. It would be his second appearance on the island of Barbados; the first had been sold out some seven years prior. The people of Barbados had been waiting for this return engagement with eager anticipation. Visitors from neighboring islands, the United States, Canada, and Puerto Rico were also in attendance, with the jazz festival drawing music lovers from around the world each year. Even the seasoned press could feel the electricity in the environment.

The tour buses had been allowed to deliver their

precious cargo to the south gate, where press badges were checked and each member was allowed entry and then escorted to a special area marked PRESS ONLY. This arrangement gave photographers easy access to the stage area. It also gave journalists a clear view. Their descriptive narratives would include each nuance of tone, inflection, and gyration they witnessed, helping to make their readers feel as if they'd been there as well.

"Please remember to only take photographs throughout the first two songs—and please, no flash mechanisms are to be used," Deirdre instructed. Those who were veterans of their craft expected such instruction. Some artists tried to get out of the grueling minutes of hordes of paparazzi all juxtaposing and positioning themselves for the best possible angle for their photos, which could certainly be a distraction for any artist who was not a seasoned and consummate performer. But they also knew that photos placed in the right magazines and newspapers would provide invaluable coverage and mean a concerted boost in the public's consciousness. That boost translated into significantly higher dollars spent both at retail outlets where CDs and tapes were sold, as well as at any of their upcoming concert appearances, so they generally agreed to grin and bear it for all of about five to ten minutes at the most. Not many artists relished the photos taken after they'd begun to perspire, or when the sheer magnitude of energy expended in the course of their performance began to show in their faces, their demeanor, or in their delivery.

Sloan had taken her seat and was busy reloading her camera with 1,000-speed film. In the darkened environment, and without a flash, it was the most assured way of capturing as much light as possible.

And with the f-stop set at its smallest aperture number, she would be essentially opening the lens to its widest range. The only drawback was if the artist moved around a lot, the photographs would record the movements in a blurred shot. She'd neglected to bring a tripod, not willing to carry the additional weight. It was one of the drawbacks to being a dual entity. Photojournalism came with its own required equipment list: cameras, lenses, flash equipment, tape recorder, writing pads, plus extra batteries for each electronic component.

Jodi, seated next to her, was busy making notes in her journal. She didn't need photos for the piece she would submit to the Associated Press but she always made it a point to sit as close to the stage as possible. That way she rarely missed any of the song titles, was able to document all the nuances of the performance, and also enjoyed the full measure of the concert.

Norwood, Lorenzo, and the two writers from England, Trevor and Glenn, were seated farther to the right. "Hey, let's go outside and get something to drink before this thing gets started," Lorenzo said.

"Good idea—I'm with you," Norwood said quickly, pulling his equipment bag onto his back.

"Why don't you leave that behind—we'll be right back and those two look like they will be here all the while anyway," Lorenzo said, pointing to Sloan and Jodi.

"Not on your life—my equipment goes where I go. I learned that a long time ago. Photography equipment is too expensive to leave to other people to take care of. I lost an irreplaceable camera, lens, and flash equipment when I had walked away from the bag at an Earth, Wind and Fire concert. That experience taught me a valuable lesson—don't take a chance when you don't really have to."

"Maybe you're right," Lorenzo said, quickly reaching for his bag also. "You don't think they would leave our stuff or let someone else walk away with it, do you?" he asked as soon as they were out of earshot of the two female journalists.

"Not at all, I just don't like to ask other people to handle any of my responsibilities—the army teaches you to be totally self-sufficient. Never expect the other guy to do what you're supposed to have taken care of. That's one of the first lessons taught at Fort Carson, in Colorado Springs."

"Wow, did you see any action or were you just a career recruit?" Lorenzo asked suddenly, not really understanding the difference between the two but suspecting that Norwood could definitely give him enough information so he would be able to make the distinction from this day forward.

"I actually saw a little of Desert Storm and was eager to have that chapter of my military career over with. There is nothing like looking at miles and miles of sand, for as far as the eye can see, and realizing that you cannot get away from it. At least not until your tour of duty is up. Man, I remember, it got so bad that I actually dreamed of sand storms hitting the States, Chicago, Detroit, Los Angeles. I remember one night a PFC woke up screaming that the sand was all over the place and it was disrupting Mardi Gras. The dude was from New Orleans. That was far out. The next day, he was so embarrassed, he could hardly make eye contact with anyone in the unit. But we all understood. Each and every one of us had dreamt something bizarre, but with that damned sand in the middle of each one." Even now, as he spoke of the memory, his hands shook slightly.

"Dog, that sounds like a nightmare I wouldn't wish on my worst enemy. I'm glad I never had to experi-

YOU REMIND ME   123

ence that war game stuff in a way. Then sometimes I wish I had had the opportunity to show my patriotism for my country. I know if we have to settle up any more scores with that Osama cat, I want to be in on it 'cause he's definitely got one coming. The West Coast did not appreciate what they did to the Twin Towers," he ended as they exited the building.

"Hey, I hear you and agree one hundred ten percent. I even gave a brief moment of thought to reenlisting when September eleventh happened. Then I realized I was probably too old, that there were enough young cats to do the job, and that I could probably make a more important contribution by staying right here."

They'd reached the concession stands, set up outside the amphitheater for the convenience of attendees who wanted to purchase refreshments. Soda, beer, rum drinks, as well as small bags of potato chips, popcorn, and even some island fare would be available throughout the concert. Nothing could be taken into the building, so many people remained outdoors enjoying the night, reacquainting themselves with friends who were just arriving, and consuming whatever they had most recently purchased. Many local residents, who had purchased season tickets to the entire jazz festival lineup, supported the event annually. The movers and shakers of Barbados were in full attendance, proud to be Bajans with a cultural conscience, as well as an appreciation of good music.

Norwood watched as Sloan and Jodi exited the amphitheater, walking toward the concession stand. He smiled for the second time that evening. Now that their luggage had been located, both women were dressed more in tune with the island's seventy-five- to eighty-degree temperatures, and he realized what he'd missed in the two days gone by.

Sloan had chosen a lime-green silk wrap skirt, which ended just at the knee and was accompanied by a matching green cardigan that she'd casually thrown around her shoulders. The pale silk halter top she wore under it clung to her breasts, creating a visual effect that caused Norwood's throat to restrict. A single strand of pearls adorned her neck and his eyes kept returning to the spot where they dipped into the cleavage displayed by the sinfully revealing top. Attempting to collect his thoughts, change the direction of his view, or at least redirect his mind, he turned toward Lorenzo quickly.

"Hey, would you ladies like something—I'm buying in honor of our newly found bags and the contents," he offered gallantly. The white rum he'd ordered had hit the bottom of his stomach like a one-hundred-pound weight. And although he'd enjoyed a substantial lunch, he realized that when you were drinking one-hundred-proof rum, also called overproof, lining the stomach walls some six hours earlier might not have been sufficient. It was like trying to burn high-octane gasoline in a vacuum.

"Sure, I'll have a Diet Coke with lime," Sloan answered. She had come to the conclusion that the best way to deal with any of the men on the trip was to be as cordial as possible, remain impartial, and to be noninteractive. Although she exchanged some minor conversation with Norwood earlier in the afternoon as they retrieved their lost luggage, she also remembered how he'd behaved in the first few days of the trip. She recognized that people didn't normally change overnight. All in all, he reminded her a little too much of Karsten.

"I'll have a glass of white wine, thank you," Jodi said then. Lorenzo stepped up, smiled at her, and offered his arm. "I'll take you up on that order—I was hoping you'd come out and have a drink with me anyway."

"Well, thank you. I'd love that." They both walked toward the solidly packed concession stand, leaving Sloan and Norwood to their own devices.

"Well, let me see what I can do about that Coke with lime. Is it okay with you if I leave this equipment here? It'll be difficult to juggle drinks and this stuff, too," he offered, his earlier conversation with Lorenzo coming to mind immediately.

"Sure, go on ahead. I'll keep my eye on everything. Good luck with that crowd—it looks as if it's about eight deep from here," she observed. Truth be told, it was more like ten deep, but the concession managers were doing their best to handle the crowd quickly, knowing that once the concert began, the lines would dwindle significantly.

"Be right back." Norwood approached the stand, decided to try one of his tried and true maneuvers, and stood as straight and tall as possible. Looking ahead, he attempted to gain eye contact with one of the vendors, and waited until that mission was accomplished. It didn't take long. A young Bajan woman looked up, saw his commanding stare, and subtly acknowledged him. That done, he moved forward and mouthed the words "Diet Coke with lime" and was supremely surprised when she smiled in recognition. He'd done it. Several of his fellow thirsty bystanders gave him a second look as he reached across, pushed three Bajan one-dollar coins forward, and thanked his coconspirator with a wink.

He returned so quickly that Sloan thought he'd forgotten his mission. Either that or perhaps the stands had closed down. Norwood smiled triumphantly and handed her the soft drink.

"How did you do that? Jodi and Lorenzo are still standing there waiting to be served," she noted.

"Let's just say that I know my way around. Most people can be approached, dealt with, and negotiations handled without the usual formalities. You just have to know how to do it."

"Well, you obviously know something most of us don't. I'm serious, how did you do that—do you have friends here or something? That or you must have had a stash of soda with sliced lime just waiting for you. Either way, I am impressed." She wanted to say that his unexpected display of hospitality and chivalry was almost suspect, given his original behavior, but figured it would only create waves where it wasn't really necessary.

"I'm not going to divulge my innermost secrets but let's just say that if you're impressed, then mission accomplished." His smile disarmed her, made her want to believe he sincerely meant what his words implied, but she felt too vulnerable to allow him access. She'd been there before, and the memories were too fresh in her mind to allow her to simply throw caution to the wind.

Sloan smiled briefly, took a sip of her drink, and cleared her throat. "You know, if I didn't know better, I'd think you were trying to be nice to me all of a sudden. And since there's absolutely nothing to gain by that behavior, I'd have to ask myself why."

She delivered the last line of her deadly speculation with a coy toss of her auburn-highlighted hair, a glare of defiance in her eyes, and the self-assuredness of a woman who really didn't give a damn.

Norwood once again felt a tightening at the bottom of his stomach. He realized that he wanted her. Wanted to feel her temperament change from cold to hot, from defiance to complacency, and from the distant air she portrayed to one of pure involvement. He also recognized that it would take time and more than a little concentration. Smiling again, he looked deeply into her eyes and stepped closer to her so that his whispers were heard by her ears only.

"Be careful of the questions you ask—the answers may not be to your liking. You and I seem to have a score to settle and last night was only the opening act," he added. He watched as she did everything in her power to retain her composure, although he knew she was livid. He waited for her to refute his last statement but Jodi and Lorenzo, having just been served their drinks, walked up at that moment.

"We thought we would be there forever. The are no real lines and the service is unpredictable. We almost gave up," Lorenzo said, shaking his head.

"Yeah, how did you get your drink so fast? Is there another concession stand?" Jodi asked, noticing the cup in Sloan's hand.

"No, actually Norwood got me a drink. He refuses to divulge his methods but I suspect he has some kind of unconventional way of jumping ahead of the masses."

"I guess that's one way of putting it," he added, wondering how she could appear to be so calm. He knew she was probably still spitting mad.

"Look, what do you guys say we make a pact that throughout the trip, we'll cover for you and vice versa. Sort of a special forces within the ranks so to speak," Norwood stated. It made perfect sense; it also played into his objectives without making them obvious.

"Sounds good to me—four heads are definitely better than one. Even my mother used to say something along those lines although I think it was two heads," Lorenzo added, laughing at his own joke.

"Yeah, it can't hurt, that's for sure. If your ability to be served ahead of everyone else is any indication of

your capabilities, I'd say we have ourselves a winner.
Now we just have to see what the rest of us can do to
pull our weight." Jodi delivered the line much as a
joke to complement the entire concept. She had no
inclination either way. Norwood, Lorenzo, and Sloan
were her colleagues committed to the same goal—
getting the story, the photos, the true essence of the
Barbados Jazz Festival. And if, along the way, friendship and comraderie developed, then it was all the
better.

"Well, if it's all right with the newly formed 'jazz
pact,' I'll be returning to the concert arena. Things
should be getting started in a couple of minutes,"
Sloan added, looking at her watch. She was not at all
sure of what Norwood's intentions were. But she did
know that he'd already stated one goal that did not sit
well with her.

"Yeah, thanks for the drink, Lorenzo," Jodi said,
taking his arm warmly. She knew he had a slight crush
on her, but wasn't sure if it was the location, the intensity of the atmosphere, or if it had any shred of
genuine feeling. It wouldn't be the first time during a
press trip that someone had gotten carried away.

Both women headed back into the arena, while the
men finished their drinks and arrived just before the
British national anthem was played. As the entire audience rose to their feet, tradition, coupled with
respect and hundreds of years of history, was clearly
evident.

Jarreau's performance was in high gear from the
moment he walked onto the stage. Decorated with
balloons spelling out the "Paint It Jazzy" theme, it was
a picturesque environment highlighted by the ceiling
spotlights. The photographers each jockeyed for position, their main objective to catch the artist in a
position of pure artistic delivery. Facial gestures, bod-

ily gyrations, anything that would capture the moment was the goal and what the public back at home would be most interested in.

Sloan realized that with the lighting coming from overhead, and the spotlight changing every couple of seconds, the best vantage point would be stage right. She moved to the area and quickly reeled off almost twenty shots in rapid succession. Reloading the camera, she quickly made the transition to her notepad, jotting down as much of her impression of the overall atmosphere, the singer's demeanor, the elements of his backup band, and so on. Hastily scribbled notes on her slim reporter's notepad would serve as a major portion of the story. She never trusted herself to remember every nuance of any performance, much less the titles of the songs performed or the intricate details of the artist's delivery. Thoroughly engaged in her craft, she didn't notice Norwood's entry into the area until he almost moved into her viewfinder. He set up his monopod quickly, attached his Nikon, and began shooting.

Professional courtesy and years of jockeying for position at similar events caused Sloan to simply move over, allow him the necessary space, and wait her turn for the remaining shots. That was how it was done, though very often, it could become a battleground. She thought of the hastily agreed-upon pact they'd just made and decided he was either extremely sure of himself, or just plain obnoxious. The latter seemed to fit and she smiled.

"What's so funny? And why aren't you shooting? You realize we have only this song for photos and that's it. After that, they want us to pack it in." Although the stadium was darkened to illuminate the performance going on onstage, he could still make out her features. In his mind, she looked good in the dark, she was gorgeous in the sunlight, and would probably be especially beautiful in the nude.

Sloan ignored his comments, proceeded to focus her Canon AE, and began taking shots.

"Listen, with the aperture and shutter speed you're using, it's going to be next to impossible for you to get a solid, steady shot. Why don't you try my equipment?" he asked. He almost smiled at the double entendre, caught himself when he realized she would probably slap him if he did, and waited for her to respond.

"Okay—thanks. I actually have one at home but I couldn't bring myself to lug it here." She realized what he'd said, but would not dignify him with that recognition. If he wanted to resort to being gross, he'd have to do it on his own.

Norwood quickly dismounted his camera, placed it on a nearby unoccupied seat, and reached for Sloan's camera. "May I?" he asked. She handed the camera to him quickly and their hands touched briefly. In the darkened atmosphere of the air-conditioned concert hall, the warmth of his touch unnerved her. It was only a split second of contact. Neither spoke as Norwood carefully connected the two pieces of equipment. Somehow, even that seemingly insignificant act took on more meaning as he slowly wound the camera around the grooves on the monopod's top. Sloan turned away. *My God, what is happening to me? It must be the heat of the tropics—or maybe that I haven't slept with anyone since Karsten moved out more than a year ago.* Her thoughts were interrupted by Norwood's voice.

"There is another method you can use to stabilize yourself and the camera. Maybe I'll show it to you one day if you behave yourself," he responded, unable to stop himself from flirting with her. "Okay, you're good to go now," he added as he held the mounted camera for her to take over.

Sloan reached, took the offered equipment into her grasp, and remained silent—not trusting herself to respond. The man was either diabolically egotistical or substantially reckless. Either way, she refused to stoop to his level by giving in to an exchange of wills which was exactly what he seemed to want.

Norwood continued to shoot now, holding his Nikon F90 in his hands, carefully monitoring both his aperture openings, as well as his shutter speed. As Jarreau launched into the well-recognized theme from the hit television series *Moonlighting*, Norwood lowered the camera and looked over at Sloan who was busy getting in her last shots. She was perfectly poised, concentration apparent, and seemed intent on closing out the world as she carried on her assignment.

"Thanks again. I'm sure I got my best shots with the mono."

"No problem. You know, practice makes perfect. I've been involved in photography for as long as I can remember and have definitely improved over the years. We should back each other up. I mean that on all fronts," he added, smiling.

Sloan recognized his meaning but chose to ignore his insinuation. His words only made her even more determined to put space between them as she realized that although she was more than two thousand miles away from her last set of demons, her "player" magnet was working overtime in attracting what would most definitely be her next problem.

Norwood, who'd gotten his shots and relaxed into his seat, was busy grooving to Al Jarreau's "Searching for a Superfine Love." He found himself smiling in spite of himself as his thoughts drifted over the past year's occurrences and he suddenly realized that he no longer harbored the profound resentment he'd carried for much of that time. As the final strains of the megahit being belted out by the star now drenched in perspiration filled the amphitheater, Norwood looked over at Sloan. Caught up as she was in the applause and mesmerized by the sheer talent and energy exhibited onstage, her face was bathed in the multicolored lighting coming off the stage. Animated and exhibiting unreserved excitement, she was unnervingly beautiful. Instinctively, he picked up his camera, readjusted the focus, and began to shoot. Even in profile, she was beautiful.

Sloan turned toward him then and he lowered the camera slowly. Neither spoke, the emotionally charged atmosphere speaking volumes without words. And neither noticed the look on Johnson Dade's face as he witnessed the silent exchange from the seats just behind them.

Ten

WNEK Channel 12 News coverage broadcast daily with its signal reaching the metropolitan area of New York City, and its affiliates in neighboring Nassau, Suffolk, and Westchester Counties. Whenever possible, feed coming in from as far south as Virginia, Atlanta, and the coastal peninsula of Florida was displayed in an information band which would accompany regular programming. Depending on the urgency and range of the breaking news, this informational news band of sorts was often accompanied by instructions to the viewers to stay tuned for local upcoming newscasts.

Anita pushed away from her desk, took the reports which had just been faxed in from the FOXX Miami affiliate, and headed for the general manager's office. Braden Douglas would want the opportunity to make a judgment call on this one. His position of authority gave him that flexibility because the "suits" at the top trusted him and the twenty-five years of experience he brought to his job.

She knocked once, waited a brief moment, then walked in. He always kept the door closed, but the unwritten rule was an open door policy, especially in matters of importance or in times of great consequence.

The silver-gray head was bent in concentration, the most recent advertising report spread out on the desk in front of him. His computer monitor displayed the latest tally of the network's ratings. He was surrounded by data that was all his to handle, including what Anita was about to reveal to him. She silently put the papers on top of the ones his gaze had just left, tentatively sat down, and waited for him to absorb the information. It did not take long.

"Did this just come across?" he asked, his voice gruff with an edge of controlled urgency.

"Yeah—if the tracking is accurate, we may have a problem in the next twelve to twenty-four hours. Do you want me to prepare a weather alert or should we just sit tight for another couple of hours?" Anita needed to know so that she could begin to prepare the alert bands which would be broadcast at the bottom of the station's telecast.

"Right now it's still graded as a storm watch. I don't like the fact that it's moving so quickly, gathering speed while it's still way off the shore of Martinique." Braden quickly hit a couple of buttons on his computer keyboard and a map of the eastern Caribbean appeared.

"If it continues on the same path it's currently on, St. Lucia will be hit pretty hard as well as the other islands in its wake." Pointing to the brightly colored display, he showed Anita what he was looking at. "Barbados is right next door, with Trinidad and Tobago in the same wake of weather patterns," he added. "Get me somebody from the Miami weather bureau on the line. We may want to include this in the six o'clock P.M. broadcast. And, yeah, prepare a bulletin just stating that a storm with hurricane potential is brewing off the coast of St. Lucia in the eastern Caribbean."

"Sure, I'll get right on it. By the way, how are the week's ratings? I hear we almost had a forty percent share on Saturday evening with 'Honor Thy Father.'"

"Better than that, the final numbers look to be about a forty-four percent share. Who would have thought a show highlighting a former priest and the orphaned kids he takes on would go through the roof, especially with all the controversy over recent events in the Catholic Church?"

"I know—it's probably a form of backlash. People can't seem to reconcile their feelings so they fixate on an imagery that is at least positive, if not altogether plausible. Go figure," she added, heading for the door. "I'll take care of this right away. Is the Miami general manager okay, or do you want the resident meteorologist?"

"Either one. I just want to make sure we don't have a category-two hurricane on our hands before they alert us again. We need to stay on top of this."

"Consider it done."

Half an hour later, Anita had connected Braden with the Miami station's senior meteorologist, had the weather bands prepared, and given instruction for them to be aired simultaneously with regularly scheduled programming. She had also instructed her counterpart at the Florida station to personally keep her informed of any additional developments.

Busy double-checking the schedule for the following week's morning programming, she automatically picked up her desk line on the second ring.

"Anita Charles here," she said crisply.

"Hey, girl—I meant to call you a couple of days

ago, but I've been so busy, so caught up, and so confused that it's difficult to describe. And on top of it
all, I really meant to thank you for your input on the
director/photographer you helped me to audition
for."

"Hey yourself. And you don't have to thank me for
any of it. I told you, I really wanted to hook you up
with the dude anyway, but didn't know how to con-
nect the dots. Then, I got word of his new project.
Somebody said they were looking for an 'it' girl for a
new music video. The rest is history."

"Well, I just wanted to thank you for doing whatever
you did. Not only did the audition process go
smoothly, but the first couple of days on the set have
been a dream come true. The director is a talented
guy. Really talented," she added. The laughter in her
voice made Anita realize there was more to her statement than the obvious.

"What's all that for? I mean, I know homeboy is fine
but I also know that when it comes to photography,
this guy is about as serious as they come. Kassandra,
please don't do anything that would have him take
you less than seriously."

Kassandra laughed then, knowing that Anita would
really flip if she gave her the details on what had really
occurred. "Listen, girl, you know that I am a complete
professional when I'm on the job. And you were right
about him. He is definitely all that and then some.
He's also all pro when he's behind that camera. It's
just when he's not behind the camera . . ." Her voice
drifted off and she left the sentence incomplete.

"Okay, what the heck is going on 'cause I know
you're holding out on the info. Look, things here are
intense with all kinds of breaking news and stories
that have to be rewritten, edited, and stuff so cut to
the chase. What happened?"

"You know, you're a little too impatient for my taste. And to answer your question, nothing happened. I'm just saying that Mr. Battle is a little more than meets the eye. And don't worry, when there is something to tell, you'll be the first to know. I just wanted to thank you again for all your help, sister dear. The video is going well and I'm really glad you gave me a heads up on the audition. Even my agent is excited that I got the assignment."

"Well, it all just came together. It's like it was supposed to happen. Destiny. Fate. Kismet. Just don't forget me when you move to Cali to star in your first series," Anita added, laughing.

"No doubt, girl. Look, if I blow up like that, hell, I'll move you out there with me. You and Marc, too. We'll all be riding down Wilshire Boulevard, living up in the Hills and drinking to the good life. I'm gonna let you go 'cause I know you're busy. Call me when you can, okay?"

"Yeah—and congratulations again. Love you."

Anita realized immediately that there was quite possibly more than had been discussed going on. She was sure of it. She was also sure that Kass would keep it under wraps until it absolutely had to be discussed or revealed. That was her nature and always had been. Secretive, and able to keep things of great importance to herself for great lengths of time: these traits had a selfish quality in Anita's mind and fit Kassandra's personality profile to a tee. But it had never stopped Anita from loving her. She understood Kass's need for privacy. Some people just needed that separate space, air of suspense, quality of mystery. In Anita's mind, it was just one more facet in the unmistakable allure of Kassandra's personality.

* * *

   And on the other side of the city, Kassandra admitted to herself that no matter what happened, she'd have Anita to possibly thank or blame for bringing her into the world of one Karsten Battle, photographer extraordinaire. And one fine brotha.

Eleven

Barbados

"*I know you're not ready to admit it, not ready to acknowledge and unwilling to surrender to it, but you're already mine.*" Norwood's lips were only inches from her own. She struggled with herself, silently vowing to move away from the nearness of him, yet unable to bring herself to take the first step.

The concert had ended, the buses had been boarded. They sat only inches from one another in the darkness. "Please—you don't know what you're asking. I promised myself that I wouldn't get involved with anyone until one year after my divorce. You were the last thing I expected to find on a press trip," she uttered, her confusion evidenced by the unsteadiness of her tone. His arms tightened, pulling her closer, reducing the distance between them.

"Yeah, well, I think a year is about three hundred and sixty-two days too long, if you ask me. Quite frankly, I can't wait that long—and neither should you." He quickly closed the distance between them, giving her no opportunity for further protest. His lips closed upon hers, demanding a response, gentle and urgent, at the same time. Sloan melted into him, her resolve suddenly weakened in spite of her earlier protests. Their kiss deepened as Norwood explored every crevice of her mouth, trailing kisses from her neckline to her temple. No longer predictable, things were spinning out of control. It took *every ounce of her strength, both mentally and physically, but she managed to put both hands against his chest and push herself away.*

"We have to stop this. I never meant to let this happen," she whispered through lips swollen with passion.

"Neither did I. But now that we've come this far, there's no way that we can turn our backs on it. I'm not giving up on you, Sloan. It may take a little time, but I always get what I go after."

His words echoed in her ear and sent a shiver of excitement up her spine. She knew he spoke the truth . . . knew it was just a matter of time. . . .

Sunlight streamed through the expanse of windows as the sounds of early morning sunbathers, swimmers, and others frolicking on the beach awakened Sloan. She stiffened, then relaxed. It had only been a dream.

She stretched languidly as a sigh of relief flooded her body. *Thank God . . . only a dream,* she thought as she headed into the bathroom to shower. The fact that thoughts of his presence had remained with her throughout the night was totally unacceptable. It was also a cause for real concern.

Norwood had sat across from her as the bus wound its way through the curving hillside parishes leading to Christ Church where many of their hotels were located. Their conversation centered more on photography than anything else. And although he was at least six feet away from her, his concentration could be felt closing the distance without ever physically making a move. In the two days since their arrival in Barbados, Norwood had become a daily expectancy, a ritual, an unwelcome and dangerous habit. His ability to assist her in getting great shots and even his tidbits of valuable photography insight had, at first, been annoying. Little by little, Sloan also became aware that it was his way of actually offering a truce. The problem was that no war had been officially declared, although she readily accepted the fact that they'd been on different sides from the very beginning.

What she couldn't accept was the way her body responded every time he was in her presence. The kisses she'd dreamed of were a product of an overactive imagination; the desire she felt each time he was near was very real.

In the darkened atmosphere of Sir Garfield Sobers Gynmasium on the previous night, their hands had touched accidentally as he'd mounted her camera on the monopod, and Sloan was at a loss to explain the immediate rise in her pulse rate or the sudden, urgent racing of her heart. She knew it was ridiculous, but she also knew it was useless to try and define any of it. In another three days, she'd be on her way back to New York; Norwood would be headed to the Midwest and the point would be a moot one. Or so she told herself as she brushed her teeth, showered, and made ready for another day in Barbados.

As she entered the outdoor restaurant of the all-inclusive hotel, Jodi waved to her from a table in the farthest corner which faced the ocean. Blue skies, pearl-colored sand, and a cooling breeze created an atmosphere of pure paradise proportion and Sloan took a deep breath of ocean air, glad to be exactly where she was.

"Well, you sure look like the cat who swallowed the canary this morning," Jodi said as Sloan sat down.

"I am happy. And you should be, too. Look, we're able to enjoy a fabulous morning like this in the month of January. At home it's probably only thirty-five or forty degrees, if that, with threats of snow, rain, or blustery winds the most common forecast. We should be celebrating every moment of being here 'cause we could be in turtleneck sweaters and snow boots."

"You're absolutely right. I'm having a Bloody Mary to salute the day. I'd suggest you do the same or order something else that's festive and island inspired. Each time I accept an assignment here in the Caribbean, I pay homage to the total beauty of the islands and the fabulous climate. We are indeed lucky. We deserve to celebrate."

"Most definitely. I think I'll just order a fruit platter this morning and maybe have a virgin passion fruit punch. I like the way they make it here," Sloan said while positioning her sunglasses to block out the intense rays of the sunshine. Although the morning was a beautifully fantastic one, the initial brightness often took some getting used to and almost everyone on the beach and at the restaurant's tables wore sunglasses in varying styles and hues.

As Sloan relaxed into her seat, sipping the wonderfully exotic mixture of juices, she spotted Lorenzo walking toward their table.

"Don't look now but I think you have company," she said as he reached them.

"Hey, don't you two look cozy and ready for a day of leisure? Mind if I join you?" he asked, quickly pulling up a chair. Neither young woman answered; the same question was on both their lips though.

"How did you get over here this morning—I know your hotel is farther down into Christ Church," Jodi managed to get out. She was also clearly pleased to see him.

"Actually, Norwood asked me to meet him here this morning. I'm thinking he'll show up at any moment, but if he doesn't, I'll have the front desk call his room. In the meanwhile, I like having the company of my two favorite ladies on the island."

"Oh, well, thanks for the compliment. We're just ordering breakfast—will you have something or do you want to wait for your friend?" Sloan asked. She was unable to keep herself from being slightly annoyed. Although she had nothing against Lorenzo, his mention of the other name made her slightly uncomfortable.

Her fruit platter arrived then and Lorenzo ordered a glass of orange juice. Only a couple of minutes passed before Norwood could be seen coming toward their table.

Dressed as he was in all white, with brown leather woven sandals on his feet, Sloan had to admit that he was one exceptionally fine brother. The two days of sun had only managed to compliment his milk chocolate complexion, turning it a burnished bronze. And the darkness of his hair and mustache had only deepened, which accentuated the richness of his skin. Sloan felt her pulse begin to race, remembered her dreams of the night before, and played with the cantaloupe on her plate as he approached.

"Well, good morning, group. It seems the gang is all here," he announced jovially as he pulled up a chair. "Is it all right if we join you ladies, or should we banish ourselves to a separate table?" he asked quickly, ready to retreat in defeat if need be.

Sloan's quiet demeanor was registering as a step backward, which he recognized immediately. He realized that she was probably never going to welcome him with open arms and readily accepted that, too. For the moment.

Jodi laughed then at the ridiculousness of the situation. "You guys might as well stay and have breakfast right here. We'll only be here for a little while longer anyway," she offered. Sloan's plate was almost empty. And Jodi had only ordered toast and juice anyway.

"Well, we don't want to make ourselves welcome where we may not be. I'm just saying that if you want us to get a separate table, we will." Norwood's offer sounded just fine to Sloan—but she couldn't bring herself to raise her eyes to meet his and say that. Instead, she waited until she heard Lorenzo declare, "Truce."

"We're staying right here with you ladies. We admit it, we don't like to eat alone. All the statistics say that men are much better off with women. We need you," he stated finally and with much fanfare.

Norwood laughed then. "Damn, I feel as if I've been sold off without even so much as an opening bid," he offered. But his smile indicated that he, too, was pleased to be exactly where he was. Sloan quietly sipped her fruit drink, mindful of the group spirit, but also totally cognizant of feelings she desperately needed to suppress.

Jodi and Lorenzo beamed at one another—glad to have successfully negotiated the one thing they both wanted—to be in each other's company.

"So, what did you guys think of last night's concert? The boy was in good shape, wasn't he?" Lorenzo added in a quick assessment.

"Most definitely—and you know Al's no new jack on the block. But you can see that he takes extremely good care of himself. His voice is in fantastic form, and so is his physical stance." Norwood prided himself on the ability to assess an artist's temperment, level of genuine commitment, as well as overall stance. The camera never lied and with the use of a telephoto lens, the view was almost microscopic.

"I thought he was fantastic. His band was off the hook," Sloan offered, remembering many of the songs he'd performed. "The classic hits stay with you. When you see them performed live, it only makes them stand out even more distinctly. And yes, I, too, was amazed at the wonderful condition the man is in.

He definitely takes fantastic care of himself," she added.

"You know, not only was the band tight, but if you consider the repertoire of music he's performed over the past two decades, you come to the realization that he's somewhat of an American icon. Jazz, R and B, blues, and his refined version of scatting have put Jarreau into a class by himself. Name one other artist that is able to deliver a song like he does and I'll buy dinner," Norwood offered. The challenge remained in the air and on the table for some minutes.

Lorenzo jumped up, spun around theatrically, and hit the table with the palm of his hand then. "Nancy Wilson has her own unique style, definitely has the time in, and also can twist a tune into a pretzel, still delivering it with finesse and real star treatment." Sporting a look of supreme pleasure at having out-foxed his colleagues, Lorenzo had his competitive spirit in full gear.

"Yeah, but Al writes most of his own stuff. You have to come up with an artist who is also a songwriter. But not a musician though 'cause that changes the playing field totally," Norwood added. He was beginning to thoroughly enjoy the exchange going on at the table. Mental calisthenics agreed with him and he couldn't help but notice that Sloan seemed slightly annoyed. *Well, that's too bad for Miss Priss,* he thought inwardly. A little challenge wouldn't hurt her and if it did, so be it.

Jodi, who had been relatively quiet throughout the exchange, was deep in thought. "I've got it. Lauren Hill—she writes, she sings, she does it all. And yeah, she's young and not really part of the classic jazz scene, but you were really talking artistry, not longevity," Jodi quickly pointed out.

Lorenzo laughed then and shook his head. "I don't

know about you, Norwood, but I don't think Lauren Hill has compiled the body of work we're talking about. Right?" he asked, eager for his compadre to confirm his theory.

"Lorenzo has a point. The young Miss Hill is a talented songwriter and producer, but we're also talking performance and character. I don't think she's reached the top rung on that ladder. Any other suggestions?" His question remained unanswered for the next several seconds.

Sloan, who appeared to be elsewhere, in spirit anyway, suddenly leaned back comfortably, clasped her hands behind her head, and smiled. "Anita Baker is my counterclaim. And although she hasn't made an album in more than five years, any one tune from any album she's ever recorded still makes my heart beat faster. How about you?" she asked the group. Her eyes locked on to Norwood's defiantly.

"Yeah, she is bad. I wish she would make another CD 'cause the ones I have are practically worn out I've played them so much," Jodi offered.

"Tell me about it. My brother borrowed *Rapture* and never brought it back. By the time I realized he hadn't returned it, months had passed. It's now into years and that sucker still won't give it up," Lorenzo confessed. The look of genuine pain on his face said it all. He obviously missed his music.

"Your candidate does have chops but I'm not sure she knocks Al out of the box. Just to be a good sport though, I'll honor my original offer. That's dinner for all present on me. And don't anybody get cute. Now, what's the best night and where should we dine?" he asked.

"Hey, guys, let's move this discussion to the beach. I want to work on getting some shots of the boats and stuff," Lorenzo said.

"Yeah, and I can work on my tan. I have one of those pocket-size island tour books, too. I'm sure it has quite a few restaurants listed," Jodi offered.

"Great—let's move this to the next level then," Norwood said, as he grabbed his gear and they all headed toward the beachfront. Lounge chairs, towels, and several striped umbrellas were available for use by hotel guests.

Sloan had worn a pair of white terry cloth shorts over her bathing suit, pulled her hair into a ponytail, and thrown the remaining items she needed into a striped canvas bag. Jodi, too, wore a bathing suit and quickly stripped down to it as they reached the beachfront area. Red and white polka dots adorned the top half, and the matching bottom was done in alternating red and white stripes. Jodi began to apply sunscreen immediately. Although she didn't normally burn easily, she knew that at this time of morning, the sun's rays were at their most vibrant and she wasn't taking any chances. Lorenzo, browned already from the California sun, as well as from his father's Mexican blood, reached over. "Here, let me do that for you," he said, taking the tube of spf 40 sunblock from her and applying it to her back and arms.

Norwood, after having secured a chair, towel, and a space under a nearby tree, removed his miniature CD player from the bag, and loaded it. The sounds of Earth, Wind & Fire could be heard, and Sloan smiled.

"I'd say you come well prepared," she said, removing her shorts to reveal a lime green halter one-piece. It fit her snugly, with the top portion accentuating the well-proportioned bosom it contained. Her legs, long and slim, only accentuated the trim waistline and gently flaring hips. She had model-like proportions, but would probably photograph as voluptuous.

Norwood's breath caught in his throat and he

turned away. Unable to disguise the feelings he was experiencing, he donned his sunglasses, reached into his bag for a bottle of water, and waited for his respiration to return to normal.

Lorenzo started snapping shots of everything around them. Jodi looked through the island restaurant guide while Sloan continued to listen to the music emanating from the CD player. Marvin Gaye's recording of "Ain't No Mountain High Enough" was playing and the pairing of his rough, urban voice with the sweetness of Tammy Terrell was pure perfection. They were quickly becoming a circle of friends. Norwood admired Jodi for her talent and stance in the industry. Associated Press didn't hire just anyone for its coverage. Lorenzo was just the type of photographer he'd been only a few short years before—talented, hungry, and willing to put his ability on the line for anyone interested in testing him. Sloan was another story. Stubborn, beautiful, and a pain in the butt, but he instinctively knew that although she feigned indifference, challenged him at every turn, and appeared to the world as if she didn't give a damn, underneath that nonchalant exterior, there was a passionate woman.

Norwood knew she couldn't continue to ignore the chemistry between them. Somewhere down the line, the timing would be right. He'd be able to put just the right moves into place and she would have to make a decision. Sooner or later, there would be a payoff—it was inevitable. It came to him suddenly that he wanted nothing more in the world than to be the sole beneficiary. And if he had his way, it would be soon, very soon.

Twelve

New York City

The third day of the shoot proved to be an even greater challenge than one and two. Wind machines, fog producers, and several "blue screens" set up to create a blank canvas were placed on the set in strategic locations. Special effects and uncharacteristic movement would be added to this canvas in postproduction.

Karsten looked forward to working with Rory Scotto, the special effects choreographer chosen for the assignment. His talent in pulling together what was real and unreal, merging them into one seamless entity, was legendary. He was all of twenty-nine. Incredible imagination still intact, he worked quickly and efficiently, often with the headphones to his CD player in place. The world he intended to create for this most current video was enhanced by the music he listened to. It was usually the artist's work. That way he was always in sync. New Deal's latest CD, *Destiny Knows No Doubt,* was loaded on this day, ready to be experienced as Karsten directed the beginning scenes.

Increasingly amazed at the sheer amount and complexity of equipment used to create atmosphere and provide the necessary backdrop for them to later instill details she couldn't even conceive of, Kassandra waited patiently for her set call. The dressing rooms, small and cubelike with one large light in the center of the ceiling, wardrobe racks lining the sides of both walls, and a standing mirror in one corner, left a lot to be desired. She sat awkwardly on the only chair in the room, her mind on the day before.

The shoot had taken place in the quaint, quiet, private Long Island village of Roslyn. Not normally give to traffic, congestion, and hoopla, it had only been through close ties with a member of the village's board of trustees that the permit had been obtained. That and an exchange of an undisclosed sum. It was how business was done and only through Karsten's many ties in the industry had it been even possible. Privilege had afforded him the opportunity, but it was not a free pass. It was a favor which would be repaid over and over again in the future and he knew it. But he'd had no choice. The location was perfect and he knew it would give him just the atmosphere and the results he needed.

The early morning lighting had been perfect. The sun's rays, filtering through the special polarizer he'd used, created a look of purity. Shots of the various members of the group, interspersed with Kassandra in different poses with the lake glistening in the background, spelled tranquility.

Wardrobe had dressed her in a white crochet and knit dress, her hair pulled up into a high ponytail with wisps falling softly around her face. The look was one of honesty, simplicity, and most of all, that of untouched beauty.

Karsten's camera caught both the stillness of the lake, the family of ducks which drifted aimlessly by, and the dazzling beauty of his subject. Five hours of shooting brought them into the early afternoon, when the sun became more potent and the shots more difficult. With lighting no longer emitting the same softness of the early morning, Karsten gave the order to pack it in. His sole purpose had been to obtain the softness of the early morning light which he felt would convey the freshness, the fragility of a new relationship.

The staff began to break down the set, and Kassandra headed for the costume trailer to change. The production staff consisted of several veterans in the industry, all of whom were only in their early twenties or thirties. Television, video, and film were all they knew, having grown up with it as a steady medium.

As a veteran of the business, Karsten considered himself the senior among the crew. Although he played it to his advantage, everyone, from the production assistants to the technicians and second string photography staff, was aware of and acknowledged his talent. He was an industry legacy, having made his mark on the sets of industry giants WNBC and WFOX. They realized, from the time he walked onto the set until it was time to shut down, that he would demand from each and every one of them only the best and purest form of their respective crafts. He, in turn, would deliver a superior product, one which they knew would ultimately satisfy the client and possibly set a new industry standard. That being the forum, no one thought to question his authority on any aspect of the business at hand. Not on the surface anyway.

They headed back to the city and dispersed. And although Karsten was tempted to offer Kassandra another ride, when he stopped by her dressing room, she had already left. He didn't realize it until later that evening as he painstakingly edited the film from the day's shoot, but he'd been looking forward to that possibility throughout the day.

As he watched the scenes, weaving them together to create an end product that would both reflect the artist's point of view, as well as appeal to their music buying public, he made a decision. One that would change everything.

Kassandra's performance of the day before had been exceptional. So much so that in the rushes developed and critiqued immediately after shooting, she'd come off as an element to be focused on rather than melded into the subsequent scenes. Her initial outfit as a schoolgirl gone temptingly bad was replaced by a spicy tangerine V-neck cropped to reveal her tiny waistline and impeccably toned abs. White biker shorts accentuated and revealed long, long legs. Neutral colored sandals, with straps which laced up around her ankles, completed the look of an extremely enticing young woman. Her hair remained in two long pigtails, signaling a child in a woman's body. Today's shoot would have her interact once again with each member of the singing group, virtually causing a chaotic situation in their everyday lives. "Faithful," the title cut, would be represented by a video which questioned the suggested integrity of each and every one of its crooners, as well as the overall validity of such a concept.

Kassandra's makeup, hair, and wardrobe complete, she was led onto the set once again, directed to her entrance area, and placed on her mark. Her nervousness of the first day had been replaced by a determination to get through the assignment—no matter what the cost.

Karsten, just finishing a meter reading on the available lighting for the scene, looked up at that moment. His reaction to her was instantaneous, although unintelligible. No one around him was even remotely aware of it; he checked himself, got behind the camera, and focused on the task at hand. Never mind that his hands were less than steady or that every muscle in his body was being infused with adrenaline.

He inwardly acknowledged that he'd had countless numbers of affairs with girls who were more beautiful, shaped better, and who probably could teach this one several lessons in the art of making a man happy. So why was his reaction to her so strong? What did she possess that turned his brain to mush and his hands to mittens?

Professionalism. Kassandra was a study in good old-fashioned professionalism. Even from the first day, he'd noticed that she was indeed a "pro." Not only did he admire and respect that, he championed and encouraged it. The industry was fraught with people only too happy to take advantage of the dreams of inexperienced young hopefuls.

She'd been genuinely reluctant to accept a ride from him, then done everything in her power to discourage him from dropping her in front of her home. He realized then that she was now doing everything in her power to keep a semblance of order on what had taken place only two days before. She'd effectively avoided him the day before. And although he was thoroughly accustomed to skimpy and often suggestive costumes, picture-perfect models in his viewfinder, and almost anything else which went hand in hand with the industry, there was something both striking and compelling about her that he couldn't quite put his finger on. She filled out the shorts to perfection, giving credence to the phrase "baby got back." Her legs, both long and well shaped, were accentuated by the three-inch stiletto heels, and the cropped V-neck brought attention to a waistline that was incredibly small, with the gently flaring hips and full bosom of a full-grown woman.

Annoyed somewhat by his inability to focus on the task at hand, Karsten yelled "quiet on the set." Everyone immediately took their places. Some three hours and several reels of videocassette later, they'd managed to capture most of the necessary scenes. It was well past noon when they broke.

They were scheduled for a full day's shoot, and today's lunch break was catered by Diamond's, a company that prided itself on good, solid, authentically prepared Caribbean foods. They also offered a variety of gourmet cuisine, including both a hot and cold buffet, organic salads and fruits, natural cheeses and yogurt, and homemade muffins. Juices, coffee, tea, and bottled water were available throughout the shoot for anyone who needed a quick pick-me-up.

Kassandra, having removed the heels and put on her own set of flip-flops, selected a chicken Ceasar salad, iced coffee, and a granny smith apple. She was starving, not having had the time to eat breakfast, and knew there would only be an approximate hour break for the hastily downed lunch.

"Hey, I think you took the last green apple. Those are my favorites, you know," Karsten said as he walked up, his cap turned to the back in its usual form.

He looked relaxed, casual, and something else that she couldn't quite put her finger on. It had not been easy focusing at times while he shot the scenes, sometimes giving direction as to how and where she, as well as the other cast members, stood or interacted. She was totally aware of him as "the man in charge" but she was also aware of him as a man, which was even more unnerving.

"Well, had I known, I would have left it. But as it stands now, I think you're out of luck," she added. What she was really thinking was that perhaps her flippant attitude would cover the way he really affected her.

"Okay, well, you don't really have to worry—I wasn't going to demand that you turn it over to me. Actually, I was just messing with you. Where's your sense of humor?" He couldn't help himself from chastising her. Her reaction reminded him so much of Sloan. Always on the defensive, always ready to do battle. He suddenly realized what it was about her that both attracted and repelled him at the same time. In some small, obscure way, something about her demeanor, her persona, and her attitude brought his ex to mind.

She certainly did not look like her. Nor did she even remotely sound like her. But there was a nondescript sort of mannerism that they shared and Karsten inwardly acknowledged that there was, albeit uncanny, something almost painfully comforting about it. You knew the turf you were on immediately. He realized that Kassandra had stopped eating and was watching him. Probably putting together the strings of his last statement, trying to add two and two together and coming up with ten.

He took a plate, filled it with salad and a healthy serving of jerked chicken, rice and peas, and several plantains. Kassandra watched him and couldn't help but laugh. His plate was piled high with food, and even though he had not one ounce of excess weight on his body, the sheer amount was laughable.

"Wow, if I ate like that I don't think you'd have wanted me to be in this video," she offered, picking up a bottle of water.

"Well, the creative juices need to be fed, you know. And I'm very fortunate. I obviously have a high metabolism 'cause I never put on a pound. By the way, I like the way you laugh. It doesn't sound forced or contrived," he added as he headed for one of the tables.

Unable to stop herself, and afraid it would appear as if she really were afraid of him, Kassandra followed.

"Thanks, it's probably my Brooklyn upbringing. A lot of my friends were real comedians when we were kids. Pulling pranks, acting up, just plain cutting the fool," she added, pulling out a chair. They both sat down and two key grips, already halfway through their lunch, nodded as they continued eating.

"So, you grew up in Brooklyn, too. What school did you go to?" he asked, curious as to how he'd missed meeting or ever seeing her anywhere in the neighborhood. Brooklyn was the fourth largest city in the United States, but everyone seemed to have crossed paths at one point. And if you were of the same age group, that was even more the case.

"Well, I went to Brooklyn Tech, then graduated and went on to the University of Chicago on a scholarship. I stayed in the Midwest until it got a little too hot for me," she added.

"The Midwest too hot? I thought it took the middle of summer and a real heat wave for that to happen." He realized that he was curious about her past, her present, and maybe even her immediate future.

"Actually, I meant that more in the philosophical sense of the word. But that's a long story. You know, I wanted to tell you thank you for expanding my part in the video. I was only assigned to be on the set for the first part and it looks like I'm now in the next day's shoot also."

"Don't thank me. It's your relationship with the camera, your ability to follow direction, and give a credible performance that's gotten you the additional assignment. Thank you for being so professional. It's made my job that much easier." He wanted to add that her beauty and her natural acting ability would probably take her much further if that's where she wanted to go, but caution made him stop. He would only regret it if he created a full-blown diva before he was even finished with his current assignment.

"Listen, I don't usually make it a habit of doing this, but you're funny and kind of cute, in a conventional sense."

Her laughter caught him off guard, but it also made him feel more comfortable in his next statement.

"What I was going to say before you laughed in my face was, are you busy tomorrow night? I'd like to see you off the set, if that's okay with you." He waited, knowing that she could blow him out of the water if she wanted. He was more than prepared for that to be the case, knowing that photographers hit on models all the time. It was an industry truism and he could no more defend himself than the next man. Beauty was beauty—in the eye of the beholder, in the lens of the camera, wherever . . .

"Karsten, I don't want you to take this the wrong way but I don't think it would be a good idea for us to go out. Don't get me wrong—I think you're great and all that, but you know we're working together. I'm just not sure it's such a good thing for us to mix business with whatever. . . . She faltered then, looking away because although the words were coming from her own mouth, they were a lie. She wanted to accept, wanted to see where it would take them, but fear stopped her cold.

What if she liked him, what if he liked her? What if they didn't like each other? And what if, God forbid, something happened? The assortment of fears running through her mind had been there for the past couple of days, and had propelled her to damn near run from the set the day before, not knowing if she'd have the strength to refuse another invitation from him. But now, sitting with him after having shared a meal in a public forum, with assorted cast members and technicians, she realized that she was fighting a losing battle.

"Are you sure you've thought this out? I mean, I know it's just a date and all but isn't that the way most things start?" Her question hung in the air and Karsten turned his hat around to the front, pulling on the front of it in a reflex gesture.

"If you mean have I been thinking about it all my life, no. But if your question is more in line with do I understand the underlying possibilities, the answer would be hell yeah." He laughed then and Kassandra did, too, the tension of the moment broken by the absurdity of the concept. They were both healthy, mature adults—unattached in a world of possibilities.

"Well, I guess I don't have to give you the address," she said, still smiling.

"No, I think I can find it. I'll pick you up around seven-thirty. See you on the set." He stood up, turned his cap backward again and walked off, mission accomplished.

Thirteen

St. Lucia

Castries, the capital city of the geographically diverse island of St. Lucia, was in imminent danger. The storm, which had been upgraded to a category two hurricane only six hours before, was headed straight for its shores.

Tiny pellets of rain bombarded the island, the sun an apparent fugitive for the past twenty-four hours. The interior rain forest, known for its dense foliage and striking trees, was awash in moisture. Unyielding and slowly gaining in momentum, the steady downpour increased in volume as the accompanying winds picked up speed. An upgrade in status would be designated if current conditions continued. Category two demanded immediate precautions, and most of the island's inhabitants were thoroughly aware of the possible ramifications. They remembered only too well the wrath of Hurricane Alan which had unleashed its ire unmercilessly back in 1979.

St. Lucia's Ministry of the Interior issued an official warning via radio station 93.7, also known as "The Wave." Radio St. Lucia and its local television station continued to monitor the storm's progress and its path. Headed west, packing winds of more than eighty miles per hour, the current path, if consistent, would bring it to the shores of St. Lucia within the next twelve to eighteen hours.

Pidgeon Island, a national landmark park as well as a popular gathering place for tourists and locals and a recurring site for the St. Lucia Jazz Festival, was awash with the high tide which now bombarded its shoreline. Waves of record-breaking heights were being reported as the residents prepared for the worst. Surrounded by the Caribbean and the Atlantic Ocean, it was awash with the high seas it literally sat in the midst of. Bombarded now for the past thirty-six hours, police markings reflecting the St. Lucia Police Authority prevented entrance from the main road. Residents living anywhere in the vicinity were being evacuated in an attempt to avoid further distress.

Properties throughout Rodney Bay and Gros Islet, two of the more popular tourist areas, also braced themselves. Business owners boarded their windows and reinforced their doors, hoping that they would be spared the full wrath of Mother Nature.

In the south of the island the rain forest was thick with humidity and awash with the accumulated levels from the constant barrage of driving rain. Normally vibrating with the voices of the many varieties and species of its natural inhabitants, the overall area had been overtaken by quiet. The only sound to be heard was the driving rain and the blustery winds which shook the leaves from the trees and upended many an unstable branch.

Located only seventy miles off the coast of Barbados, St. Lucia was in the throes of an indomitable force. Weatherwise, the two islands usually shared the same seventy-five- to eighty-degree temperatures year-round with an occasional rainy season occurring in early spring.

Hurricane Grace, seemingly intent on unleashing

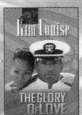

A SPECIAL "THANK YOU" FROM ARABESQUE JUST FOR YOU!

Send this card back and you'll receive 4 FREE Arabesque Novels—a $25.96 value—absolutely FREE!

The introductory 4 Arabesque Romance books are yours FREE (plus $1.99 shipping & handling). If you wish to continue to receive 4 books every month, do nothing. Each month, we will send you 4 New Arabesque Romance Novels for your free examination. If you wish to keep them, pay just $16* (plus, $1.99 shipping & handling). If you decide not to continue, you owe nothing!

- Send no money now.
- Never an obligation.
- Books delivered to your door!

We hope that after receiving your FREE books you'll want to remain an Arabesque subscriber, but the choice is yours! So why not take advantage of this Arabesque offer, with no risk of any kind. You'll be glad you did!

In fact, we're so sure you will love your Arabesque novels, that we will send you an Arabesque Tote Bag FREE with your first paid shipment.

Call Us TOLL-FREE At 1-888-345-BOOK

* Prices subject to change

THE "THANK YOU" GIFT INCLUDES:

- 4 books absolutely FREE (plus $1.99 for shipping and handling).
- A FREE newsletter, *Arabesque Romance News*, filled with author interviews, book previews, special offers, and more!
- No risks or obligations.

INTRODUCTORY OFFER CERTIFICATE

Yes! Please send me 4 FREE Arabesque novels (plus $1.99 for shipping & handling). I understand I am under no obligation to purchase any books, as explained on the back of this card. Send my **FREE Tote Bag** after my first regular paid shipment.

NAME _____

ADDRESS _____ APT. _____

CITY _____ STATE _____ ZIP _____

TELEPHONE ( ) _____

E-MAIL _____

SIGNATURE _____

Offer limited to one per household and not valid to current subscribers. All orders subject to approval. Terms, offer, & price subject to change. Tote bags available while supplies last.

Thank You!

AN073A

ARABESQUE

Accepting the four introductory books for FREE (plus $1.99 to offset the cost of shipping & handling) places you under no obligation to buy anything. You may keep the books and return the shipping statement marked "cancelled". If you do not cancel, about a month later we will send 4 additional Arabesque novels, and you will be billed the preferred subscriber's price of just $4.00 per title. That's $16.00* for all 4 books for a savings of almost 40% off the cover price (Plus $1.99 for shipping and handling). You may cancel at any time, but if you choose to continue, every month we'll send you 4 more books, which you may either purchase at the preferred discount price. . . or return to us and cancel your subscription.

* PRICES SUBJECT TO CHANGE

THE ARABESQUE ROMANCE BOOK CLUB
P.O. BOX 5214
CLIFTON NJ 07015-5214

its fury on St. Lucia, was on a direct course with its neighboring island of Barbados. That was a certainty. The only thing as yet undetermined was the level of strength she'd still have upon arrival. And that would only be determined by monitoring the next twelve to twenty-four hours of activity.

Through all of it, the rain never slowed, the winds continued to pick up speed, and the storm itself grew more powerful, gaining additional strength as each hour passed.

This preordained date with a weather destiny appeared to be unavoidable. And the people of both St. Lucia and Barbados would be at its mercy.

Fourteen

Barbados

Heritage Park was lit up like a miniature Christmas village. A working distillery whose product ESA FIELD rum was enjoyed the world over, the setting was magnificent. Center stage for the evening concert was Marcus Miller, guitar wunderkind, arranger, and composer extraordinaire, and one of the most successful young musicians on the jazz scene. His band was always tight with the legendary Hiram Bullock on bass. Known for playing in his bare feet, Bullock was undoubtedly one of the finest bassists on the planet.

Norwood's senses were on heightened alert. He was more than aware of the value of the featured artist, having photographed him in the past. These shots would be monumentally important to his assignment and a key element in the final product to be delivered.

Heritage Park's nighttime setting was exquisite with tiny lights adorning the many trees framing the walkways. Many of the buildings, as well as the distinctive brick architecture, were also adorned with simple white lights illuminating every facet. And although it was most certainly beyond reproach in its delivery of ambience and beauty, the venue itself was a photographer's worst nightmare. The lack of light, the variations of color, and the strategically placed back lighting did not make for an easy shoot. Norwood's challenge would be a test of his skill. The creativity needed to capture photos that would highlight his subject, including the environment in which he performed, was definitely on the line. That was photography at its best. But then, Norwood was genuinely gifted so he was actually looking forward to the evening on a professional note. On a personal note, he had several reservations.

Sloan was doing everything in her power to keep an even balance between work and whatever her feelings were concerning Norwood. Once Pandora's box was opened, its contents were irretrievable, unpredictable, and often regrettable.

She and Jodi boarded the bus, greeted everyone warmly, and then sat across the aisle from Norwood and Lorenzo. Deep in conversation concerning the merits of lighting filters, the two photography buffs continued their heated discussion.

Johnson Dade, who sat directly behind them, listened intently to every word, wondering how they could be so involved in something so mundane. Photography had always bored him. It had too many gadgets, too much precision, and not enough of a paycheck attached to it for him. Not until you reached the top of the ladder, anyway. Advertising, on the other hand, paid handsomely once you had your accounts set up. And the residuals were just gravy. He'd leave the bells, whoops, and whistles to guys like the two in front of him any day. They were amateurs in the scheme of things and in the arena of life, where it really mattered. Discussing technical equipment like two lab partners in a high

school class. He dismissed them mentally and focused on the ladies sitting across the aisle. For some
reason, which he couldn't for the life of him understand, they'd apparently formed a foursome. For
now anyway. If he had his way, they would soon be
missing one of the major components—Miss
Whitaker. And tonight was the night, in his opinion,
that he should and would make his move. Quietly,
within the darkened confines of the tour bus, he
cultivated what in his mind amounted to a master
"plan."

Sloan, wearing a long denim prairie skirt, white eye-
let camisole top, and suede belt which matched the
natural tone of her sandals, looked relaxed and casual. She'd pulled her hair up, pinning it at the back,
leaving soft ringlets falling around her face. It accentuated the planes of her neck and the angles of her
cheekbones. Norwood watched her as she'd entered
the bus. He wanted to play with the ringlets, unbutton
the camisole top, and take shots of her looking di-
sheveled. He settled for photographing Marcus Miller
instead.

The humidity, thick and out of character for the
area, was definitely rising. Several audience members
waved makeshift fans and commented on the increased moisture in the air. It wasn't altogether
uncomfortable, yet its effects could be felt and seen in
the attendees and in their behavior. Many waved programs incessantly. Others opened yet another button
on their shirts, blouses, or whatever they were wearing. And although the forecast had not included a
prediction of rain, you could feel it, almost smell it, in
the air.

Norwood focused on setting up his equipment, and

was poised to commandeer the vantage point which would result in the most poignant photos. He was hot. The humidity aside, an afternoon of seeing Sloan in her bathing suit, laughing and talking with her as she nonchalantly went about the business of lunch, leisure, and life, had begun to get to him. And when they'd parted just before five o'clock, he'd vowed to put a little distance between them for the remaining days of the trip. In his mind, it was the honorable thing to do. It was also the safe thing.

With the sleeves rolled up on the white collarless shirt he wore, head bent in concentration, he didn't realize Sloan had taken a position beside him until he caught the distinct scent of her fragrance. By now, it was recognizable to him and he inwardly groaned, the discomfort he felt increasing with every moment she remained so close to him. He'd imagined, over and over again, how she'd probably feel in his arms, his senses reeling from the nearness of her. He managed to look at her, smile innocently, and then look away again. If she were able to read his thoughts, she probably would have had him arrested. With that thought, he laughed to himself, unable to contain the hilarity of it all.

"Private joke?" she asked. She'd begun to remove her wide-angle lens, anticipating that the evening's artist would command close-up shots whenever and wherever possible. She realized that a photo of Marcus Miller would make a great cover shot for the newspaper and was already thinking ahead in giving herself the best possible advantage by use of the most appropriate equipment.

"Yeah, you could say that. You look nice, very nice," he added, noting the long graceful sway of her skirt, the way she filled the blouse out, and, in particular, the tiny pearl buttons which he counted to be exactly eight. He realized, at that moment, that she looked good in almost anything. But then, she would probably look particularly good in absolutely nothing at all, too. He mentally chastised himself for not being able to control his thoughts. "Hands off," he told himself for the one hundredth time that day.

"Thanks—so do you," she responded. Sloan realized that she liked the way he dressed. Neat, not preppy or thuggish, and extremely conservative. And although she hadn't really noticed it before, she liked the way the salt and pepper of his hair was accentuated by the stark white of his shirt. Black pants and a black snakeskin belt which matched his loafers completed his outfit. His only jewelry was a Tag Heuer watch, the epitome of both precision and style. The collarless shirt he wore reminded her of a minister and she smiled thinking that Norwood was as far from being called to religion as Karsten had been. And with that thought, Sloan realized that there were many obvious similarities between the two. She also realized that she'd been comparing them the entire time. The realization both annoyed her and made her wonder just how far the similarities went.

Watching Norwood painstakingly set up his equipment, remembering the helpful hints he'd passed on to her during previous concerts, and thinking of the earlier portion of the day and all that had transpired, she realized that he was as different from Karsten as night and day. The only similarity was that they were both handsome, incredibly talented, and highly motivated, successful photographers. Karsten's medium was motion pictures; Norwood excelled in still photos.

The evening's lineup was announced and the audience waited in eager anticipation, ready to bear witness to a phenomenally talented individual. Marcus Miller walked onstage, his band struck up the beginning chords of "Jazz in the House/Represent" and it was on. Members of the press had been given no restrictions on this evening's event and went about capturing as many photographs as possible, eager to catch the young, energetic talent in a self-defining pose. It was that "one great photo" which they all sought.

Norwood's experiences of the past had primed him. He was a pro at knowing just where to stand, what angle to shoot from, where and when and how to look for that perfect shot. Miller's band, along with the man himself, provided countless such vantage points. The concert itself was even better than Sloan had anticipated. Marcus Miller, born in Brooklyn and raised in Queens, had more funk and soul than the law allowed, and the West Coast had obviously not changed him at all. They performed several cuts from his latest CD and then went on to perform "vintage" Miller from his days with legendary trumpeteer Miles Davis. Miller's credits also included producing David Sanborn's *Backstreet* album. His performance brought the house to its feet time and time again.

"That was so incredible—I am going to buy all his CDs when I get home," Sloan exclaimed, clapping enthusiastically. Her face glowed in the diminished lighting and Norwood found himself reining in his natural response to her presence.

"Yeah, Marcus is a bad boy—always has been. Is this the first time you've seen him perform live?"

"Yes—I had no idea he was so good. It just goes to show that New York puts out some top notch musicians—he could only have gotten that attitude and that polish from the East Coast."

"Well, I don't know if I'd go so far as to say that. After all, what about New Orleans, Memphis, and even St. Louis? There are lots of musicians who came out of all those places—cats that have been in the spotlight for years but maybe you just haven't heard of them before either." He definitely didn't want her to develop a preferential attitude based on insufficient data. There were too many other people in the world who had taken on that assignment. Norwood continued to repack his equipment while waiting for her next comment. He knew she was formulating a stinging retort because she took her time before speaking.

"Look, I didn't mean that just because Marcus Miller grew up in New York that it gave him some special advantage. But you do have to admit that his brand of jazz has a definite attitude and you can't buy that anywhere else," she fired off without looking at him. Busy making some final notations on her notepad, Sloan never took her eyes off the page. She was still into the final moments of the performance. The concert had contained so many nuances, so many high points and features that she wanted to point out, she almost wished she had a laptop at her disposal right then. But with her handwritten notes and a good memory, tomorrow would be soon enough for her to put together the final version.

Norwood smiled then, though she missed it with her head bent in concentration. She was intelligent, opinionated, and made him want to close the door on the outside world when she was in his presence. What a deadly combination.

"Don't try to clean it up now, Sloan. You New Yorkers are always ready to champion the cause for your state thinking the rest of the world is somewhere out there doing nothing," he said then. But inwardly he reasoned that if Miller had been a fellow Chicagoan he probably would have felt the same way.

"No, see, you're not getting it. It's not that we don't

recognize the rest of the country—it's just that New York is the capital of the country—you'd better recognize, my brotha," she said in distinct street language. He laughed then, good and hard, and she joined in. Looking up at him, Sloan knew something was developing that neither had full control over. They enjoyed more than each other's company—they enjoyed the challenge, the intelligence, the thought processes which seemed to come about with each encounter.

At that moment, Johnson Dade walked up and, true to form, stood in between them. "Pretty good concert, don't ya think?" he offered.

"Yeah—Miller's the man all right," Norwood offered. His lack of enthusiasm was apparent to Sloan, but Dade seemed to be unfazed.

He turned to Sloan and she felt his gaze burning a hole through the sheer gauze of her blouse. "Are you coming to the jazz jam they're having at the St. Lawrence Gap tonight? Some of the musicians from Miller's band are supposed to show up—maybe even the master himself. Why don't you let me buy you a drink?" he asked quickly, as if by saying it fast enough, he might get the answer he wanted.

"Well, I'm not really sure what I'm doing just yet," she answered, putting her notepad and camera away. "I really should go back to the hotel, straighten out my story, and have it ready to file tomorrow morning in the press room."

"Hasn't anyone ever told you that all work and no play makes Sloan a dull girl?" he responded.

Norwood listened without commenting, carefully repacking his photography equipment, unable to move from the spot. He felt as if he needed to protect Sloan at any cost from the predator that he knew Dade to be. Hell, the man reeked of lust and if she didn't watch herself, there'd be another scene like the one from the first night. He felt the first stirrings of anger and tried desperately to control it. Sloan was a grown woman capable of handling herself, and definitely able to handle Dade. Or so he told himself.

She laughed then and Norwood felt his anger rise to another level.

"Look, can't a girl want to do a good job? My editor will be extremely pleased to receive feedback from the past two days' concerts while I'm still here. That means he'll have current news from a Caribbean music festival while the concert is still ongoing. That's what we call 'hot' news."

"*You* are what I call hot news," Dade responded, unable to keep his fangs covered for even the most minor conversation. With that statement, Norwood, who was still standing within earshot, nearly lost it. He waited for Sloan to respond, decided it wouldn't dignify her to respond to the comment, and dove in—head first.

"Listen, man, Sloan already agreed to come to the Gap with Lorenzo and me. Jodi will be there with us, too. We'll probably catch you there later—maybe I'll even spring for a drink or something," he said, summarily dismissing Dade.

Johnson Dade realized that he'd just been trumped. He looked at Sloan, silently willing her to refute the geek's claims, but she just gave him a pathetically weak smile.

"I see, well, I didn't know you were spoken for," he said, sarcasm dripping from his every word.

"We're just having drinks together tonight, old man. The invitation to the wedding should go in the mail in about a week," Norwood added. He'd been unable to refrain from throwing the last nail into Dade's coffin with his sarcastic comment.

Sloan looked up in surprise then, caught off guard by how far Norwood was obviously willing to go to get rid of the pest.

"Listen, we'll see you all down at the Gap. Everyone's going to end up there anyway, so what's the big deal?" she asked, not wanting to hurt Dade's feelings any more than she had to. It had been humiliating enough when they'd both argued and almost gotten into a physical encounter only two nights before. She wanted to avoid any additional drama.

"So that's how it is—okay. Well, I guess I'll see all of you around then," Dade said. He avoided meeting Norwood's stare, which was burning a hole into his back as he walked away.

Dade headed back toward the exit from the park as the concert attendees left the venue. He was disappointed, annoyed, and, most of all, determined. Determined to show Mr. Hotshot a thing or two about women. And Miss Hotshot a thing or three about men.

Lorenzo was hell-bent on getting to the St. Lawrence Gap. Jodi simply wanted the night to never end and both Norwood and Sloan wanted to avoid any more encounters with Johnson Dade.

"Listen, I promised you guys dinner today. I think you should take me up on it. After all, I could decide to welsh on it, cheating you all out of the one unprogrammed evening of the entire trip," Norwood said. His amusement was obvious, his offer genuine.

"So, where is it that we should have this feast for the ages?" Lorenzo asked. Clearly, he was not thrilled at the prospect of missing out on more jazz from the band he'd enjoyed so thoroughly throughout the evening. In truth, he didn't care where they went as long as Jodi was there, too.

"The Southern Palms is supposed to have an excellent restaurant. It's in the same vicinity of the Gap—within walking distance. Once we're finished with dinner, we can walk over. Those guys will still be jamming into the wee hours of the morning. Trust me—once they get going, they don't stop. I know 'cause that's how they do it in Blues Alley back in my hometown. We have some awesome jazz clubs right in the heart of downtown Chicago," Norwood offered convincingly.

"I don't care what we do as long as we do it somewhere away from here. It's so humid tonight and if I didn't know better, I'd think it is actually hotter than it was today," Jodi said. She was right. The barometric pressure had risen substantially with the humidity approaching close to 97 percent.

"Well, I'm with Jodi on that. 'Let's get to steppin' as Martin would say. I should be going back to my hotel and putting this stuff together but you guys are so entertaining I wouldn't miss this for the world. Not to mention a free dinner," she added. Norwood laughed then, knowing that the line she'd used on Dade was just that. He also knew that she definitely preferred his company, even if she pretended otherwise.

"Come on—if we hurry up, the bus will probably even drop us off close to our final destination," Norwood said as began walking toward the many vehicles which filled the parking lot.

Once onboard, the two women sat together deep in conversation. Norwood sat alone, thinking of the evening ahead, and analyzing the moments before. Lorenzo had taken the seat behind him directly across from Johnson Dade. No longer in a friendly mood, he ignored the entire group, quiet and morose, his mind intent on getting to their destination. His next drink was calling to him and he had no intention of allowing that call to go unfulfilled.

The Southern Palms, a beautifully exotic hotel located in one of the most popular tourist areas of Barbados, the St. Lawrence Gap, also contained one of the island's finest restaurants—the Southern Coconut.

After browsing the wine list, Norwood signaled the waiter. "Bring us a bottle of the ninety-eight Chardonnay due Blanc de Rothchilds please."

His guests for the evening, undoubtedly impressed, signaled their approval. They actually applauded, to which Norwood stood up, took a stiff bow, and returned to his seat beaming. He then proposed a toast, raising his glass and looking meaningfully toward Sloan. "To new beginnings, new friends, and a renewed future," he said. The words hung in the air, with Lorenzo clearing his throat suddenly.

"Yeah, to all of that," he deadpanned, then laughed. Jodi joined him, with everyone touching their glass to that of the others. Sloan reached out to clink glasses with Norwood and he reached in closer, linking his arm with hers. Intertwining their glasses, he brought them within inches of each other. Jodi and Lorenzo looked on in amazement. Real or imagined—the chemistry in the air was not to be denied. And though they were still feeling their way tentatively toward whatever was in development between them, they couldn't help but champion their two fellow journalists.

"And to you," he said, looking deeply into her eyes. Sloan's heart beat faster as she sipped slowly from the glass. Unsure of her response, she said the first thing that came to mind.

"To East Coast versus West Coast," she responded, her laughter issuing a challenge.

"And to all that lies between," Norwood responded. His meaning, unclear, but his statement highly suggestive, made Sloan pause. Looking into his eyes, she saw a distinct challenge there. She sipped the wine slowly, never waivering in her gaze.

They ordered then, appetizers, entrées, and even a Barbadian specialty—pepper pot—for the table, which everyone would share. A spicy stew, the mixture contained native vegetables, cooked with exotic spices, and was especially tasty with small amounts of ginger.

It was almost two in the morning when the last traces of dessert, a coconut custard pie, were consumed.

"I'm still committed to seeing those guys wail again—where is the club where they are supposed to play?" Lorenzo asked. His memory, though dulled by the wine he'd consumed, would not allow him to forget that they were in the vicinity.

"Man, you're like a dog with a bone. . . . Come on, you guys. We're on our way to Time Out at the Gap. Let's walk—it's only a short distance," Norwood offered. After the two bottles of wine they'd consumed, the walk would do them good, he reasoned.

They heard the music well before they reached the hotel/restaurant/bar known for its late night jazz jams. Time at the Gap had a reputation: great atmosphere, good food, and the best of the island's live jazz. Crowded, with many members of the press gathered at the tables both indoors and out, as well as various noteworthy locals, the bar area looked more like a mob scene than a well-run establishment. Lorenzo led the way to a small table in one corner. There were no chairs available.

Norwood offered to find seats for them but doubted if he'd really be able to successfully find four available. So they stood, like most others, and tried to order drinks.

"Why don't you use that same technique you did at the concert the other night, Norwood?" Sloan asked. "You guys should have seen it—he was able to move through a crowd at least seven deep, order a drink, and come out of it alive. I was impressed but I'll bet you can't do that again," she added.

"I'm not sure the same will hold true here—it's a different world in a indoor setting. But I'm willing to try. What's the incentive?" he asked then, looking directly at Sloan. For a moment, she almost backed down. Then ego, instinct, and the three glasses of wine she'd consumed kicked in.

"You name it—if you can get through that crowd, you deserve pretty much anything you can come up with," she said recklessly.

Jodi and Lorenzo, deep in conversation and unable to hear over the music, the overall noise level and their own words, missed out on the exchange. The challenge was strictly between Norwood and Sloan, which only added to the intimacy.

"You obviously don't know the meaning of a challenge like that. Haven't you ever heard of the marines? We don't believe in backing down. And especially when the stakes of the reward are so high. Listen, I'll be right back. Don't you move one inch." His last words were issued with authority.

Sloan looked at him, smiled seductively, and issued her own set of final orders in a whisper, "Hurry up, I'm thirsty." Norwood needed no further instruction. Employing the same tactics he'd used successfully only two nights before, he accomplished the mission in less than record time.

"No, you didn't—how the hell did you get those drinks so quickly? And what's up, my brotha—why didn't you let us know you were making a drink run?" Lorenzo's questions made both Norwood and Sloan laugh. Totally oblivious to and unaware of both their conversation and the heightened sexual tension in the atmosphere, he was the perfect straight man.

"I know you know how to take care of business so I figured I'd leave you to your own devices."

"Mmm, what is this?" Sloan asked. "It tastes great but it's definitely not white wine."

"Specialty of the house—it's called a 'White Charger.' A splash of overproof white rum, Vanilla Coke, and lime. If you don't like it, let me know and I'll get you another glass of wine. Whatever you want . . ."

"No, actually this is fine. It's delicious. And the rum is mellow. Not harsh or strong. Why do they call it overproof?"

"It's actually the best rum the island has to offer. Aged and prepared with great finesse, it's one of the finest products they manufacture. I thought it would be nice to sample some native spirits." He had ordered the same thing, figuring what was good for the goose was even better for the gander.

The music dominated the atmosphere, with various musicians taking center stage from time to time. Now well into the early morning hours, there was an endless stream of players, eager to sit in on a set they knew would be talked about from Barbados to New York— from Jamaica to Canada. Lorenzo and Jodi found seats at the bar and Sloan and Norwood were eventually able to find two chairs.

"So, are you going to live up to your promise or are you gonna welsh on that bet you made earlier?" he asked suddenly. He wanted to see just how much guts she really had.

"What bet—I thought your efforts were gallant and certainly proved you know your way around a bar crowd. We didn't actually bet though. You were just being funny, right?" Sloan's memory, fuzzy at that moment and not able to focus on the subject, caused her to wonder just what the hell was going on.

"Okay, so now you're gonna try and play it off. I distinctly remember you flossing. I knew you weren't game. It's the old bait and switch—New York style," he added. Norwood laughed so hard he almost bent over.

Sloan was amused but not at all sure if the joke was really on her or not. She half remembered saying something really gangster like "whatever you say" in the stakes being raised for his getting the drinks in record-breaking time. But that seemed like yesterday now.

Jodi brought over a plate of golden brown codfish cakes, raving about how good they were. She and Norwood thanked her and devoured them in record time. Sloan stood up then, looking for the rest room, and the sensation of being unsteady on her feet surprised her. *This is ridiculous,* she thought and she looked at Norwood and felt an overwhelming sense of happiness. Things were really going well. She was actually happy for the first time in a long while.

"Hey, let's order another round. This one's on me 'cause I'm celebrating."

"If you're sure you can handle it. I know you had at least three glasses of wine. Sure you don't want to play it safe and call it a night?" Norwood's question fell on deaf ears as Sloan signaled the waitress. She ordered two White Chargers, which were somehow delivered in record time now that the crowd was thinning out.

"The bar must be slowing down now," Norwood said as he sipped the drink.

"Yeah—well, the party is not over yet." Sloan tried to pay for the drinks, but Norwood wouldn't let her. "Not on my watch," was his reply.

"So, what are we celebrating?" he asked, his curiosity getting the better of him.

"Oh, that." She hesitated. "My divorce. It was finalized two weeks ago. Great timing, don't you think?" she said, her voice sounding as if it were coming from far, far away.

"I see—well, don't take this personally but I think you should slow down a little. Those White Chargers are not for the faint of heart. I didn't expect you'd want to reorder within the same night. I just wanted you to sample some local product."

"Well, as it turns out, I like your choice. I like you, too. In fact, I like everyone in this club. They're all nice people. I'm going to the bathroom—excuse me." And she was up again.

Norwood waited for her to return, realizing it was probably time to call it a night. His thoughts were with Sloan's last words. So, she had just gone through a divorce. That would explain her reluctance to open up to him. It also let him know that she was more like him than he'd imagined—emotionally vulnerable and wary.

"If you don't mind my asking—what happened? You were talking about your divorce. I can't imagine anyone not wanting to be married to you. Unless you're one of those women who looks great on the outside and is a pain in the neck in the real sense of the word," he said. She'd returned, sat down, and was now looking at him as if he had two heads. Her drink remained on the table, untouched.

"Why are you trying to make me feel as if I have to defend myself? I thought I could share something of a very personal nature with you and not be judged. And to answer your question, nothing happened. That was the problem. Nothing that was supposed to—happened," she added defiantly. Sloan didn't know why but suddenly she was angry. Angry with Norwood, angry with herself, angry with the world.

"I don't mean to pry, but that doesn't make any sense. You just told me that your divorce was finalized only a couple of weeks ago. I suppose your husband was inconsequential, a no-good rat bastard, and a liar and a cheat," he flung at her. He was tired of women who made everything seem as if life had dealt them the only rotten hand. He was a living, breathing testimony that men also got the short end of the stick.

Sloan looked as if he'd slapped her in the face. She didn't respond, just got up from her chair and walked over to the bar where Jodi and Lorenzo were sitting.

"I'm leaving now—you two have a good night or whatever is left of it," she added, heading outside to hail a cab. Lorenzo knew Norwood would go after her. He figured they'd work it out so he just sat back down and continued listening to the music. He also cautioned Jodi, who almost got up to leave, too. "Let them work it out," he advised.

Norwood, realizing that Sloan was not coming back to the table, cursed under his breath, then got up quickly, leaving some crunched bills on the table, and rushed after her. He got as close as taking her elbow when she whirled on him, anger and fury apparent in her face.

"You don't know anything about me, my ex-husband or what I've gone through. You obviously assume that every woman you meet is one with major problems. I don't have to prove anything to you or anyone else for that matter. And to answer your question, yes, he was all that and then some. A no-good rat bastard, a liar, and a cheat." Her fury unleashed, she wrenched her elbow away from him and quickly approached a waiting taxi. Several were lined up waiting for the remaining patrons to come out and head for home, their hotels, or wherever they would end up for the night.

Norwood followed her, not making any statement.

He'd managed to eradicate the entire mood of the evening with one inconsequential statement. That had not been his intention. They rode in silence, arriving at their hotel's entrance in record time. They had traveled through the now deserted streets of each connecting parish without any traffic. The normally bustling villages and towns were quiet now waiting for the dawn of another day.

Norwood paid the driver as Sloan rushed ahead, eager to get to her room. He caught up to her though, her heels a definite disadvantage when it came to covering ground quickly.

"Sloan," he called out in an attempt to get her attention. But she was having none of it. They were almost poolside when he finally caught up to her. The moonlit night was punctuated rhythmically by the sounds of the crashing waves. The shoreline was only a few feet beyond the perimeter of where they now stood, with the ocean stretching out for miles and miles beyond.

He quickly closed the distance between them, grabbed her arm firmly, and said her name softly, "Sloan, please let me explain."

She turned then, tears having formed in her eyes, and looked at him. He hadn't realized that his words would sting her so sharply, hurt her so thoroughly, or wound her so deeply.

"You have no idea what you said to me back there, nor how on target you were. And you had no right to even go there. . . ." She took a deep breath and tried to turn away. But his grasp on her arm stopped her. He reached out and cupped her chin with one hand, tilting her head upward so that he could look into her eyes.

"You're right and I am sorry. I guess I was testing you. After all, you flirted with me and I bought it. You had no intention of living up to any of it. It was all a big bluff. I guess I was angry," he ended, his disappointment now more than obvious.

Sloan took one step forward, closing the distance between them, looked deeply into his eyes, and whispered, "Who said I was bluffing?" Norwood gathered her into the circle of his arms. Her lips were softer than he remembered and the kiss started out as a test. He enclosed her in a circle of warmth and reassurance.

The resentment she'd felt only moments before dissolved as indignation and anger gave way to pure passion. Softly and slowly, he kissed his way from her tear stained eyelids to the edges of her lips. Testing, teasing, it became increasingly evident that she was waging a battle with the passion which was building with every passing moment. Sloan wound her arms around him, grasping the back of his neck, as his kisses became deeper and more insistent. He explored the inner sanctum of her mouth, their tongues teasing and wrestling in a mating dance. Sloan forgot where they were, who they were, and what they were. Thought was slowly and irrevocably being replaced by need.

Norwood kissed each eyelid closed, then slowly trailed kisses from her forehead to her lips again. She trembled as she realized that he had taken control, something she'd wanted to avoid. Sloan slowly molded her body to the length of his, feeling his response, sharing his passion.

"Do you know what you're doing, Sloan?" he asked. Her face was unreadable in the moonlight, though her breathing was heavy and her eyes were no longer filled with tears.

"I'm losing the bet," she answered and kissed him boldly. She could feel his restraint and knew he was unsure of her intentions. Slowly, their bodies molded together in a battle from which no one winner would emerge.

Sloan pulled his shirt from its tucked-in position, slipping one hand up his back to caress the smooth skin there. The muscles felt like smooth ripples of solid rock in her hands. Norwood's response was immediate. He murmured her name, unable to squelch his response to her. "Baby, I don't think this is such a good idea," he managed to say between kisses, caresses, and the passion that was slowly threatening to overtake them both.

"I don't want to think about anything right now. Except this. . . ." Sloan kissed him again and time ceased to exist.

Slowly, Norwood stepped back, took her hand, and brought it up to his lips, kissing each fingertip tenderly. The sensation sent shock waves through her body.

"I want to come to your room," Sloan said.

Moonlight from the glass terrace windows facing the oceanfront bathed the entire room in a blue-tinged light. Norwood wanted to reach for the light switch but Sloan was in his arms and he couldn't bear to make the transition. His hands were full.

Their kiss deepened as passion and need erupted full force. Norwood slowly, gently, lifted the long prairie skirt she wore, his hands searching for the warmth and strength of the legs which had been branded into his brain from earlier in the day. Toned and well defined, she was silky and strong at the same time.

Sloan backed away from him, boldly held eye contact, and removed her belt. Norwood couldn't take his eyes off her and she reveled in the fire she saw reflected in his eyes. It only mirrored and intensified the smoldering passion that she felt within herself.

She stepped out of the skirt, kicked it away and in one movement, entered his arms again. Norwood slowly began unbuttoning the tiny buttons which had teased him all evening. Easing the tiny straps of the camisole down her arms, he gently pulled her to him. The strapless bra she wore shone brightly in the moonlit room. Its tiny pink polka dots reminded him of innocence and purity. But the woman he held in his arms was surely no saint. She continually surprised him, first with the boldness of her challenge—then by backing it up with substance. He'd never dreamed that she'd see any of it through and had fully expected her to wiggle out of it. Instead, she was now wiggling out of her clothing.

Sloan opened the last of the buttons on his shirt. Her hands roamed the planes of his chest, feeling the hardness of it, loving the solid landscape she'd encountered. Norwood groaned as her touch held him in her power. Standing before him in matching pink polka dot panties and bra, she was astounding in her beauty. Slowly, he took both her hands in his and placed them in a prayerlike position, kissing each side. Filling his memory with the sight of her, he held his breath, indecision overcoming him. He knew she'd never have expected them to be where they now were. Yet, on another level, he knew he was more than ready to take on whatever she was capable of giving. He kissed her again, forgetting all thought.

Sloan raised one of Norwood's arms above his head, holding it in a grasp that was both firm and sure. Slowly she raised the other arm and stepped into him. The feel of her scantily clad body against the length of him, the perception of powerlessness she'd invoked by her actions, threatened to overtake him.

He remained immobile against the wall, the blood racing hotly through his veins as Sloan took her time kissing her way down the expanse of his exposed chest. She unbuckled his belt and reached for his zipper. No longer able to remain impassive, he brushed her hands away.

"Whoa, whoa—when did you become such a little hellcat?" he asked, circling her waist with one arm. With the other, he cupped her chin and met her lips with his own. Their kisses only heightened the passion and Norwood's fingers traced their way down one side of her arm, coming to rest on her breast. He circled it slowly, trailing kisses from her mouth, her neck, teasing her with his tongue. When his mouth found the tip of her breast, Sloan's sighs encouraged him. And as he unsnapped the clasp, freeing her, she moaned with desire, his lips preventing any further sound.

His hands held her, his fingers brushing across the tips of her breasts in a tantalizing motion, increasing her need and fueling his own desire at the same time. Sloan turned around then, leaning against the length of him, feeling the evidence of his desire against her hips, his hands encasing her now engorged breasts. His kisses at the back of her neck almost made her whimper and he removed one hand as he slowly unzipped his trousers. Just before stepping out of them, he removed a tiny foil packet from one of the pockets, remembering the first rule of responsible sex.

Taking Norwood's hand, Sloan led him to the nearby bed. There didn't seem to be enough time to do all the things they each wanted to. Norwood wanted to kiss her forever and would have been content to do just that. Sloan wound her legs around him as they lay face to face, touching, caressing, need becoming a tangible element as they explored each other. Time ceased to exist and indecision was replaced by sheer passion.

Norwood kissed his way slowly, tantalizingly from her lips to her neck. He placed feathery kisses on each of her breasts, his tongue loving them until Sloan almost cried out from the sensation. Waves of pleasure rippled through her body and she felt hot moisture between her legs. She knew she wanted to feel him there, and signaled to him. But he ignored her urgings, continuing with his own plan of action.

A man of pure dedication, Norwood explored Sloan's body thoroughly, causing her to cry out time and time again from the sensations his mouth, his lips, and his tongue created. When his mouth found the core of her womanhood, she exploded in a dynamic meltdown. Slowly, he caressed her body again, stoking the fires until Sloan wanted more than anything to be joined with him.

"Here, let me," he whispered as he protected them. He entered her slowly at first, but Sloan could not wait. Raising her hips to meet him, she coaxed him in, and he entered her deeply, relishing the heat, the feel, and the fit of her. Sloan moaned wantonly, knowing that she did so. She couldn't help herself. They gave to one another as they if it were the first, the last, the only time ever. The fire, once ignited, would not be extinguished until the first light of dawn, which brought an entirely new day into play.

Fifteen

New York City

Kassandra dressed, undressed, redressed, then sat down and had a stinging mental monologue with the only person present. *What's all the fuss—it's only dinner. So what, he's your boss, the director, the photographer, and perhaps a key element to your future in video. Just go out, be yourself, and have good time.*

The words, once spoken, filled her with even greater trepidation. Karsten held the key to so many of the doors in her world at the moment that she was truthfully afraid to be in his company outside the realm of business. Why she'd given in to his request and allowed herself to say yes was beyond her immediate comprehension.

"Dinner, no drinks, no hand holding, no kissing, no nothing," she repeated to herself for the third time as she applied lipstick. The dress she wore, though understated, did nothing to detract from the alluring curves of her body. It was a Donna Karan matte jersey, with a boat neck, long sleeves, and knee-length skirt. Kassandra's body did things to the fabric that even the designer hadn't anticipated. It clung to her at the hip, indented with her at the waist, and vividly accentuated her more than ample bustline. She'd chosen it because it was the most demure thing she owned. No plunging neckline, thigh-high skirt, or cutouts strategically placed which would have sent a message of seduction.

She'd pulled her hair up into a French twist, secured it with two Japanese combs constructed from black mother-of-pearl, and placed tiny pearl hoops in each ear.

Gucci's Rush, a favorite scent of hers, was sprayed lightly, accentuating the lotion she'd applied earlier. The bell rang just as she was placing the first foot into her sling-back black pumps. "Damn, he's prompt," she muttered, grabbing her bag as she turned off the lights.

Karsten waited patiently curbside after ringing the bell. He had no intention of entering her apartment. Although he was looking forward to spending the evening in her company, he didn't want any complications. And to be truthful, he'd even had some second thoughts after asking her out. But he'd sensed that she had given serious consideration to his invitation, and that made him curious. Obviously, she wasn't into "consorting" with the crew. He liked that. In his experience, models who carried themselves like whores were often treated even worse. And their careers never seemed to take on the polish and the flare for success that might have been possible had they behaved a little more responsibly. He had no intention of "testing" Miss Algernon. Just a little light conversation, dinner, and some downtime. He'd been working seven-day weeks for the past month and a half. The time away from the work cycle would do him good, or so he told himself.

Kassandra closed the front door to the building, walked down the steps, and Karsten got out to open the car door for her. She was wearing a long, military-style black wool coat with brass buttons. With the collar turned up, she looked both elegant and authoritative.

"Hey, you look great. I don't know whether to salute you or kiss you," he said, quickly coming around to the passenger side.

Kassandra laughed as she got into the car. Its warmth immediately hit her and she began unbuttoning the heavy wool coat. "Neither will be necessary," she offered quickly. By the time he got in on the driver's side, she had removed the coat and sat back in her seat, fastening the seat belt.

Karsten let out a low whistle, taking in her fragrance, the alluring curves he could just make out in the darkened car interior, and the flash of leg he saw as she crossed them.

"Wow. I thought you looked good in that schoolgirl outfit we had you in on the set. Baby, the law shouldn't allow you to walk around looking that innocent. You're like an unlit stick of dynamite," he offered, his eyes lingering on curves he could clearly see even in the limited lighting.

Kassandra laughed, in spite of her initial reservations. He looked like a small boy who had somehow stumbled on a great and magical secret. "You know, if I didn't know better, I'd think you were making a pass at me," she said, looking at him quizzically.

"Pass—no, that would lead to other things and I have nothing in mind. Not at the moment anyway." Karsten knew she was just playing with him, knew she was not game or up for anything. He suspected that if he did try and hit on her, she would have clobbered him with her pocketbook, run screaming from the vehicle, and called the local authorities.

"So, where are we off to, Mr. Battle?" she asked.

"We're off to a little spot up in Harlem that I like. Have you ever been uptown? I know you're from

Chicago so you may not have visited that part of New York yet," he said.

"Actually, there's a little shop that I was turned on to by another model a few months ago—it's called the Brownstone. Great clothing, funky jewelry, and even one-of-a-kind household pieces. I probably spent more than I intended but came home happy."

"Okay, and where was this little oasis of a shop?" he inquired.

"Right on Fifth Avenue and One-twenty-fifth Street. It was great. I even had lunch while I was there."

"Well, even though I can't say I introduced you to Harlem, I'm sure you'll find the Sugarhill Bistro a very interesting uptown enclave. Live music, great food, and an art gallery. It consistently draws a clientele that's eclectic and trendy. I think you'll like it."

They pulled up in front of the restaurant at 145th Street. As luck would have it, they found a parking space just as someone was pulling out. The three-story brownstone, whitewashed and redone to reflect the finer nuances of its interior characteristics, was alive with music and people. A three-piece jazz combo was in full throttle, sending out a clear-cut message that was undeniably solid. Patrons filled the first floor, each table occupied by at least three persons. The bar, which was located toward the entrance to the outdoor area, was also filled to capacity with men and women enjoying the ambience, the social comraderie, and the music which blasted its way throughout the entire space.

"Reservation for two—Battle," Karsten said to the young woman maître d'. They were shown upstairs to a quiet dining area, tables covered by white cloths. The entire building was devoted to promoting good vibes, through the music, the food, and the general social interaction which took place on a daily basis.

Kassandra looked around, taking in the richness of the environment. The brownstone had been restored with diligence and great care. Most of the original features were in place although in several places modern updates had been melded in, causing the original features to stand out even more. She began to remove her coat and Karsten quickly assisted her.

He'd worn a sport jacket over a black turtleneck and dark gray wool pants. The baseball cap had been left at home. It occurred to Kassandra that he was a good deal more mature than he'd originally appeared. She liked that. Minus his signature cap, he was very handsome. That caused her some concern. She wasn't totally prepared for the reaction she was experiencing. She unfolded the menu, scanned it quickly, closed it, and then reopened it. For the first time that evening, Kassandra realized that she was nervous. The man sitting across from her was undoubtedly fine. There was no other way to say it, no other way to characterize it. He was also powerful, her immediate boss, and in charge, at least for the next couple of weeks.

"Now, don't tell me that you're going to totally change character on me and become quiet and subdued. It's the last thing I'd expect from anyone in your profession," he said. What he really wanted to say was "Relax, I'm not going to hit on you—not tonight anyway."

"Well, I can't speak for everyone in 'my profession' as you so aptly put it, but there are times when I am a little quiet—reflective, if you will. I was actually just observing the character of the restaurant. I love old buildings and this one has been restored and upgraded really nicely. The building my apartment is located in was also gutted and restored."

"I see. That's pretty common for a lot of the buildings here in New York. I live in a loft in Brooklyn Heights. When I first bought it, it was an old hatmaking factory. The millinery machines were still in place and I had to have everything removed. Six months of living with the skeletons of ancient machinery, and the remnants of thousands of hats. It was a wild experience," he ended, shaking his head.

"That sounds like a great environment though for a living space. How'd it turn out?"

"So far, so good. I'm still living there. I actually had a decorator come in after the first year. The renovation work had been completed and I was ready for some comfort. During the year of all the heavy work, I was working out the details of a divorce. The general disarray and the construction pretty much matched my mood." His personal revelation, intertwined with the conversation on the construction, held her attention. Kassandra realized he was revealing the "real" Karsten bit by bit—in tiny increments.

They ordered drinks and appetizers then, and some of the initial reservations they'd both held dissipated with conversation.

"So, you're divorced. I've never been married. Close, but no cigar," she added. "Do you have any children?"

Kassandra hadn't thought about Norwood and the things that occurred in Chicago for a long time, a very long time. Now sitting here with Karsten reminiscing about the past, attempting to find a path to the future and a firm foundation in the present, he suddenly came to mind. And just as suddenly, the memory was gone.

"No, no children . . . almost but something happened." As Karsten uttered the last words, he shook his head as if trying to ward off the thoughts going through it. "We were in college, best friends in college. I thought it was the right thing to do—you know, but it just didn't turn out well. Anyway, that's ancient history. What should we drink to?"

"How about the completion of the video. Or to the creative process—either one sounds good to me," she added, picking up her glass of chardonnay.

"Fine—to video, the creative process, and to restoring old structures," he said, a smile playing around his mouth. Karsten held up his merlot and looked deeply into her eyes. There was an unmistakable challenge there. Kassandra recognized it, did not flinch, and clicked his glass. Taking a small sip of her wine, she picked up the menu.

"I was almost married once. I got cold feet, messed things up, and fled. To this day, I don't know exactly what it was that I was so afraid of." Her revelation, once spoken, shed clarity on the event. She'd never meant to hurt Norwood, never meant to tread into waters so deep. But the thing with Jordan had happened so quickly, leaving her shocked, ashamed, and mainly, confused. She'd realized that it couldn't be undone and decided to just turn and walk away.

"You sound as if you have some serious regrets. Are you sure you can't change any of it? Love on the rebound is never a solution," Karsten advised. Hell, if she was looking to replace an old love, or to reinvent something that happened before he ever knew her, she was asking for nothing but trouble. And he wanted no part of that scene.

"No, it's not about trying to go backward. It's sometimes about recognition though. I've come to the conclusion that you most definitely have to be able to identify what went wrong, how you contributed to it, and just what it meant to you, before you are able to become one hundred percent again. You know, two halves do not make a whole in a relationship. You both have to come to the table as whole individuals—it's only then that you are able to complement and mesh with one another," she advised.

"You remind me of someone I once knew. She was wise beyond her years but I was a young hothead, hellbent on making my presence known in the world. It seems like it was a really long time ago, but in fact, it was only a few years ago. We got married, separated, and divorced just recently." His candor both surprised and invigorated him. He hadn't meant to unload such personal information, hadn't planned to share anything so intimate, but found himself unable to withhold anything which would allow her to know him better.

"Ah, so that's the reason for your being relatively shy and somewhat reserved. I didn't know anything about your past." She wanted to add that a recent divorce might make him somewhat jaded, and at the very least, cautious toward the opposite sex. But Kassandra also recognized that it was probably not the most optimistic information to pass on and decided to leave it out.

"I am definitely not shy. You've only known me in the work environment—shooting video calls for a lot of concentration. I have to make sure the camera angles are exactly dead on to produce the best possible shots. And though, if I may say so myself, the artists and models we've been working with are extremely talented, and very good looking, it still requires my total concentration."

Compliment delivered, he sat back, laced his hands together behind his head, and looked directly at her.

Kassandra smiled, thoroughly accustomed to being the center of attention and the target of much assessment. She spent most of her days being scrutinized by people just like him, so it felt right.

Looking at her now, in the subdued lighting of the restaurant, Karsten was no longer looking through the lens of a charged coupled device or CCD, a videotape camera. He noticed her skin, its texture, its smoothness, its rich brown clay color. He also noted the fit of her blouse, the angle of her breasts, and the rise and fall of her chest with each breath she took. His reaction was purely male, purely physical. He realized that he wanted her. But he also knew he did not want to jeopardize their working relationship. One took definite precedence over the other in his mind.

"So, I remind you of your ex. Is that a good thing or have I just cut my own throat?" Her question, direct and totally without guile, caught him off guard. He'd been deep in thought on how to make his next move—his best move. Switching gears mentally, he recalculated the evening. If it was not meant to be, so be it.

"When I said you reminded me of someone, I actually meant that in a good way. My ex was extremely talented, thorough in anything she did, and was also very good to look at. It was through my own shortcomings that the marriage fell apart. I only made the comparison based on positive attributes, believe me."

Kassandra listened, absorbed, and remained silent, unsure of the validity of his words. If he was lying, it was a moot point anyway. Only time would tell.

The waiter arrived with their orders, which they'd placed earlier. Kassandra had ordered the grilled tuna with mango-dressed salad. Karsten's ravioli, filled with porcini mushrooms and accompanied by grilled vegetables, looked delicious. They both continued making light conversation as they consumed the meal, each more willing to divulge a little more of themselves now that they'd gotten some basic information on the table and out of the way.

Karsten decided to order a bottle of Cabernet Sauvignon 1999 from the Sonoma Valley. The waiter, undoubtedly impressed, went off to the wine cellar. "I noticed that you seem to know a lot about wines. I love the stuff, but never seem to know what goes with what. Other than red with meat and white with fish, how do you determine what's best to order?" Kassandra asked then.

"Well, back when I was in school, I did a little bartending. That always helps and you get to know the different brands and such pretty quickly. An old barhop, that's what we call those guys who've been tending bar since the flood waters receded, schooled me in the finer points of liquors, wines, and even some liquers. And then because I was interested in the stuff, I started to subscribe to *Food and Wine* and *Gourmet* magazines. There is a wealth of information in those publications."

"Wow, I'm impressed. So you never took any wine appreciation courses, or any gourmet food classes?" she asked then. Her food was delicious and Kassandra realized that the restaurant, located in the heart of Harlem, was probably at least a four-star establishment.

"No, although I've always wanted to take a culinary class. I don't think you can appreciate food properly without wanting to know a little about its preparation," he added.

"Yeah, back in Chicago, I took a couple of classes and it helped me to become more well rounded in the kitchen. I still prepare pretty basic stuff but I feel more confident when I am putting things together. I'm no gourmet chef, but I can hold my own," she laughed.

"Well, we'll have to put you to the test one day. Maybe you'll invite me over so that I can sample the goods," he said then. Once said, he couldn't retrieve the words but quickly realized that the double entendre had not been lost on his dinner companion.

"I see—and just when is it that you had in mind? After all, I wouldn't want it to be said that I was holding up your schedule." The look she gave him was chilling. Karsten felt its coldness from where he sat. If arctic winds blew fast, the temperatures would be felt by half the city in the next moments.

"You've misunderstood me."

"Really."

"Listen, I didn't mean anything by that—relax, your virtue is intact." He held his hands up in a gesture of submission. He felt as if he'd set off the timer to a nuclear reactor.

"Hey, I realize that you probably are used to treating women like sluts; the industry you work in helps to promote that attitude anyway. But just remember, although you may be the director, the cameraman, the head honcho on the set, tonight is not a video shoot. And I refuse to allow you to talk to me in a denigrating, derogatory way. I didn't work my way up the ladder of fashion, move halfway across the darned country, and struggle to make a name for myself here in New York City to allow you to treat me like I am some subspecies. And thanks a lot for the dinner," she said, sarcasm clearly evident in her voice as she rose from the table to leave. Grabbing her purse and coat, which was thrown across the back of her chair, Kassandra tried to quickly walk away. But Karsten was faster—and stronger.

He reached for her arm and held tight. "What the hell has gotten into you? I said I meant no disrespect. You've totally misconstrued my meaning. I wouldn't ask you out to dinner and then insult you like that. It was a poor choice of words—nothing more. Why are you blowing everything out of proportion?" His question, once uttered, hung in the air unanswered for what seemed like an eternity. Everything seemed to have stopped—all motion ceased.

Then Kassandra realized that they were making a scene. Not everyone in the restaurant realized what was happening, but those seated closest to their table did. That made Kassandra want to just disappear. So, she sat down.

Karsten, not able to believe what had almost happened, sat down also. "Look, if you really want to leave, we can. I'll drop you at home. But I think we should at least finish our dinner first. And I promise not to say anything else that sounds like a proposition, an insult, or a negative comment," he ended.

The remainder of dinner was consumed in silence. Karsten didn't trust himself to say anything—his luck seemed to have run out in terms of conversation. Kassandra just wanted the evening to be over with. Not only had she jeopardized her reputation in the industry, but the remainder of the video now had to be done under a cloak of discomfort. She chastised herself mentally for having made a mistake no first-year model would have made. And she certainly didn't have that excuse on her side.

They left the restaurant, both wrapped in their own thoughts, and walked to the vehicle. As Karsten watched her walk toward passenger side door, her head held high, anger and disappointment written on her face, he came to a hastily made decision.

"Look," he said, placing both hands on her shoulders and turning her to face him. "This will probably be the last time you'll ever go out with me so I have nothing to lose." And with that statement, he lowered his lips to hers in a kiss that was at once demanding, yet gentle.

Kassandra's reaction was swift and decisive. She pulled back, wiped her mouth with the back of one hand, and cursed under her breath. "Just what the hell do you think you're doing? I must have been out of my mind to agree to go on a date with you. You have the hormones of a sex-starved teenager and the manners of a baboon," she spat out, as she tried to move away from the vehicle. But Karsten had anticipated her reaction and now stood between her and the vehicle, her elbow in tow.

He laughed then, knowing that she was madder than he'd seen anyone in a very long time. "Listen, that was only a joke. I didn't seriously expect you to kiss me after the night we've had. But you looked so irresistible, I couldn't help myself. Come on, let me drive you home. And don't even think of trying to say no. I won't entertain the thought of you jumping into a cab or any other mode of transportation. I brought you here, and I'll take you home. No hands, no kisses, no kidding," he ended. His conviction was apparent as he held up his hands in testimony.

Kassandra eyed him warily, not wanting to trust him, not trusting herself to judge him any further. He'd made a fool out of her and that was something she wouldn't allow herself to forgive or forget.

"I want you to promise me that you will not do that again. Also, promise that you'll drive me straight home—no detours or funny stuff, Karsten. Your professional reputation is on the line—swear it," she demanded. She stood warily beside the Range Rover, unsure as to her next move.

"I swear—no funny stuff and straight to your house. Scout's honor," he added with one hand held up in the traditional sign.

Although she couldn't for the life of her explain why she believed him, she reached for the door handle. Wary and suspicious, Kassandra practically cowered in the corner all through the drive back downtown to her apartment building. When Karsten reached her block, she let out an audible sigh of relief, knowing she was safely within walking distance. He'd kept his word, upheld his promise.

"Thank you," she said in a small voice. Relief flooding her every pore, she now felt as if she'd made too much of his kiss, overreacted to his ridiculous statement, and blown the entire evening out of proportion.

"You're welcome. And again, I apologize if we got off to a bad start. Sometimes I rub people the wrong way. It's always been a shortcoming of mine. Just forget about everything that happened this evening. Don't forget—you have an eight o'clock call on the set tomorrow morning. No excuses," he finished pointedly.

"I'll be there. And thanks for an interesting evening," she added as she exited the vehicle. Her emphasis on the word "interesting" was not lost on him. He wanted to say something but figured nothing would really do any good. He'd blown it. So why did he feel something akin to exhilaration?

Kassandra's heart was pounding as she unlocked her door. She could still feel the slight pressure, the soft brush, and the distinctive feel of his kiss. She removed her clothing, washed her face, and got into bed. Thinking of the evening's occurrences, tense moments and all, she suddenly laughed. *What a handful—so he really earned that reputation and probably plans to live up to it for as long as possible. Someone needs to teach Mr. Battle a lesson,* she thought.

It was a long time before Kassandra fell asleep that night.

Sixteen

Barbados

The *Tamarind II*, a seventy-five-foot catamaran sailing vessel, was scheduled to leave port in downtown Bridgetown at 11:00 A.M. Forty-nine members of the press, scheduled to cover the seventh annual Barbados Jazz Festival, would have their first full day of real leisure activity. Journalists, photographers, and publicity personnel from as far north as Canada, as far east as England and Germany, as far west as California and from the neighboring islands of Jamaica, Trinidad, Venezuela, and Puerto Rico were all present.

A "welcome aboard" drink, made of champagne laced with fresh-squeezed orange juice, was issued along with a laminated boarding pass at the dock. In the midst of the early morning sunshine, the fruity but potent drinks had the desired effect on the passengers clad in bathing suits, shorts, sunglasses, and carrying canvas bags which had been distributed by the Tourist Board. Barriers came down and bonding was instantaneous. Everyone boarded, shoeless and looking forward to a day filled with adventure and great fun.

Sloan, wearing a large black straw hat, dark sunglasses, and a black two-piece bathing suit covered by a black and white polka dot pareo, was in pain. Both mental and physical. Her sandals in hand, she immediately approached the bartender on board. "Do you have anything for a headache?" she said quietly.

"Sure, let me get out the medicine box for you, Miss," the young man behind the counter responded politely. It was not the first time he'd seen a tourist who had obviously had too many rum punches, or more than their share of Caribbean nights.

Sloan waited patiently while he sorted through several boxes within a cabinet under the counter. He finally stood up with a smile and produced a packet of Advil.

"Thank God," she said, smiling for the first time that day. Awakening somewhere around 7:30 that morning, she'd almost panicked when she realized she was in Norwood's bed, his leg thrown intimately over hers. Being careful not to awaken him, she'd slid out from underneath the weight of that one limb, only to find that in response, he threw an arm possessively over her shoulder. She almost reached out and lifted it but was afraid it might awaken him. Instead, she slithered her way out, holding her breath the entire time, afraid any unusual sound to accompany her movements would be the final straw. As luck would have it, Norwood was a heavy sleeper.

Her clothing was strewn from the bed to the entrance and she picked up the items gingerly, her memory of what had transpired abundantly clear and confirmed by the trail outlined by each piece. The memory of the night gone by—the seduction, the passion—all were vivid in her mind. And although she wanted to use the bathroom badly, Sloan did not trust her luck to hold out any further. She eased her way to the door, pulling the various items of clothing on, while holding her breath as she quietly turned the knob. She felt like a thief leaving the scene of a crime. Outside his doorway, she breathed a huge sigh of relief. The maids were already milling about, knocking softly at any door not earmarked DO NOT DISTURB. She quietly made her way across the corridor to the stairwell. Her room, only one floor above, would be easily accessed by the stairs. She didn't want to take the chance of running into any of their group in clothing she'd been seen in the night before. Any one of them would be able to put two and two together.

Once inside her room, Sloan stripped off everything, took a quick shower, and lay across the bed naked. Her body still throbbed with the passion which Norwood had awakened, satisfied, and rekindled throughout the night. Memories of their lovemaking, his caresses, his kisses, and her response to them were only too fresh in her mind. She turned over and pulled a pillow between her legs, her thoughts in direct conflict with her body's urges. *What the hell have I done, and how am I going to face him today?* she mused as she realized that in less than two hours, they were all scheduled to assemble for a catamaran cruise. She tried desperately to fall asleep, hoping that the additional rest would help her mind focus more sharply, but tranquility evaded her. Finally, she rose, put on her bathing suit, gathered her gear, and headed for the restaurant. Perhaps a strong cup of coffee would at least help her to gain some clarity.

Norwood awakened abruptly, crossed one arm over his eyes, and instantly sat up. He looked around, realized that Sloan was nowhere in sight, and cursed under his breath. She was doing just what he'd expect. Running and hiding. He had no doubt that she'd awakened in a panic and gotten the hell out of there. Well, she could run but she definitely could not hide. The island was too small for that and they still had a couple of days before the concert series was scheduled to end. Until then, she'd have to face him and what had transpired. And although he hadn't expected that the rest of their time together would be a honeymoon, he certainly hadn't expected her to desert him and his bed so abruptly.

He showered then, knowing he had only a short time before the transportation was scheduled to arrive. Their pickup time would be 10:00 A.M. and it was only a little after 8:00. He promised himself that he'd let the chips fall where they may, not stress about Sloan, or what had occurred the night before, yet all through breakfast he found himself looking for her, listening for her voice, and wondering where she was.

When Norwood boarded the bus, he greeted everyone jovially, moved to the back and sat down. Sloan was nowhere in sight and he wondered if she'd blown off the day's activities just to avoid him. His curiosity was satisfied in the next moment. He could make out both Sloan and Jodi strolling toward the vehicle. Sloan had worn a straw hat which shielded half her face, and her hair was pulled back into a ponytail. She looked young, hip, and extremely beautiful and Norwood felt a knot form in the bottom of his stomach. He thought of their lovemaking only hours before and wondered what it would be like to make love to her again—in the daylight with the sun shining brightly on their bodies, its warmth only adding to the temperatures they'd generate as their passion built. He had to put his beach towel over his lap at that point. He also put on his sunglasses, hoping that by shielding his eyes, perhaps some of his thoughts would be hidden from anyone's most direct view.

Sloan walked onto the bus and Jodi, wearing a red bathing suit with a sheer mesh cover-up, stopped to say hi to Lorenzo. Their evening had also lasted well past 2:00 A.M. with the jazz at Time Out at the Gap not finishing up until sometime after 3:00 in the morning. They'd jumped in a cab, come back to their respective hotels, and were looking forward to spending the day in each other's company. Jodi took a seat just across from Lorenzo. Within minutes, they were deep in conversation, laughing and teasing each other like lifelong friends.

Sloan stopped to talk to a public relations agent from Toronto and then wound up taking a seat next to her. She had planned to sit as far away from Norwood as possible anyway; this would do just fine.

Although she'd managed to avoid him by taking her coffee and a carton of yogurt back to her room earlier, there was no doubt in her mind that as the day progressed, it would be increasingly more difficult to avoid interacting with him. When they reached the dock area in downtown Bridgetown, ready to begin boarding the huge catamaran, Sloan breathed a sigh of relief. *So far, so good,* she thought inwardly.

Setting sail, instructions were given for the whereabouts of life vests, snorkeling gear, and the intended day's activities. Many of those onboard chose to sit alongside the outer rim of the vessel, soaking up as much sun as possible. Some rode the starboard hull of the ship, glorying in the feel of the wind at their faces, the sun on their bodies, and the spray which the catamaran issued as it cut through the water. Sloan chose to sit below deck, chatting with a group of journalists from Toronto, then the two writers from England who were both funny and knowledgeable. She drank only water, resigned to giving back as much of its normal equilibrium as possible in a short time.

Norwood, on the other hand, chose to ride in the front of the sailing vessel. He realized from the time Sloan had boarded the bus that she was keeping her distance. Although he wasn't altogether sure of her reasons, he understood the indecision that plagued her. Hell, he felt the same way. He had no real "category" to put their actions of the previous evening into; it had just happened. And as such, he was willing to deal with it. But, if she wanted to behave as though he had the plague, or that he had somehow taken advantage of her, so be it. No problem. Easy come, easy go.

A public relations account manager from Washington, D.C., who also happened to be originally from Chicago, was introduced to him. Short and pretty with long red hair, Alisa Arlington had just arrived the day before. Loose ends on several accounts had kept her at the agency delaying her departure for a trip that would now last for only two days.

"So, tell me—just what is it that has kept you in Chicago all these years? Didn't you ever have the inclination to head either east or west? I know I couldn't wait to relocate, not that there is anything wrong with Chicago. I just couldn't take the bitterly cold winters. Lake Michigan was beautiful in the spring and summer, but is frozen for more than half the year, if I remember correctly," she stated, laughing at the memory.

"Yeah, I know it's pretty cold but you have to admit that Chicago also holds some of the finest restaurants, museums, and culturally expansive institutions in the country, right?" Norwood coaxed.

a laughed, her red hair blown by the wind, the reen two-piece bathing suit enhancing a body that was shapely and devoid of any excess due to an incessant focus on diet and exercise. She worked out with a personal trainer three times per week and went to the gym on at least two other days.

"Yeah, all right, the cultural thing is great. And what they've done with Navy Pier and the "gold coast" of Lincoln Park is fantastic. Lake Shore Drive has always been my favorite part of the city but if you take all of that away, what do you really have?" she asked, smiling invitingly.

"Lake Michigan," they both said at the same time, laughing uproariously. It was at that moment that Sloan looked in their direction. Her heart almost stopped in her chest. So, he was going to play it off, too. Already, he looked as though he was moving in on some redhead with an hourglass body and breasts that were practically falling out of her bathing suit top. *I should have known better,* Sloan chastised herself inwardly.

She headed for the rest rooms located in the bowels of the ship. There were no mirrors and the mariner lavatories held latrines with pump handles for the flushing mechanism. While below, she took the time to reapply her lipstick, mentally stabilizing herself for whatever was to come in the remaining day. Sloan leaned her forehead against the wall, closing her eyes briefly. The coolness of the metal helped her refocus and regroup.

Men, she thought as she returned to the small group she'd been sitting with. Thank God she'd been able to find shelter with an entirely new group of colleagues, far away from the likes of Mr. Norwood Warren. Glen Yates, a senior editor with the *York* *Times,* made room for her to sit in the midst of Thanking him, Sloan reached over, tou sleeve of his shirt, and whispered, "You' though you are part of the Queen's England." The entire group laughed and Norwood watched as Sloan seemed to make herself quite at home with a group of strangers. Inwardly, his gut tightened. Hell, if she wanted to pass herself around, so be it. He hadn't pegged her for a slut, but her actions were definitely suspect.

He turned to Alisa, asked if he could refresh her drink, and headed toward the bar. *The hell with Sloan—I should have known she would be trouble from the very first night,* he thought as he stood waiting for the drink order to be filled.

From where she sat, Sloan could make out Norwood's profile. It was unmistakable. Try as she might, she couldn't tear her eyes away from him. He was wearing navy blue and white striped bathing trunks, and his back was to her. Her mind remembered only too well the feel of the muscles now on display; she felt as if her hands had somehow recorded that familiar landscape. Sloan's heart pounded, and she prayed that Norwood would not turn around and discover her visual assault. She swallowed hard, picked up her glass of Coke, and drank from it. Someone asked her a question. "I'm sorry, what did you say?" It took all of her concentration to try and focus on the conversation but she willed herself to do so.

They reached the first stop of the day, in the middle of the Caribbean Sea, and anchored so that they could snorkel and dive in search of the huge turtles known to inhabit that particular part of the sea. Almost everyone participated, with only a few choosing to remain onboard.

Norwood dove in, realized the water was unbelievably warm and calm, and floated on his back for several moments. As he looked upward at the sun, his ⸺d again came to rest on Sloan. He realized he wanted her by his side, wanted to swim with her, make her laugh, hear the richness of her voice as they frolicked in the blue-green waters which were so clear, you could almost make out the bottom even in more than twelve feet of depth. He thought he could make out her image on the bow of the ship and quickly turned away. The last thing he wanted was for her to think he was looking at her, searching for her, pining for her company.

Alisa swam over, playfully splashed water in his face, and laughed as he wiped it away. "This is great, isn't it? Did you see any turtles yet?" she asked.

"Yeah, they are just under the catamaran and to the right—over there where everyone is swimming," he pointed out.

"Why aren't you over there with them?" she asked then. Although they'd just met, he seemed to be pretty okay. Maybe a little stuck in his ways, but that was to be expected. People from the Midwest were solid, staunch, nonwaivering, for the most part anyway. She was that way, too, although D.C. was fast allowing for subtle changes in her personality and outlook. Although she'd never dated interracially before, the man swimming before her made her want to rethink that whole subject. He was intelligent, obviously talented, and definitely fine.

" 'Cause, for the most part, I'm a loner. Always have been. What about you?"

"No, I'm what is known as a 'people person.' That's why I'm in public relations. Right now, I'm definitely going to attempt to swim with the turtles since it's something I've never done. I was just getting used to the wonderful feeling of swimming in the Caribbean Sea. I'll catch up with you later." And with that swam off.

Norwood realized that the trip could b

complicated if he allowed it to and knew he wanted no such thing to happen. He'd already blown his original plans of not interacting with anyone and look at what had occurred.

The swimmers reboarded the boat some twenty minutes later, excited at having completed a swimming experience they would all remember and talk about for months.

Sloan had finally put on the snorkeling gear, left the catamaran at the rear, and experienced the sight of the huge sea turtles for herself. She couldn't believe the size of them or their tolerant nature. It was an unbelievable experience, one she was glad she'd participated in. And she'd made sure to steer clear of Mr. Warren, swimming only on one side of the catamaran.

A buffet-style lunch had been laid out and the sight and smells of the dishes quickly reminded everyone that it was, indeed, time for lunch. Flying fish, beef stew, jerked chicken, macaroni pie, rice and peas, salad, and small crusted rolls were all aligned alongside the bar area. Additional drinks were served, with rum punch and Bacardi mixers being two of the favorites consumed.

Both Sloan and Norwood, unbeknown to each other, stayed away from those two choices, deciding to request Diet Coke, water, and orange juice for the most part. It seemed that alcoholic spirits were to be blamed for much of the behavior of the evening past. Neither wanted to reexperience clouded judgment or impaired thinking ever again.

As the day progressed, the spirit onboard the sailing vessel became more relaxed, more partylike. Music blaring, feeling no pain, the crew members encouraged their guests to enjoy themselves. Dancing to one particularly catchy beat, several members of the sailing group finally got many of the other members of the group to join in. By the time they reached the second docking location, everyone was having an incredibly good time.

Known to the local mariners as a spot where a historic shipwreck had occurred, they anchored and instructed their guests as to what to look for. It was also only several yards to the shoreline beaches of the west coast of the island of Barbados, one of the most respected parts of the island. The famed hotel and guest spa Sandy Lane could be seen from the boat, its reputation well known among world travelers.

They swam for about half an hour; the waters were a little more choppy than their earlier frolic in the surf. The wind had also picked up somewhat and even the captain of the *Tamarind II* noted its increase.

Giving the crew the order to call everyone back to the vessel, Captain Robinson radioed back to the base. "Yeah, this is the *Tamarind II*—we're getting a hell of a trade wind out here—what's going on? The radar scope shows a decided increase in the pressure area to the south. Tell me something," he added, flicking the over switch on the microphone.

"Captain Robinson—the winds have been picking up steadily all morning. You can finish your day cruise but you'd better head on back. There's a storm off the coast of St. Lucia and it looks like it might be headed our way," the port master advised.

"Okay, Smith. We're headed back now. Over and out."

The captain set a direct course for the port in Bridgetown. His crew was only slightly aware of a small degree of urgency; their passengers onboard knew nothing of the impending storm. They did recogn a sudden shift in the winds—both in speed an tensity. The sailing vessel, manned by exp as well as those who were accustomed to the climate of the region, cut a direct path to its original port. And although it was definitely a rougher ride than four hours earlier, and several of the guests had the uncomfortable feeling of being almost seasick, it was still the culmination of an unforgettable day.

Norwood, militarily trained and staunchly fearless by nature, rode the squalls like a true sailor. Several of the other journalists were not so fastidious and did experience bouts of nausea, unable to quell the uneasiness which came with the fierce rolling of the vessel. Only one vomited though.

Maybe it was the drinks of the night before, perhaps it was the tension she'd experienced since the day began, but Sloan couldn't stop herself from heaving up the small amount of lunch she'd consumed. Thank God, she made it to the lavatory in time though she still looked green when she emerged some fifteen minutes later. Accustomed to almost any emergency, two of the ship's first mates quickly sat her down, offered her ginger ale, and a stomach-settling antacid. She declined the antacid and tried to diffuse the fuss, not wanting to draw attention to herself or her plight. She just wanted to get back to the hotel, lie down, and never board a catamaran again in life.

Norwood, witnessing the entire drama play out, hesitated. He realized she'd avoided him the entire day and didn't want to complicate matters. But he also wanted to help her. Throwing caution to the wind, he walked over to her.

"Hey—are you okay?" he asked, concern in his voice and etched into the planes of his handsome face. Sloan looked at him, realized that she'd missed talking and interacting with him, and shook her head no.

"I'm fine—just a little too much rocky road, if you

know what I mean," she responded, sipping the ginger ale slowly.

"Yeah, I do know. Look, try this," he said. He put his hand on the back of her neck, the warmth immediately jolting her. But instead of caressing it, he gently pushed her head down until it was close to her knees. "Stay like that for a couple of minutes and close your eyes. It'll help restore your equilibrium," he said. Sloan did as she was told, and he kept his hand in place. The heat from it seemed to burn its way through her, spreading to her chest, then to her stomach, creating a calm which she welcomed intensely. Then that same warmth found its way to her loins. Totally unexpected, totally unacceptable—there was no way that she could be feeling like this after vomiting her guts up, but she did. His hands felt so good—so warm. She wanted him to never remove them.

A few moments passed and she realized that he hadn't moved. He sat down next to her, leaned over, and said softly, "Okay, is it any better?"

Opening her eyes, Sloan took a quick swallow of the ginger ale she'd been given and whispered "Yes." She didn't want to admit it, but she indeed felt better.

"Thank you." She didn't trust herself to say anything more—but surely couldn't bring herself to say anything less.

"No problem—you're obviously not cut out to be a sailor. Stick to dry land," he said then, his meaning covering much more than the obvious situation. Sloan smiled weakly, unable to formulate a formidable response. Her bout with nausea had taken a toll, her strength was diminished.

Norwood, satisfied that she was okay, stood up. "I wouldn't advise you to drink anything stronger than that for the next twenty-four hours," he added, walking away. He was torn between leaving and wanting to stay by her side, but not if she didn't want him there. All day long she'd avoided him, after leaving his bed without so much as a note or a backward glance. Then, she'd spent the entire day avoiding any contact with him. Her behavior was rude and totally unacceptable.

So why did he still feel the warmth from the back of her neck in the palm of his hand? Why did he feel compelled to glance backward, even as he walked away, making sure that she was, in fact, okay?

Despite the questions he asked himself, the nagging feeling of recognition he'd experienced as he watched her mingle and flirt all day remained in place. It brought to mind a scene which he had, until now, successfully erased from his mind. Kassandra—he hadn't thought of her in a long time, but watching Sloan in all her glory brought the memory of that disturbing episode back with crystal clarity. The pain, disappointment, and betrayal were like a fresh open wound. Norwood hastened his step. He didn't want to be anywhere near her, or the memories she brought to mind.

Sloan watched him as he walked away, feeling worse as each moment passed. She had no excuse for her behavior, no explanation for what had occurred. She only knew that she regretted the way things had turned out. She saw Norwood glance back at her and wondered if he, too, was thinking of the night they'd spent, the intimacies they'd shared. *No, his behavior today suggests that he's moved on already. The redhead would probably be his next casualty,* she thought. Gathering her things, Sloan realized that her stomach was still churning, but it was her heart that felt the most pain.

Across the expanse of the vessel, a pair of eyes shielded by sunglasses took in the scene being played out. Johnson Dade recognized opportunity when he

saw it. Killer instinct was his best and most effective
quality. He prided himself on it. In his mind, whatever
fling those two had begun was obviously now finished,
kaput, over. It was definitely time for him to make his
move.

Seventeen

New York

Eight o'clock came around too soon for several of the people on the set that morning. Unfortunately, though they arrived on time, their dispositions left something to be desired.

Alton, who'd spent the night with a friend playing cards, drinking Bombay gin with lime squirts, and swapping stories of the time he'd spent in Brixton, England, after leaving Jamaica, definitely felt it. He was on his third cup of coffee by 8:45, believing the myth that the caffeine would help somehow help him focus. All it really did was rev up his metabolism and make him more irritable.

After not falling asleep until the sky began to lighten, Kassandra felt like she'd been dragged through the town on a horse with no name. That is until she saw Karsten. Then she figured the horse's name must have been "torture." There was no other way to describe the feeling of seeing him on the set, in charge of her every move, wearing that ridiculous cap turned backward, and in possession of that smile.

Karsten, having slept like a baby, was in rare form. He knew exactly what the day's frames should hold, what every scene would reflect, and was fully aware of what the finished product should be. He was also aware that his second-string photographer was not operating at 100 percent efficiency. It wouldn't be the first time that he'd had to compensate for someone else's shortcomings. It just meant that everyone else would have to be a little better, a little sharper, and more on target. Alton was the day's charity case, his concentration shot.

"Ready on the set. Okay, listen up. We're going to shoot one of the final segments today and I want everyone to be sharp. We have to be crystal clear on what it is that we're doing here. Let's try and execute this without having to retake the shots over and over again. We're spending money here—let's do this right," he ended. His pep talk delivered, he reached down for his daily water bottle. It was nowhere in sight.

"Shelley—can I get some water over here?" he yelled. The day was definitely starting off on the wrong foot. Shelley, in charge of odd jobs and general goferlike assignments, quickly retrieved a cold bottle of Dasani. Although she'd never witnessed it firsthand, she'd heard stories of people in her position being fired for much less than missing water.

The set had been designed to resemble a neighborhood street scene. Actual footage of a Brooklyn neighborhood would be used to fill in and enhance today's shoot. There would also be more close-up shots of the various members of the singing group interacting with several females. Kassandra's shots would hold a key spot in those taken; she had become one of the principal characters in the video being filmed.

A pink chiffon blouse, with ruffles down the front, complemented the pink shorts Kassandra had been instructed to wear. Beige mules highlighted the current trend in urban summer wear, accentuating the length of her legs, the brevity of the shorts, and the pure essence of female form on display. Her hair, left long with the ends turned upward in a playful flip, convincingly confirmed the message. Wardrobe had done an excellent job; her hair and makeup were flawless, effectively hiding the lack of sleep. The over-all unease she felt was also well hidden by a steel veneer. Accumulated years in the industry had taught her well; the camera never lies, so keep it under wraps until the lens is not in your face.

Karsten was operating on autopilot. His mission was to accomplish the full day's shoot, without wast-ing time or film because they both equated to dollars. By bringing the finished product in on time, he would save the producers thousands of dollars. It would also create a reputation that would serve him well in the future, securing his reputation as a crackerjack director.

Everyone was in position, the camera rolling, on the second scene of the day. All four members of New Deal were seated on the false steps of the building's façade. Kassandra, as instructed, walked slowly by, giv-ing them a seductive look, a toss of her hair, and nothing more. Camera one, operated by Karsten, recorded her every movement. Camera two, operated by Alton, recorded each group member's response as she passed. The scenes would be integrated in the editing room. Suddenly, Alton's voice could be heard. And that was not part of the script.

"How the hell did this happen?" he asked, his hands reaching for his head in desperation. He walked away from the camera, then walked quickly back as everyone on the set watched in amazement.

Karsten yelled "Cut" and took off his headset. "What the heck is going on, Alton?" he asked, won-dering what else could go wrong. He was doing everything in his power to avoid acknowledging the stress he was under with what his viewfinder was locked on to. There was no way to describe looking at someone you wanted through the lens of a video camera. It only intensified those feelings and right now he just wanted to get the day's work over with. He also wanted more of what he'd seen the evening before, but he knew that was out of the question. At the moment, she was avoiding him like the plague and he figured it was probably well deserved. He'd behaved abominably, insulted her by suggesting something demeaning, and then followed it up with the manners of a cad. But it had felt good. Somehow, he figured if they could get past the hurdle of a horrible first date, let the chips fall where they may. His thoughts were brought back to the present crisis.

Alton walked over, led him aside, and stated, "I forgot to load the tape and I think we may have to reshoot the entire first scene. I'm sorry but I had a really rough night," he ended.

"Al—my man—that's the first rule of photography. You have to load the camera. The next thing you'll tell me is that you forgot to turn it on. Damn." Karsten's voice raised at that point and several members of the cast and crew looked over, somewhat surprised to hear him curse. Obviously, whatever was going on with Alton had obviously affected something. They all waited, holding their breaths, wondering when the next shoe would fall. It did not take long.

"Okay, people—I want you to assume the original positions you took earlier today. We just want to make sure everything was done right so we're gonna do it again," he added. He'd be damned if he'd let them know that his assistant cameraman was falling down on the job.

Kassandra walked back to her position off camera, ready to enter at the signal which would be given by

Shelley. It encompassed a long shot of her walking for several quick seconds before she entered the range of the group's members. With that long shot, the camera focused on her from her feet to the top of her head. Karsten had already gone through this torturous routine once. Having to do it again was a bit much, but he knew that the scene was crucial to the video's texture. As Kassandra came into view, he thought he detected a slight swagger she seemed to have added to her walk. It actually was a good addition, creating a more streetwise type of young woman for the formidable group of men she was about to pass before. But it suggested something more to him personally. Unable to pinpoint if she was aware of this change in her demeanor but not willing to acknowledge it, he just continued taping. He also made up his mind to ask her out again.

Alton noticed the change, too. Uncertain as to how it would affect the final editing process, and on the edge because of his earlier screwup, he signaled Karsten.

"Cut—now what," Karsten said, as Alton closed the distance between them.

"Our prima donna has developed an 'attitude.' The model is coming on too strongly. Didn't you notice it?" His voice lowered, he glanced quickly in Kassandra's direction, then looked away, not wanting her to know that she was the subject of his discussion. But Kassandra's tenure in the industry had given her many useful tools, one of which was instinct. She sensed the discussion was about her, although she didn't know exactly what it entailed. After the events of the night before, she figured a pink slip could be in order by the end of the day anyway. It wouldn't be the first time a model had refused to give in to the attention of a hotshot director and gotten fired. She watched and waited.

Alton's assessment was insightful, yet Karsten knew he was the director and, as such, should be the one to make the call. Not his assistant.

"Yeah, Driggs, I noticed but thought it added character. I would've called 'cut' if I thought it needed it. Can we get back to work now?" The irritation in his voice was evident. He'd obviously spoken louder than he intended as several of the crew looked over to see what the new drama and interruption was based on. It suddenly became very quiet on the set.

"Yeah, sure. I just figured I'd bring it to your attention."

"My camera lens is just as clear as yours—I see it just as quickly as you do. I chose not to stop the scene because it was playing to the end product anyway. The model, the swagger, the scene stays. Everybody, get back to your marks. We're picking it up at frame fourteen," Karsten shouted. Cast, crew, and talent all returned to their previous position, holding their breaths collectively. This one day had held more tension than all the others combined; they all felt as if they were working and walking on eggshells. And though no one knew to what it could be attributed, somehow the key characters seemed to point to Kassandra, Karsten, and perhaps, Alton.

The remainder of the day passed without incident. They wrapped at 6:45 P.M. with only one final day of taping to be done. Karsten had given instruction for them to report to the studio at 7:00 A.M. They would then be transported to the location, a spot just below the Brooklyn Bridge. Chosen for its view, the ambience, and the feel of expansiveness, the location would prove to be challenging as well. The early morning light, combined with the water in the background, would present its own set of problems. But Karsten was not concerned with any of that. He was, at the present, concerned with getting another date with Kassandra.

The wardrobe area was more of a storage area separated by a long black curtain than anything else. It provided the rudimentary elements of privacy—nothing more. There was no door. Kassandra had just removed the pink blouse and matching bra when she heard her name being called.

"Yeah—just a minute," she replied but Karsten was already standing before her. He'd forgotten that this was not only the hair and makeup area, but the dressing room as well.

"Oh, damn—I'm so sorry," he sputtered as Kassandra crossed her arms before her exposed breasts.

Karsten, wanting to be a gentleman, knew he should turn his face away. But the simple truth was he could not. Instead, he held eye contact hoping that he wouldn't break down and ogle her unclothed torso. She was absolutely beautiful, standing before him wearing nothing but her dignity and the pink shorts and mules. Her skin was flawless and even. He immediately noticed that although she was not wearing a bra, her breasts were high and firm, despite being mostly hidden by the two hands being stretched across her chest.

"Do you think you could have knocked first, or yelled out or something?" she asked quickly. She couldn't believe that he hadn't moved from the spot.

"There's no door. And I did call out your name. You should have said something to let me know you were still dressing. Anyway, I only came back here to let you know that you did a fine job today. You caused some turmoil with the change in your attitude but on tape it was pure perfection. You can get dressed now," he added, turning away.

He'd wanted to ask her out again, but with her in a

half-undressed state, wearing emotional armor, her arms crossed in a defensive mode, he couldn't bring himself to pursue it. Desire rolled over him in waves as he headed toward the front entrance of the building. For the first time in a long while, he felt challenged by something he could not control.

Pulling out of the parking garage, he thought he heard his name being called and stopped. Rolling down the window, he saw Kassandra walking toward the vehicle. She'd dressed in her own clothing, a pair of jeans and a white hooded sweatshirt.

"Yeah, what have I done now?" he asked, sure that he was about to receive a reprimand for his latest transgression.

"Well, where do you want me to start?" she retorted, not willing to let him off that easily. His compliment, though delivered under compromising circumstances, still meant a great deal to her. And she wanted him to know that, barring the events of the night before, she still respected and recognized his talent, his ability, and most important, his position in the industry.

"Look, I just wanted to let you know that what happened back there wasn't any big deal. I mean, I undress all the time in front of people—on the set. I know you didn't do it on purpose and I appreciate your taking the time to let me know about the day's shoot. It means a lot to me."

Karsten was silent for a moment then cut the motor of the car. "It was probably the highlight of my day actually." He wanted to laugh but thought better of it. "Look, do you think we could start all over again? I mean, I'd like to take you out again. Last night was such a monumental disaster that I want to rectify everything I did and said. Even if it goes no further than the second date, at least I'll know that I got a chance to make a second impression." He wanted to add that the sight of her nearly naked had only added increased his desire to get to know her better but knew she'd never speak to him again if he did. Knowing he was being driven by lust did nothing to quell his desire; it did, however, cause him to censor the things he said.

Kassandra stood beside the vehicle wondering what she should do. He'd obviously displayed a portion of his true personality yet she also knew he was trying his best to be charming, irresistible, and convincingly sweet.

"Look, how about this—you agree to go out with me after the shoot tomorrow. The video will be finished—from the taping standpoint, at least. The pressure will be off on that side and we'll just get to know one another as human beings. That way, you won't feel as if you're dating your boss, I won't have to worry about your respecting my judgment after we've been in each other's company in any compromising way, and we can all live happily ever after," he ended, smiling.

"Well, it certainly seems as if you have it all wrapped up with a nice neat bow," Kassandra said. "What happens if we hate each other?" she asked quickly.

"Look, first of all, why don't you get in? I'll drop you at the train, or at your doorstep—whichever you prefer. It's your call. We can talk about it on the way," he added, reaching across to push the door open in invitation.

She hesitated for a moment, then walked around to the passenger side.

"I'm glad you weren't afraid to take that step. It would have made the rest of what I was saying a moot point," he added, starting up the vehicle.

"Anyway, I just wanted to explain what happened last night. I am sometimes challenged by demons. Most of the time I manage to overcome them. Just know that at no time were you in any real danger." His shrewd summation delivered, he turned the vehicle and headed uptown.

Kassandra was stunned by his attitude. He obviously wanted to apologize but couldn't. It wouldn't be the first time a man was unable to take responsibility for his actions.

"Look, I understand what you're trying to say—I think. It's okay, it's over, and we can move on. We only have one more day of shooting and that's it. Finito!"

Karsten heard her words and knew he had his work cut out for him. Nothing was finished—not the video, not his work, and most certainly, not whatever it was that had gotten started between them.

"I think you've missed my point. What I'm trying to say is that I want to see you again. Now, I know you may have some reservations, may even be inclined to turn down my offer, but just think about it. You don't have to give me an answer right now. Tomorrow when we wrap up, let me know then."

Listening intently to his words, Kassandra suddenly realized that he was on the way to her house. He'd bypassed the train station, taken the most direct route and was only blocks away from where she lived. The familiarity and ease which he displayed wreaked havoc on her senses. She was torn between what her better judgment called for and what she felt sitting beside him.

"Please don't take this the wrong way but I do have to think about it. I broke a cardinal rule by going out with you and look where we ended up. I am not willing to jeopardize my professional reputation, nor my personal life in that way," she stated vehemently. She wanted to add "it's just not worth it" but that would have been untrue. He was worth the risk and she knew it. Hell, he probably knew it, too. That's why he was being so persistent.

"That said, just sleep on it. I guarantee that tomorrow morning will shed new light on the entire subject of Karsten Battle," he said, laughing. He pulled up in front of her building, miraculously found a space, and began parking the Range Rover.

They sat in the car for the next hour, talking, exchanging ideas, laughing at the incidents which had occurred on the set, and reaching a comfort level which had been nonexistent beforehand.

Karsten, a lover of music from the time he was a teenager, kept the radio on. WQCD 101.9 was his favorite station and, although he owned a slew of CDs, he allowed the station to play, filling the vehicle's interior with the sounds of smooth jazz.

The sun, which had begun to set when they pulled up, cast a burning orange glow against the backdrop of Manhattan buildings. As Kassandra prepared to leave the vehicle, she turned to him, touched his arm, and whispered, "Thanks."

"For what?"

"Just for being who you are. I'm sure I could have had a director who was much more difficult, not even half as much fun, and not anywhere as good to look at," she added, laughing.

"Oh, so are you trying to tell me that you find me attractive?" His question hung in the air. If answered, it would give him all the ammunition he needed to do what he really wanted to.

"I didn't say that—I just said you were good to look at."

"Come here," he commanded, taking hold of her arm and pulling her toward him. Kassandra stiffened, then went with the flow. His lips pressed against hers softly, and slowly became more demanding. Unable to break the contact, not wanting to lose the connection, she found herself kissing him back with a small de-

gree of hesitation. Theirs was a test of wills; he knew
what he wanted from her and she wanted the very
same thing, but was not willing to risk her career to
get it.

Karsten traced a trail of soft kisses from her mouth to
her neck and earlobe, then back again. This time when
their lips met, there was no resistance, no hesitation on
Kassandra's part. She met him with a pent up passion
that encompassed the past six months. Placing both
hands softly on his face, she kissed him with an energy
borne of restraint, months of deprivation, and newly
built hope. Their lips melded, their tongues meshed,
each exploring the other with passion tempered by a
first kiss. Leaning into him, her soft breasts crushed by
the tightness of his hold, Kassandra grasped the back of
his head. His hair felt like soft, silky baby's curls and she
found her hands tangled in its midst.

Karsten, surprised by her sudden abandon, needed
no further encouragement. Reaching out to pull her
closer, his hands wandered to her back but the bulky
sweatshirt impeded his need to get closer. His hand
found its way beneath it where he explored the
smooth expanse of her back. Kassandra moaned,
leaned closer, and Karsten knew the meaning of true
torture.

Breaking the connection, he whispered softly, "See,
I knew you liked me." They both laughed then, the
sexual tension still present but clearly defined.

"I think it's time for me to go in now," she replied,
unwilling to acknowledge what had just transpired although her body was sending a clear message that she
was unable to deny or ignore.

"Fine—so we're set for tomorrow night and I'll see
you on the set at four P.M. Remember, it's a night
shoot under the Brooklyn Bridge. We should wrap
by about ten or eleven," he added.

"Thanks for driving me home—and yes, I'll see you on the set tomorrow afternoon." She purposely left her answer to his first statement unanswered.

Now that she knew what she was really up against, Kassandra definitely wanted to think about it. Another date with him would mean two things—one, that she really wanted to go out with him even though she knew he could be difficult. And two, a continuation of what they'd just started. There was no doubt in her mind that as long as they didn't get into an argument that reached World War III proportion, she'd end up in bed with him.

It was a lot to think about. For the second night in a row, Kassandra found it difficult to sleep. As she tossed and turned, dreaming of his Karsten's lips, his kisses and how they made her feel, it seemed he was already in her bed.

Eighteen

Barbados

Saturday's scheduled all-day outdoor concert at Farley Hill was in serious jeopardy. Huge cumulus clouds darkened the skies, with intervals of great gusts of wind forcing umbrella closings on the beach, as runaway straw hats tumbled across the sand. Many made their way into the water, only to be retrieved by owners who still had use for them.

Normally calm seas, turquoise and clear, had become a churning wave-crested ocean, whose power was becoming increasingly apparent. Intermittent, short intervals of sunlight pushed their way throughout the day and gave hope to all that the storm brewing would somehow bypass the island of Barbados. But the clouds prevailed, with the winds picking up and the humidity increasingly steadily.

The weather center, operated by the Ministry of the Interior, watched and waited. They issued a "storm" warning, knowing that it would at least cause shop owners to prepare for the worst and local inhabitants to be on alert also. All in all, they prayed for the best. Memories of Hurricane Marie, which had hit the island in 1997, were still fresh in their minds. Homes destroyed, business interrupted, and a coastline that had been diminished slightly were the overall lasting

effects. But the real devastation lay in the hearts and
minds of the island's local people; their inability to
control Mother Nature had left a lasting and deep
impression.

Roland Gilbert, president and CEO of RG Tours International and organizer of the festival, was in a
quandary. Most artists' contracts contained clauses
specifically stating "rain or shine" compensation. As
such, RG Tours had an immensely difficult decision
to make with Mother Nature literally calling the shots.
Spyro Gyra, led by Jay Beckenstein, was scheduled to
perform. Also on the roster for the all-day concert
venue were Chaka Khan, Barbadian guitarist Ian Al-
leyne, and the legendary Earth, Wind & Fire. All
artists were in residence at one of the island's most ex-
clusive resorts, the Almond Beach Club. They'd been
flown in two days earlier and were now enjoying the
climate, the sunshine, and the overall exotic laid-back
atmosphere which only an island can impart. Everyone was looking forward to performing at the
legendary historic park site. The remaining ruins of a
culturally rich location lent both character and charm
to the park. Tents that housed vendors featuring local
arts, crafts, and exotic dishes were set up and would
draw the attention of visitors throughout the day between concerts.

By 11:30, families with children, couples, singles and
groups began arriving. Blankets, coolers, and assorted
items needed to offer the basic comforts of home away
from home were hauled in for use throughout the day.
The parklike setting offered lawn seating only, but no
one was complaining. It was a Farley Hill tradition, one
that was well respected and eagerly anticipated. The impending rain, storm, or whatever it was to be was an
extremely unwelcome element.

Sloan, having recovered from her experience on

board the catamaran, was actually looking forward to the day's events. She'd come to the conclusion that Norwood, and all that had transpired between them, had been one huge mistake. The press trip was almost over—she'd gotten her story, obtained her photographs, and learned a valuable lesson in the process. Never sleep with the competition. Although they weren't strictly competitors having altogether different fields of communication, it still irked her that he'd behaved as if he wanted to help her in the beginning. All his offerings of information and guidance had turned out to be one big crock. She suspected his only real motivation had been to disarm her natural instincts, allay her fears, and move in for the kill.

He reminded her of Karsten—only at least her ex would have been totally honest and not hidden his ulterior motives. That was one thing about him that she remembered. Karsten had always been totally above board with his intentions—no matter how selfish or negative. He had been brutally honest in most cases, often giving excruciatingly specific detail to things she'd rather not have known. But knowing was an advantage. And at the end of the relationship, when they'd both known that divorce was the only solution, she'd come to respect him, even after all they'd been through.

Now, as she sat preparing to assemble her equipment, reload her camera, and pack the necessary items for the day's concert schedule, Sloan noticed the overcast skies. Rain would mean even more difficulty in getting the necessary shots. She silently prayed that the concert event would not be canceled, not knowing that the chances for that were remote. It would prove to be costly for the promoters and disastrous for the tourist board.

Sloan's thoughts reluctantly turned to Norwood as

she dressed. After pulling her hair into a ponytail, she put on a pair of white cropped jeans, a white-eyelet sleeveless top, and low white sandals. Silver hoop earrings adorned each ear; her watch and one silver bracelet were her only other jewelry. *Whatever happens today, I absolutely have to remember that I only came here to get a story—not to sleep with anyone, not to fall in love with anyone, and certainly not to become involved! Mr. Warren was an inconvenience, a huge error, but one that I can forget and move away from. It's only today and tomorrow—Monday we all head home.*

The next seventy-two hours would prove to be difficult but Sloan knew she could handle it. She had to. She had no other choice.

Norwood dressed, loaded his camera equipment, then decided to call Lorenzo. For some reason, he wasn't looking forward to having breakfast alone. And he for damn sure didn't want to run into Sloan. After the cold shoulder she'd given him the day before, he wanted nothing more to do with her. She'd spent the night with him, made love with him, then discarded everything that transpired between them like a stick of overchewed gum. So be it for the chick from New York. The hell with her.

But in the deeper sense, Norwood blamed himself, too. He'd originally planned to stay as far away from everyone on the trip as possible. So, how had it happened that within three days, he'd found himself in bed with a beautiful photojournalist from New York City who obviously didn't give a damn about him, was just using him for recreational sex, and who didn't even have the courtesy to retain common civilities afterward?

He dialed Lorenzo's hotel, silently willing him to

pick up when connected to his room. He was in luck. Lorenzo picked up on the third ring.

"Hey, man, what's up? I thought you had decided to bow out of our circle of friends," he said when he recognized Norwood's voice.

"No, dude—I just had some things on my mind. Listen, would you like to get together for breakfast? The bus isn't scheduled to pick us up until around ten thirty. We still have more than two hours," Norwood said, looking at the clock. It was 8:15 A.M.

"Yeah, sure. Just let me get a shower. I just came back from a nice early morning swim in the ocean. I can't sleep much after six in the morning anyway so I get up and walk on the beach every morning. Most times, I swim, too. You should have come over and joined me. It was awesome!"

"Yeah, I actually was up but doing some thinking. Okay—so where should we meet?"

"Why don't I come over to your hotel again? Your meals are all inclusive and I only have to pay a minimum. Not to mention that maybe I'll get to see Jodi for a minute before the day's schedule kicks in. That girl really does something to me, man." His laughter made Norwood smile. So, he, too, was feeling the effects of the women, the island, the sun, the heat, and the natural instincts all those things brought out.

"Sure, meet me downstairs in the restaurant area in about twenty-five minutes—is that okay?"

"Definitely—if you get there before me, order a large orange juice. I can already taste it. See you in a few, man," Lorenzo said, hanging up quickly.

Scrambled eggs, toast, juice, and coffee comprised breakfast for both men. Lorenzo ordered a side order of bacon, canceled it, then dug into the plate before him.

"You know, only two years ago, I gave up all meat. Not only have I felt better since then, but I dropped at least ten pounds."

"I stopped eating pork when I was a teenager. I still eat meat sometimes though. I can't resist a juicy steak—especially when I go out to dinner. There are some great steak houses in Chicago. God, I actually feel as if I miss it and I've been gone less than a full week." With all that had transpired in the past four days, it would probably constitute a month's worth of emotional stuff but he neglected to say so. Although he felt Lorenzo was cool and he definitely enjoyed talking with him, he wasn't sure that he was ready to share what had transpired with Sloan with anyone at this point. He wasn't 100 percent sure of what his own real feelings on the subject were either.

"I'm thinking of seeing if I can get a special arrangement so that I can get over to the eastern end of the island. I understand that's the side where the surf is really kicking. I think some candid shots of that would be awesome. You know how California likes to think they have the surfing thing all sewed up—well, I'd just like to offer a little Caribbean competition." Lorenzo also recognized that shots of the surf, with the added turbulence of an impending storm, would possibly bring big bucks. It was the only way to differentiate your stuff from that of the everyday, run-of-the-mill photos.

The remaining concerts and programs would include additional highlights of the festival, but his real interests lay in scenic photography. As yet, he'd only used two rolls of film which included any shots of real outdoor locations. They alone would complete the total picture of what he had in mind.

Things would be winding down quickly after today's outdoor concert with one additional concert Sunday evening featuring Nancy Wilson. The classic jazz diva was scheduled to close out the concert series which had included funk, soul, R&B, local artists, calypso, and classic jazz at its best. But his soul would not rest until he obtained at least a full roll of film shot on location, showing the devastatingly beautiful seascapes, landscapes, and breathtaking views which the island had to offer.

"When are you proposing to do this, man? You know today's concert series is all day, outdoors, and will probably take up most of the daylight hours. Did you speak with Deirdre of the BTA on this? The Tourism Authority seems to be really flexible but I'm sure they have stuff that's off limits. They are pretty much responsible for our safety while we're here, too," Norwood reminded him.

"Yeah, don't worry—it's all taken care of. They're going to take us to Cherry Hill. It's one of the highest points on the island and overlooks a fantastic stretch of beach. The driver will be assigned for the entire day. So, even if we're a little late, we can still catch tomorrow's evening concert."

"Whoa—whoa. . . . What do you mean 'we'? I thought you were just telling me about this. I had no idea that I had a role to play in this nature tour, or outdoor photography fest," Norwood added. He laughed then. Lorenzo looked like a kid who had just discovered Christmas. And he had to admit, it did sound interesting.

"Man, I'm sorry but you have to come. Knowing you, you'll probably take some pictures too! Come on, the car is going to pick us up at exactly ten o'clock. That gives us all day to circle the island, get the photos, and get back in time for the evening concert."

"I guess—man, with the way the weather seems to be shaping up, you'd better hope it doesn't rain on your parade. The clouds are circling like buzzards. Even today's weather looks iffy if you ask me," Norwood added, looking up. And indeed, as they'd finished their breakfast, the normally bright sunshine faded into an overcast shadow.

"Honestly, I think we'll just be playing it by ear. But on a brighter note and a totally different subject, Jodi and I have decided to keep in touch when we return home. I know it sounds crazy, but I really dig that chick. Three thousand miles is an awfully long distance for a relationship, but a friendship is fine. She's something else, though. Don't you think?" Lorenzo asked, eager for male confirmation.

"Yeah, she's great. Smart, funny, and pretty cute, too. I probably should have noticed her instead of her sidekick. The chick is a head case even though she is fine as all hell."

Lorenzo had been careful to steer clear of any conversation which included Sloan after noticing both their behaviors onboard the catamaran the day before. If he hadn't known better, he'd guess they hated one another. Even Jodi had mentioned it to him, wondering what the heck was going on.

"Hey, hey—hands off Jodi," Lorenzo laughed. He knew Norwood was just talking through his hat. The brother was probably so hung up on the New York chick that he was saying anything to make himself look like a player. But he also recognized that the last thing Norwood needed was to feel as if he'd peeped his hole card. So he kept those thoughts to himself.

"Sloan doesn't seem like a head case to me. Just a little reserved—maybe even scared. You know I hear New York is one of the most difficult places to build a lasting relationship in. It's a city that's great for your career, great for making a ton of dollars, but all that competition and fast lane activity wreaks havoc on your personal life."

Norwood was silent. His thoughts were on Lorenzo's statement and how it might explain, though not make an excuse for, Sloan's behavior. His coffee was cold. He turned the cup up, drained it, and looked Lorenzo in the eye.

"You may be right about that—Chicago's not too far off the mark either. You have to watch your back in any major city, and it does make you defensive. But that doesn't give you the right to go around acting like Attila the Hun. Then you've become part of the problem, not part of the solution."

Lorenzo wasn't entirely certain of what Norwood was getting at, but he suspected that things had gotten a little complicated between him and Sloan. If truth be told, he almost wished that he'd put more of a move on Jodi but also recognized that it would have been too soon for either of them. Theirs was a friendship that would age and mellow with time. Hopefully, it might eventually mature into something more; he was willing to wait. Especially since a long-distance relationship was even more complex.

"Hey, I don't have any of the answers, man. Just thought I'd offer what little insight I may have come across in my travels. Don't sweat it though. Between you and me, Jodi thinks Sloan likes you a lot, but just doesn't want to let on. You know how women are, man. They're more complicated than a Pentium Four computer."

They both laughed. "State-of-the-art technology—now that's what I call a real necessity," Norwood added. The way he figured it, if you had the right equipment, everything else would fall in line. Those thoughts brought him full circle to Sloan again. And although Norwood didn't want to compromise the specifics of his relationship with her, he wanted to say that she'd certainly behaved as if she liked him. Especially when they were in bed. He found himself remembering her passion, her responsiveness, and the texture of her skin. He could even remember the feel and smell of her in his arms. Norwood realized that he was torturing himself. He'd already been there and done that—knew it was to be avoided at all costs. "Okay, look—I guess I'll sign on for this trek across the island to get the scenic shots. You'd better hope that this rain holds off though, or lets loose today and clears up."

"Yeah—it'll probably rain for about an hour or so, then break out with a magnificent rainbow and sunshine for the rest of the day. That's a typical day here from what I understand. The hotel desk clerk told me earlier that even if it does rain later on today, it'll probably clear up pretty quickly."

"Well, that's a relief. It's been threatening to rain for the past day or so."

"Let's just hope that today's outdoor concerts aren't rained out. I am looking forward to it. And to sampling the local art, crafts, and the food. Bring on the macaroni pie," he added. It was certainly not a staple in California's health-conscious diet.

"Definitely. Okay, see you later."

"Yeah, listen, don't forget to bring some kind of protective gear—just in case." Norwood had a plastic outer wrap for all his equipment. He never traveled without it after having been caught in a huge storm many years before. Photographic equipment was extremely sensitive—water was not its friend and he'd learned that the hard way. His first camera, a thirty-five-millimeter Pentax, had been lost to him forever in a rain-soaked shoot. Now, whenever he spotted clouds

in the sky, he prepared for the worst—especially in any
outdoor situation.

Everyone on the bus was eager for the day to begin.
The clouds overhead cast an impatient pall on each
member of the entire group. No one wanted to believe that the darkening clouds overhead would
actually develop into rain. Their threat seemed exaggerated. Jodi and Lorenzo were in conversation about
the uses of different filters and whether or not their
effects represented authentic photography or some
altered hybrid. Neither really cared but were happy to
be in one another's company just the same.

Norwood, sitting again in the back of the bus,
watched Sloan as she conversed with another journalist
from England. At first, he felt a slight annoyance and
nothing more. If she chose to continue to behave in an
immature fashion, who was he to intervene? It was her
choice whom she spent time with. Obviously, she had
completed whatever her mission had been with him.
That much was clear. What was abundantly unclear was
just who the hell she thought she was. His annoyance
grew with each passing moment—he wanted to approach her and set the record straight. But pride kept
him in his seat. *The hell with her*—he'd thought that before, he realized. It seemed he needed to repeat it
several times to have it become part of his psyche. The
bus continued on through the Barbados countryside,
beautiful rolling hills dotted with homes, then entered
the main business district of Bridgetown and continued
on toward their destination.

Farley Hill was beautiful. The historic park was
filled with tall, forestlike trees and the remnants of
several structures still stood as a testament to the island's historic past. Tents and tables filled many of the

areas where local vendors displayed their wares. Local artists, native artifacts, and Caribbean-inspired wares adorned the many tables. Food vendors were disbursed throughout and the scent of jerked chicken being roasted filled the air. Rice and peas, macaroni pie, flying fish, fried breadfruit, and many other national favorites were also available. Haagen Daz, a frequent sponsor, also occupied one tent, offering its deliciously rich desserts throughout the day.

The main stage, set up adjacent to the ruins, presented an excellent view from all points. And the breathtaking drop-off crowning the top of a steep incline offered a view of Barbados that stunned all who saw it. It was a day filled with incredible possibility and undeniable potential.

Chaka Khan took center stage first and the crowd went wild. Hit after hit, many of which she'd recorded with the group Rufus, sent a ripplelike effect through the attendees, many of whom remembered vividly the era Chaka represented.

"Sweet Thang" brought them to the barricades chanting for more and Norwood, Sloan, Lorenzo, as well as many of the other photojournalists on hand, were inundated with capturing the enthusiasm on film. The photos taken would serve to reconstruct the atmosphere of the day in vivid detail.

Meanwhile, Jodi was content to record each nuance of the concert in her journal: the crowd's enthusiastic response and the surrounding elements. She was an excellent writer and prided herself on bringing back a story that was replete with visual imagery aided by powerfully descriptive paragraphs.

Johnson Dade, content to browse through the many stalls present, and not given to either photography or journalism, took stock of the situation. He'd already come to the conclusion that Norwood and

Sloan's former friendship was obviously on hiatus. And though he didn't altogether understand why, he really didn't give a damn. He saw it as a renewed opportunity.

Sloan was busy reloading her camera, having taken a seat to do so. There was an air of excitement which permeated the entire perimeter where the journalists and photographers were in operation. She had been so involved in getting her shots, taking notes in between, and keeping track of what she was doing, that she'd had little time to think of Norwood. For that, she was grateful. He, too, seemed determined to also avoid contact or confrontation.

Johnson Dade walked up, sat down next to her, but remained silent. Sloan continued to load her camera, checking the flash for optimum strength. The sun was beginning to set which would necessitate as much light as possible for each shot going forward.

"So, how's the photojournalist doing? Are you getting everything you need?"

Sloan hesitated, then smiled slowly. "Yes—and you?" she asked. She really wanted to stand up and walk away, ignoring him would be the kind thing to do. But instead, she turned politely waiting for his answer.

He took her hesitation and her smile for acquiescence. "I'm having an okay time. It would be a lot better if you and I could get back on the right foot. I think you misunderstood me before. And then, your friend blew everything out of proportion by butting in . . . " He left the sentence open, not wanting to verbalize his true feelings. He recognized that he'd have to play it smart with this one. She was no dummy— New York women were reportedly sophisticated and she was no exception. In fact, if truth be told, that's probably where he'd made his first mistake in underestimating her.

"Look, why don't we call it a truce? I'd like to get to know you a little better. It's a lovely island—a great atmosphere. I've never fallen in love on a tropical island, have you?" he asked.

Sloan almost gagged. The guy was unbelievable. They all were. She wanted nothing to do with any of them.

"No—and I don't plan to be around long enough to give it a try. Now, if you'll excuse me . . ." She closed her camera bag and stood up.

Quicker than she could have anticipated it, he reached out, grabbing her wrist. "Don't act like you're saving it—I saw you leave the jazz club the other night with that photographer from Chicago. What's the matter—things not working out between you two?" he asked with an insinuating glare.

Incensed beyond words, Sloan wrenched her wrist away, stepping back and putting as much distance between them as possible. "Leave me alone, Dade—what I do is none of your damned business," she practically spat at him. She then walked briskly toward the stage area just as they announced Earth, Wind & Fire.

The words Johnson Dade muttered under his breath were heard by no one but himself, but they were understood by a pair of eyes that watched him closely. Norwood had witnessed the scene between him and Sloan with clenched teeth. And although his feelings for Sloan were becoming more and more complex as the days went by, the rage he felt when he saw Johnson Dade grab her wrist was mild by comparison. He'd watched, waited, and almost closed the distance between them. Only a self-imposed code of honor had kept him from reacting. That and a will of steel.

Sloan, busy getting shots of the legendary act as they performed "Kalimba," tried to focus on the task

at hand. She almost felt nauseous again when she remembered the sneer on Johnson Dade's face. The
guy was a potential keg of dynamite—she wanted
nothing to do with him. But a nagging feeling of regret seized her as she realized that his observation of
her behavior with Norwood had only added fuel to an
obviously still-burning fire.

Meanwhile, Johnson Dade made two crucial deci-
sions. One, somehow, in the next twenty-four hours, he
would show "Miss High and Mighty" what a real man
was made of. And two, but not necessarily in that order,
he would also make it a point to effectively eradicate
the likes of the sidewinder from the Midwest.

They were both amateurs in his estimation. But
they needed to be taught a very professional lesson.
And he was just the teacher to do it.

Nineteen

Brooklyn's Waterfront Café, a landmark restaurant, and the surrounding wharf area provided the perfect set for the video's final scenes. The backdrop of the Brooklyn Bridge, with the lights of Manhattan visible in the distance, only enhanced the incredible skyline. Karsten was determined to capture each nuance of the location on film. The romance and escalating passion would be illuminated by the atmosphere the wharf area projected.

The group's members, dressed in the latest jeans and khakis, with casual sport shirts in pale colors completing their outfits, looked young, hip, and virile. Two of the young men had sport jackets thrown over their shoulders, expressing casual sophistication.

Kassandra, dressed in tightly fitted black jeans topped by a black pin-dot halter top, her hair pulled into a chignon at the back of her neck, looked chic, sophisticated, and very sexy. Close-up shots of her interacting with each group member would suggest flirtation, teasing, and irresistible attraction. But there would be only one of the four who would come forward, take her hand, and walk into the moonlit night.

Reynard Elgin, the tallest and most photogenic, had proven himself to be the best candidate for that characterization. Six feet two, built like an athlete, and in possession of smooth skin, great cheekbones, and incredibly large brown eyes, he also had what industry types referred to as "camera burn." Actors, models, and extras who, for whatever reason, interacted with the camera without losing the three-dimensional qualities of their features were fortunate indeed. Their good looks transcended film.

Karsten was deep in discussion on camera angles with Alton as the group members and other personnel took their respective places. He watched as Kassandra walked from the trailer to the film area, her hair and makeup impeccable, taking her assigned spot. No sign of nervousness was apparent. To the world, she appeared to be cool, calm, and collected. Through the lens of Karsten's camera, she looked delicious.

The butterflies she felt in her stomach each time her eyes were drawn to the camera area were not apparent to anyone—Kassandra's professionalism was being called to order in full force. And although the darkness enhanced by the huge klieg lights blocked out any vision she would have had beyond her immediate perimeter, she imagined that Karsten not only saw her very clearly, but also read right through to her thoughts. It made for a very uncomfortable shoot. Thinking ahead, she realized that the date could very well be a deal breaker in her career; there was no other way to categorize it. And although she didn't know what to expect, she couldn't relax and think of it as just another date. He'd made it abundantly clear that he would not take no for an answer.

Halfway through, Karsten yelled "Cut" for the third time. He called the assistant cameraman aside and they conferred for a moment. They then called in one of the set assistants and gave her instructions to restructure several things. When all was said and done, the final scene positioned Kassandra in the arms of Reynard after a rapid succession of carefully structured takes. The initial attraction already documented throughout previous footage would cement the video's message. The scene, shot from an angle showing both their faces in a side view, turned out to be more steamy than anyone originally envisioned. The last minute addition added sizzle and punch to the romantically inclined short film. It also added fuel to the fire that was already burning within the director's imagination. The images he'd seen through the lens of his camera stained his memory and infuriated his senses.

They wrapped the shoot on time and within budget. Everyone was ecstatic, everyone was excited. And most of all, they all recognized that they'd been involved with a project that would, at the very least, provide an excellent vehicle for the client's newly released album *Destiny Knows No Doubt*.

Karsten waited for Kassandra to change from the wardrobe outfit, his cap turned to the front once again. He was tired, but ultimately excited knowing that the entire shoot had gone extremely well. If things went as planned, his name would join the ranks of the talented few who were called on to photograph and direct videos, commercials, and even movies. The excitement that he'd felt while filming the final scenes was on simmer; he needed only a minor incendiary device to incite the flames.

That device was now walking toward him; he could actually feel his pulse begin to race. Kassandra had changed into a retro-style slipdress. It showcased her body in an elegant, yet subdued way. It also caused Karsten to hold his breath as she approached his vehicle. He had not anticipated his continued reaction to her. And although he could not put a finger on it, nor a name to it, the range of emotions he experienced whenever in her presence was defiantly dogged. Unrelenting, haunting, and desperately needing an outlet, he found himself smiling as she entered the vehicle.

"Hello."

"Hello yourself. You look incredibly young and naïve in that dress. Are you trying to test my will? You know, I have a soft spot for women in long, flowing dresses," he added. With the statement, he realized that it reminded him of something he'd once said to Sloan. Before they knew they had no future, before they knew there would be no baby, and before they realized that it took more than a reflex reaction to responsibility to make a successful marriage. He sincerely regretted his reaction to the miscarriage, but he also totally understood why he went on to destroy any semblance of love that existed between the two of them at that time.

Having come from a home in which love, sacrifice, and dedication were the major components of what elevated him from a life of crime and poverty, he could not or would not allow anything less than 100 percent true commitment to be his own personal legacy. And although he'd come to care a great deal for Sloan, even love her in a more conventional sense, he'd known in his heart that theirs was a relationship that did not have legs—legs to stand on, legs to support itself, or legs to go the distance!

As he now watched Kassandra adjust her skirt beneath her, Karsten realized two things. He wanted, no, he needed someone of substance in his life. Although he'd not realized it until that very moment,

Sloan had definitely left a lasting impression. The pain they had both experienced through the loss of an unborn child had been too much for a relationship so fragile, so undeveloped. But it had served to bring them to another depth in their emotional existence.

Kassandra had purposely taken her time, re-applying her own version of makeup and simple jewelry which she felt complemented the outfit she'd chosen. The print, consisting of a simple geometric pattern repeated in smaller, then larger versions, was multicolored as well. Black, beige, and sandstone pink were threaded throughout and she'd added beige sling-back pumps which made her appear at least two inches taller. It also raised her to what could simply be termed "stunning."

Karsten knew that the evening would either be a sensational success or a dismal disaster. He was hoping for the former.

"So, were you satisfied with today's filming?" Kassandra knew it would be a safe subject and wanted to ground herself in comfort before moving on to anything else.

"Yes, extremely satisfied. You made it easier just by being there. By the way, you look good enough to be the subject of an Andy Warhol retrospective. That seventies looking stuff has really come back with a vengeance and you're wearing it very well, Miss." He let out a low wolf whistle and Kassandra laughed in spite of her reservations.

"So, now that the shoot is over, we can have some time to ourselves," he offered as he turned the engine over.

"The experience has been everything I thought it would be—and more than I ever expected," she offered. She wanted to add that getting to know him was an added bonus but refrained. Uncertainty would probably be good for him—he'd probably never known the feelings associated with being less than 100 percent sure of anything, she surmised.

"So, where to?" She noticed that he'd headed toward the Brooklyn Bridge into Manhattan.

"You'll find out. I'm keeping it to myself until I absolutely have to divulge it. Tell me more about your expectations of your first film shoot. I'm eager to hear just what a beautiful woman like yourself expects when she signs on for a video assignment which will expose her to the energetic talents working in the industry today. Was it all that you thought it would be? Did you find the members of the group relatively easy to work with? What about their music, and the wardrobe? Were you disappointed or did both live up to your expectations?"

"Whoa—what did you do? Make up a list of twenty questions last night?" she asked. Kassandra laughed then. It was obvious he'd given the discussion serious thought, the only question was why.

"No, not twenty exactly." They pulled up to the entrance to the World Yacht Charter Club and a valet parking attendant approached.

"For how long, sir?" the attendant asked.

"About three or four hours," Karsten responded, reaching into the back for a sport jacket. He quickly removed his cap, ran his fingers through the tousled hair he hated to comb, and smiled sheepishly at Kassandra.

"Sorry, but I don't believe in carrying combs and such around with me. I hope it doesn't embarrass you, but I hate combing my hair."

"So, that's why you wear the baseball cap all the time. And you have such nice hair. What's the problem?" she asked. In her mind, he looked good no matter what he wore, and his hair, a tawny brown with golden highlights, was a curly mess. Looking at it now brought the feel of it to mind. The last time he'd driven her home, she'd held his head in her hands as they'd kissed passionately. Kassandra wondered what it would be like to kiss him again. She also wondered if the evening would end in anger as their first date had.

"I guess I developed a bit of a complex—I got teased a lot when I was a kid. Curly, mophead, good hair, you know. Kids do a lot of damage with that stuff and I was a definite target until I kicked a few butts. Then they left me alone. But by that time, I had become a serious rebel. One of the indications was that I refused to comb my hair. I'd wash it, throw some of my mom's stuff in it to make it nice and soft, then just let it curl up as tightly as it wanted to. I didn't comb it at all until I got to college." He laughed then at the shocked expression on her face.

"So, when did you finally come to your senses?"

"I haven't—I just washed it this morning and threw some conditioner in. I figured in honor of the video and the World Yacht, I should at least do my part to appear civilized," he said. The smile on his face belied his true intentions.

"A dinner cruise—that's pretty romantic," Kassandra said as she realized the evening's itinerary.

"Well, I thought tonight should be something special. I've just completed shooting my first music video—the execution of a longtime dream. It seemed only right to celebrate by doing something a little out of the ordinary. You're seaworthy, aren't you?" His question, once asked, brought the memory of Sloan's inability to handle the motion of a boat back to him. He hadn't thought of it for a long while. And for the second time that evening, his thoughts rested briefly on his marriage and an ex-wife whom he'd loved too little for too short a period of time.

"Yes, as a matter of fact, I love boats. Especially big ones."

"Now see, this is where our last date got a little sticky. You made a comment, I teased you, and you took it the wrong way. Can we please not allow that to happen tonight? I mean, whatever you say is fine with me, but I don't want to start another war."

"Neither do I—and especially not over an innocent comment."

"Deal."

They walked toward the ship, a large white yacht with *Spirit of New York* on its side. The three levels shaded by the smoked glass of the ship gave no hint of its interior elegance. The first level, or boarding level, held a large dance club complete with flickering lights and a disc jockey who knew all the latest hits. The second level going up contained a five-star restaurant, complete with dining room serviced by waiters committed to first-class service and a maître d' with a conscience.

An open air deck on one side encompassed the entire top level which could be used to view the incredible sights the journey offered. New York's harbor, including the Statue of Liberty, Ellis Island, Governor's Island, and the surrounding landscapes of lower Manhattan, were on display.

Kassandra gasped as they were shown to their seats, realizing the entire ship was lined by floor-to-ceiling glass windows. They encompassed the entire dining room, offering a magnificent view as each guest enjoyed the five-star meal of their choice.

"Wow, this really is a celebration. Thank you for wanting to share it."

"I can't think of anyone who understands the

· importance of what I've just accomplished—except my mother and she turned me down. It seems she gets seasick," Karsten said, laughing.

Kassandra smiled, not sure if he was serious. It was obvious that he'd chosen her to be his companion for the evening based on their work together. She wondered how much more there was to it. His reputation was that of a smooth operator. Thus far, he'd certainly held up his end. But, she didn't consider herself to be a novice either. She wondered how much further the game would go before one or the both of them would fold.

"Champagne?" His question interrupted her train of thought, and secured the importance of the occasion even higher in her mind.

"Sure. You can't properly celebrate without it now, can you?"

Karsten ordered a magnum, then excused himself to the men's room. As Kassandra scanned the menu, she realized she was starving. She'd only eaten a small portion at lunch. Now, as she looked at all the choices, her mouth watered. She had decided on an appetizer and was considering the entrée when Karsten returned to the table.

Kassandra looked up and her mouth dropped open. "What did you do?"

"Nothing—just a little trick I learned when I was a kid. Water does it every time!" His hair was slicked down now back from his face. The trademark baseball cap, the unruly curls, were all gone.

Kassandra, reluctant to show just how handsome she found him, shook her head slowly. "You are full of surprises, Mr. Battle," she murmured. She reluctantly tore her eyes away, hoping her face didn't give a clue as to her innermost thoughts or reactions. He was talented, he was successful, and he was fine. Kassandra totaled the attributes, and knew she was in, quite possibly, over her head.

"I just thought I'd better pull it together. After all, this evening is a class act, present company included." His compliment registered and Kassandra smiled as she continued to scan the menu, unwilling to meet his gaze. It seemed he was determined to be irresistibly charming. She didn't trust herself, or him for that matter. So, she kept her eyes on her menu.

"So, what looks good?" Karsten picked up the menu, scanned it for a moment and signaled the waiter. He ordered appetizers for them both after asking Kassandra her preference.

"So far, this date is way ahead of the last one. Are we actually getting along, or is it all a figment of my imagination?"

"Your imagination, from my experience, can be pretty vivid so anything is possible. But on the whole, I'd have to say that tonight's vibes are a hell of a lot better than last time. It's probably got something to do with the moon, the tides, you know. After all, we're on the water—that accounts for a lot too."

He pondered her analysis, wondering how much of it was accurate, then leaned forward. "So, if what you're saying is true, then we're more compatible when we put water into our equation—am I hearing this right?" he asked, a look of incredible disbelief on his face. A smile was lurking just beneath the exterior, and Kassandra had to stifle a laugh before she answered.

"No, you have it all wrong. You see, the water is what is holding back the confrontation portion of the relationship. When we're on land, your moon and my sun interact in a way that is negatively charged. The water disbands the negative charges and allows for a positive flow of energy."

"So, you're a soothsayer as well. A beautiful model, a talented actress, and a soothsayer all rolled into one. What have I done to deserve such perfection?" he asked, his hands held up in a gesture which called to mind divine intervention.

Kassandra wanted to laugh, held it back, then hollered. She realized that she was enjoying herself, enjoying him, and looking forward to the remainder of the evening. Their food arrived, and they continued to make small talk, feeling more and more at ease with one another as the night progressed.

After dinner, Karsten suggested they visit the lower level. Music could be heard as they approached the spiral stairwell and Kassandra realized that the ship boasted a fully stocked discoteque. Two bars lined the walls at opposite ends of a well-lit dance floor, now filled with several couples who had seen fit to take advantage of the opportunity offered. Music, dining, and dancing—the *Spirit of New York* circled the harbor of New York City, while offering the best of all three with the lights of the skyline thrown in for good measure.

It was well past two in the morning when the yacht made port again, its passengers having enjoyed an evening which would long be remembered. Karsten and Kassandra disembarked, hand in hand, laughing at some inane comment.

They were both quiet as Karsten drove uptown via the West Side Highway to Kassandra's apartment. The highway was virtually empty and the short trip took less than ten minutes. During that time, Karsten wrestled with himself mentally. He knew how he wanted the evening to end, but was reluctant to press his luck as he was unsure of Kassandra's feelings. Under any other circumstances, he would not have even given it a second thought. But, after spending the evening in her company, after really seeing her as an up-and-coming model turned actress, he realized that she was someone he could quite possibly come to care a great deal about. And with that in mind, he made a decision.

He double-parked the vehicle in front of her house, walked around to the passenger door, and opened it.

Kassandra, her mind still on the wonderful evening they'd just shared, looked up and smiled. "Thank you for the best time I've had in a long time," she said, stepping down to the curb. Karsten was still holding the door open and there was only about two inches of space between them. His natural instinct overcame his practical mind and he leaned forward, brushing his lips against hers quickly. He'd only meant it to be a brief encounter, but Kassandra leaned into him then, the contact full frontal and provocative.

Karsten circled her shoulders with one arm and leaned into her body firmly. Their lips once again connected and the kiss became intimate immediately. Both arms circled her, coming to rest at her waist. She felt incredibly soft, yet firm in his hands. He pulled her to him then, unable to control himself or the growing passion he felt.

Kassandra, hungry to once again experience the feeling which he'd ignited only two nights before, did not move away. As she felt his hands mold her waistline, pulling her hips more securely to him, she realized his passion. The intimate fit of their bodies signaled another level for them both. And although neither wanted to admit it, the sexual tension, which was now being groomed and elevated, had nowhere to go but to the hallowed halls of graduation.

The video was complete, the assignment over. So why did he have such mixed feelings about becoming involved with someone whom he probably never had to see again? Karsten realized that he was unsure about his next move. Unsure about whether or not he wanted to risk becoming involved with Kassandra. What he was totally certain of was that he wanted to make love to her, knew that she wanted him as much as he wanted her, and knew that if not tonight, then it was only a matter of time.

He raised his lips from hers, brushing them against her temple softly. "So, we don't hate each other after all?"

"I never thought that was the case—I think you were just testing me."

Karsten wanted to laugh but thought better of it. She was right in many ways. And the test results were still being tabulated.

"Listen, I kind of promised the crew and some of the cast members that we'd have a small 'wrap' party on the weekend. Are you up for it?"

"Sure—after all, I was part of the cast. That sounds unbelievably pompous but I am so damned proud of myself. Kassandra Algernon was part of the cast. . . ." Her voice trailed off. "Yes, I'd love to attend. When and where?" she asked quickly, looking into his eyes.

He kissed her again, softly, his passion obvious, but restrained. "At my place—I'll have Shelley call you with the address. That way you won't feel like I'm giving you 'special treatment.'" His meaning unclear, Kassandra ducked under his arm and turned toward him. Walking backward to her building's entrance, she smiled.

"Special treatment—now that's an ambiguous term. What exactly did you have in mind?"

"Stop flirting with the director—you can be fined heavily for that. In fact you probably should be fined with heavy penalties based on your past behavior."

"Well, it seems that I can't win for losing with you in power. What's a girl to do?" she laughed.

"I'll answer that the next time I see you—I have a feeling you already know the answer though." His statement hung heavily in the air and Kassandra found herself wondering if she should laugh or cry.

Twenty

Barbados

The sound of raindrops steadily pelting the windows awakened Norwood from a deep but troublesome sleep. He'd tossed and turned all night with thoughts of Sloan drifting incoherently through his mind. Bits and pieces of conversation either real or imagined were still with him as he came to uneasy wakefulness. The telephone rang once, then was silent. He turned over, wondering who had called. It rang again and he reached over quickly picking up the receiver.

"Yeah—I'm up." He listened for a few moments. "Man, isn't it raining? How do you expect to capture the stuff you're after in this light?"

Lorenzo explained that with the brightness of the area they were headed to, there would be more than sufficient lighting. His eagerness in the opportunity to possibly film a surf that was distinctly rougher than usual was apparent in his voice. Norwood, accustomed to a totally different venue of photography, wasn't half as enthusiastic. But the artist in him understood Lorenzo's frame of mind. Sometimes, unusual circumstances of weather, lighting, or happenstance made for incredible opportunities in picture taking. If he was able to pull it off, Lorenzo might be able to photograph the island in a way that hadn't been done or published before. It was a photographer's ultimate dream—it was also the only compelling reason to draw one out in weather that was wet, windy, and quite possibly hazardous.

Forty-five minutes later, they met in Lorenzo's lobby. A special driver had been hired to take them to the eastern side of the island. Known for its rough surf which wave riding enthusiasts often attempted to maneuver much like the West Coast of the United States, or the legendary coastline of Australia, Barbados offered its own challenges. Rocky in many places with waves normally cresting at four feet or less, the western shore was known for its challenges. This day, it was in rare form. The waves, foaming with an incredible force of turbulence, reached heights of more than seven feet. No surfers or swimmers were in sight as Norwood, Lorenzo, and their driver, Martin, arrived. Everyone was indoors watching the latest breaking weather news and preparing for the worst.

Only twenty-four hours before, the Ministry of the Interior had issued a "storm warning" which had since been upgraded to a "storm watch." Norwood and Lorenzo were unaware of the change in status, but would not have altered their plans anyway. Each was secure in his ability to handle a little wind, a little rain, and a minor weather-related challenge.

Unfortunately, they were also unaware that things were about to get a lot worse.

Even without the most advanced mechanisms in weather technology, Barbados was still capable of predicting a storm's potential strength. Cuba, boasting some of the world's best hurricane-predicting capabilities, is actually also without the most advanced technology available in the world's marketplace.

Cuba and the United States share information on weather. Dr. Lexian Avilar, a native of Cuba and one of the nation's foremost hurricane experts based in Miami, heads up the National Hurricane Center. All hurricane warnings emanate from this technologically advanced think tank and Barbados, like many other neighboring islands, also taps into the National Hurricane Center's valuable resources for weather information.

Small islands like Cuba and Barbados may lack sophisticated meteorological technology, but they more than make up for it in experience. The first hurricane recorded and predicted with precise results was in 1875. The successful evacuation of Cuba gave credence to the need for this kind of predisposed information. In October 1963, Hurricane Gloria pounded its shoreline. In October 1996, Hurricane Lily did minor damage. And in September 1988, Hurricane George reached category one status. Hurricane Michelle, which turned out to be a devastating category four storm in November 2001, devastated Cuba's coastline, destroying 923 homes. More than two thousand homes were evacuated with many business locations also demolished. The count of lives lost in those storms was minimal; Cuba knows how to prepare its people, evacuating them to higher ground before things get out of hand.

Prior to current hurricane warning systems, people living in coastal cities and countries were at the extreme mercy of these devastating storms. In 1900, Galveston, Texas, lost more than eight thousand people in a hurricane. For the first time, the United States realized the importance of hurricane prediction, as well as preparedness.

Norwood and Lorenzo decided to set up their equipment, get the shots they needed, and get back to their respective hotels. Both men were unaware of two very important things. One, the storm's upgrade had been prompted by winds gusting up to ninety miles per hour. Although the interior portion of the island of Barbados was in a less hazardous position, the entire country was now at risk of a major hurricane alert. And two, Cherry Hill, the island's highest vantage point, was in direct line with the eye of the storm.

The Office of Emergency Management, its offices located in Miami, was in the process of tracking the weather headed straight for Barbados's shores. St. Lucia had suffered and withstood its pounding winds, rough surf, and downpour of more than twelve inches of rainfall in less than forty-eight hours. But the eye of the storm, with winds topping 135 miles per hour, was headed straight for the shoreline of Barbados.

"I'm having one hell of a time keeping this tripod steady—give me a hand, will ya?" Lorenzo asked. Norwood, having pulled his navy blue windbreaker on to stave off the thrashing pellets of rain now pounding them both, gave the assistance needed. Their driver, Martin, stayed with the van, wondering why "Yankees" were so weird. His walkie-talkie, which tied him into the Barbados Tourism Authority offices, was static filled. And although he'd spoken with them only one hour before, just as they'd left the hotel areas, he'd continually tried to get through in the last minutes. Something about the wind, the rain, and the fact that they were so close to the shoreline didn't sit altogether well with him. The last time a storm like this had hit the island, he'd been a small boy. But he'd never forgotten the devastation it had caused—nor the home that his family had lost. He tried the radio again, got static instead of reception, and prayed that the two photographers he'd been assigned to drive came to their senses soon.

"Okay, hold it steady and I'll try to finish off the roll

of film. This will be awesome—do you see the height
on those waves? It looks like a wall of water," Lorenzo
said. The excitement in his voice was evident, but Norwood was having a hard time sharing it. His military
training told him that dealing with an unknown entity
like Mother Nature in the middle of a storm was not
to be taken lightly. He also didn't like the fact that the
wind had picked up substantially since they'd arrived.
The rain remained consistent, but with the upsurge of
wind, it felt as though it was slicing through the air.
Lorenzo's T-shirt was drenched, and his pants clung
to him. Norwood, no stranger to Chicago's winds,
pulled his hood up. He knew the storm was increasing
in intensity.

"Hey, man, I hope you're getting the shots you
wanted. This is getting to be insane." Norwood wiped
his forearm across his forehead. The thoroughly
soaked water-resistant fabric merely smeared water
from his sleeve across the planes of his face.

"Just a couple more—we never see this kind of
weather in California. It's incredible. Look at the sky,"
Lorenzo said, pointing upward. The clouds, blue gray
with tinges of smoky black around them, circulated
angrily. No light came from them and the sky's darkness cast an overall shadow over the island. Far off in
the distance, the storm was gathering speed. And the
eye of the hurricane was rapidly heading straight for
the island's shoreline.

*She walked up behind Norwood, circled his waist with
slender arms, and placed soft, tiny kisses behind his left ear.
Turning into her arms, he became the aggressor, lowering his
lips to hers in a kiss that scorched her soul. His lips sent tender shivers down her spine as he coaxed her to join him in a
bout with passion. Her breasts were crushed against his chest,*

the hardness instantly creating a solid contact. He kissed her neck, her throat, and her clavicle. Sloan threw her head back in sensual abandon. Being in his arms felt right, it felt complete. Norwood's hands held her to him tightly as he pressed their hips together intimately. Sloan could feel the evidence of his desire against her. His arousal matched and mirrored her own. For the first time in her life, she wanted nothing more than to be taken by the man who held her in his arms.

"What's holding you back?" she whispered. He let his body do the talking for him, kissing her lips again, their tongues becoming engaged in a mating dance that incited her to an even higher plane. His hands circled her waist, found their way upward and began to mold and caress her breasts slowly. Encircling them with his thumbs, he held each precious orb in the midst of his palm. Looking into her eyes, he whispered, "You are."

Sloan awakened, the dream having been an annoying confirmation of the desire that he'd aroused, still apparent, still in existence, still an undeniable element. She could feel the heat within her body waiting, wanting to be released. She immediately showered in cold water, then called Jodi's room. There was no answer. Looking off the terrace to her room, Sloan realized that the normally well trafficked beach front area had become a barren, deserted wasteland. As she walked to the dining room of the restaurant, a few of the hotel's guests were present. Some remained in their respective rooms; many had gathered in the hotel lobby. It seemed that people did seek the comfort of others in a time of danger or possible hazardous condition. A hurricane was no exception.

Sloan found Jodi in the lobby in conversation with a couple from Toronto, Canada. They were totally unfamiliar with anything even closely resembling the weather being experienced and were visibly concerned. Jodi tried her best to put them at ease, but the nonstop rain, driving winds, and cloud-filled skies did not help in her attempt to reassure them.

"I've been here many times when the weather has kicked up—it usually calms down within less than twenty-four hours. Not only that, they're really accustomed to changes that occur during the season. Don't worry—everything will be fine. If it makes you feel better to be indoors, you can even camp out in your rooms. I kind of like the thought of other people around me so I always come down to the lobby. That way, if anything changes, the front desk will be the first to let us know," Jodi advised sagely.

Sloan listened, nodded, and remained silent. She was thinking of all the times she'd traveled to various locations. This would be a first on several different fronts. Not only had she become intimate with a fellow journalist, but a monster storm seemed to be barreling down on the island. Maybe it was tied together—retribution for unworthy deeds. Her mind seemed to be playing little tricks on her. Thoughts of Norwood made their way through her consciousness. And the dreams . . . they were undoubtedly the worst of it all. She awakened alone, aroused, and angry that she'd allowed herself to become vulnerable. She almost welcomed the diversion the storm was creating. Now she could focus on something solid, something tangible, something other than the likes of Norwood Warren.

Jodi, hoping that she'd been able to offer some semblance of calmness to the couple from Toronto, decided to call Lorenzo's room. If the day was to be one in which they'd all be confined to their immediate hotel areas, perhaps they could spend it together. She made the call from the lobby desk phone, and was surprised when she received no answer. At one-thirty, she received a call from her editor that the trip to Trinidad, to cover the award-winning Panmasters, would be canceled. The steel band had been unable to get home after playing in New York the day before.

Jodi and Sloan, recognizing that the weather had created its own separate agenda, decided to stay in the lobby close to the phones. Any updated information, whether it pertained to the weather, the hotel, or the day's agenda, would come forth through that epicenter first. They had each brought laptop computers with them. Between updating their stories to be filed, accessing the many reading materials available at the concierge's desk, and watching the mounted television screen near one wall, they felt secure in the knowledge that any breaking news or information would be received.

As the day progressed, many staff members at the Mango Tree Hotel wanted to return to their homes. Concerned that family members, neighbors, and friends would be caught off guard and possibly be in positions of danger, one by one they left the hotel's Christ Church location and headed toward all other points of the seventeen-mile island.

Local television news, some of which was broadcast from Miami, showcased the storm's tracking. At two o'clock, the Ministry of the Interior of Barbados officially issued a "hurricane advisory." Reports coming out of Miami concurred with the warning being broadcast for the islands of Barbados, St. Lucia, and Martinique.

Sloan and Jodi watched, helpless and feeling totally useless. The people of Barbados were being assaulted by Mother Nature. There was no other way to put it. They both wondered and hoped that the island possessed the capability to wage its own war. Preparedness would mean everything.

Jodi, uncertain as to why she felt so uneasy, called Lorenzo's room for the third time that day. She'd received no answer in previous attempts. She decided to let it ring through to the front desk. Perhaps he, too, was camped out in the lobby.

"Excuse me, I am looking for Lorenzo Altazar—he's in room 105 but there hasn't been any answer all morning. We're with the press here for the jazz festival and it's unlike him to be unavailable for most of the morning," Jodi added quickly. She realized that she'd spoken rapidly. She also realized that she was nervous.

The desk clerk excused himself for a few moments and the line went dead. He'd placed the call on hold. Jodi called to Sloan, told her what she was up to, and Sloan nodded in agreement. Although she wanted nothing to do with Norwood, she didn't want to make Jodi feel as if she were some kind of compassionless monster.

"Okay—yes, I do know them both. And you say they left with a driver this morning a little after ten. Well, thank you, thank you very much. Oh, yes, you can tell him that Jodi called. Yes, and thanks again for looking. I appreciate it."

Sloan, overhearing Jodi's conversation, realized that both Lorenzo and Norwood were obviously somewhere together. She hoped it was somewhere inside; it was not a good day to be outdoors.

Jodi, her brow furrowed with concern, sat down near Sloan and sighed. "Lorenzo and Norwood left the hotel early this morning to do some shooting on the other side of the island. They're not back yet." Her final words hung in the air like punctuation points. Sloan looked up, saw the worried expression on Jodi's face, and realized she had a knot in her own stomach.

"How did they get there?" was her first question. She knew that if a local person had accompanied them, it made their situation much less damnable. If alone, anything was possible because neither of them was familiar with the island or its weather possibilities. And although Norwood had indicated that he'd been born on the island, she also remembered him saying that he'd left at the age of two and not been back since.

"A driver took them. They were supposed to be back around two and no one has heard anything from them." Jodi's factual, if not frantic, reporting told Sloan that she was desperately concerned. And although she obviously was not prone to hysterics, the way she'd laid out the circumstances raised the level of concern that Sloan had also.

"Look, those guys can take care of themselves. It's only two-fifteen now. I guarantee that by three P.M., they'll show up somewhere. We can still keep calling the hotel if you like. I'll even take a turn." Sloan, though she didn't want to appear concerned, hated the worry she could see etched on Jodi's face. Why they'd decided to venture off alone, with a storm obviously on its way, was beyond her comprehension. It was just the kind of behavior that a man, in an attempt to appear both macho and indestructible, would engage in. Lorenzo, with his part Mexican background, would definitely not want to show any sign of hesitation. And she suspected, Norwood, with the military training he'd so often referred to, also would not consider allowing the storm to have first consideration.

Sloan folded her arms across her chest, as if to ward off any further pain. She silently prayed for their quick, safe return, not knowing if they were in any real danger or just behind schedule. The one consistent thought that continued to run through her mind was Norwood's last words to her on the boat.

"Stick to dry land," he'd advised her. His words echoed in her head almost as an omen. Sloan realized that both he and Lorenzo could quite possibly be in a great deal of danger. The winds, the rain, and the unpaved Barbados roads added up to one huge hazard. She said a silent prayer, then went to the front desk.

"Excuse me, I'd like to put a call through to the Tourism Authority. Some of our fellow journalists seem to have taken a badly timed trip this morning. We're just trying to make sure they're somewhere safe. This storm looks like it's getting pretty bad," she added. Sloan then dialed the number Deirdre had given to them as a contact number and waited. The line was busy.

Twenty minutes later, after having dialed several times, Sloan realized the possibility that telephone lines had probably been affected by the gusting winds they could now actually hear blowing and whistling all around them. She voiced her concern to the hotel's manager, Carl Whitfield. He called Barbados Cable and Wireless but those lines rang busy also. It seemed the only way to communicate would be through cellular phones or walkie-talkies.

Sloan and Jodi appeared calm and resolute though each recognized the possible danger involved. They spent the entire morning in the lobby, helping to reassure the other hotel residents that everything would be fine and that things were under control. It was only when they looked at one another that the fear, the concern, and the questions they'd both internalized became apparent.

At four o'clock, the hurricane advisory was upgraded to a category two storm, with winds averaging 110 miles per hour. It was at that moment that Sloan's fear became a nagging, gut-wrenching reality. Local news broadcasts told everyone to stay indoors. They also advised putting aside drinking water, canned goods, and any other staples which one would determine to be "crucial." Jodi realized the seriousness of the upgrade immediately and approached the hotel manager again.

"Look, some of our very close friends may be out in this storm. Isn't there something that can be done before it gets any worse? Can you contact someone and find out if they are still out there? I mean, they need to know what's going on and unless they have a television or something, I don't think they do," she ended almost breathlessly. Her concern was clearly evident. Carl was moved by her plea. But there was only so much he could do. He pulled out a cell phone, dialed quickly and waited.

"Hello—listen to me. We have a sticky situation on our hands. A couple of the journalists have gone on a location shoot and we're not sure if everything is okay. Actually, they need to get back to the hotels because the storm is increasing in strength. It looks like we're in for it. I see—well, I'm glad that you were already on to this."

"Yeah, I can do that. Yeah—in about one hour. Okay. Sure, I'll make the other calls. You just bring the other equipment—you know what it takes in this kind of circumstance. Yeah—and thanks." He hung up.

"Okay, listen to me. The BTA is going to round up a couple of volunteers. A heavy duty truck will be here in one hour to take out a search party. They're only stopping here for some needed supplies."

His prayers had been answered when he'd reached one of the principal officers at the Tourism Authority. Their telephone lines were down, but cellular service was still in operation. Eager to orchestrate the fastest possible response, the Tourism Authority was now in the process of organizing several members of a search

party. They would all converge at the Mango Tree
Hotel in one hour, then head for the same destination that Norwood and Lorenzo had been taken to
earlier that morning.

Carl made several calls quickly, then hung up.
He'd arranged for two of his best workers to accompany the search party. Aside from the obvious
necessities, what was needed were people with an
uncanny sense of direction, excellent survival skills,
and possibly, equipment to pull individuals out of
sticky situations.

Thirty-five minutes later, two vehicles arrived. Driven
by local off-duty law enforcement personnel, the Jeeps
were filled with four other persons: two members of the
Tourism Authority, one journalist from Britain who
had trained with the Royal Air Force, and Johnson
Dade, who was a former member of the Air National
Guard. When the call had gone out, it specified that
anyone with background in military, security, or law
enforcement would be preferred. More than ten had
volunteered, but the group was narrowed down to
four, a more manageable size.

The stop made at the Mango Tree Hotel was only to
gather one last item of survival—water. Jodi watched
silently as they loaded up the vehicles with six bottles of
purified water. Her nerves were shot. In the last hour,
she'd imagined all kinds of reasons why Lorenzo had
not yet returned to his hotel. The fact that an actual rescue party was going out to search for him as well as
Norwood was almost too much for her to handle.

Sloan sat silently on one of the cushioned sofas in
the lobby, unable to speak, move, or display the mixed
emotions going through her mind. She'd long since
passed concern, and was quickly approaching anxiety.

She'd never before faced such a dilemma. Not knowing Norwood's fate was much worse than any news she could have actually received. And worse yet was the fact that until now, she had fooled herself into believing that she had no feelings for him. Tricked herself into thinking that if she simply walked away, never looking back, that it would all go away like a bad dream. Now, as she sat and waited, watching the most recent news and weather reports being piped in via Miami by way of satellite, she acknowledged that this press trip, no matter what the outcome, would remain in her memory for the rest of her life. And that Norwood Warren had touched her more deeply than she'd been willing to admit.

Johnson Dade realized as the truck approached the hotel that Sloan and Jodi were both residents. He'd joined the team without knowing the names of the two journalists who were involved. He couldn't believe his luck. In his mind, either way, he stood to benefit from the outcome. If they were successful in bringing the two wandering minstrels back, he'd be dubbed a hero. And that always made a strong impression on a woman, he reasoned. But, on the other hand, if the group was unable to locate the two, at least he had been part of the rescue effort.

With that issue resolved, he strode into the lobby. He spotted Sloan immediately. She looked as if she needed consoling. He slowly walked over, put his arm lightly around her shoulders, and said softly, "I'm sorry to hear about your friend—hopefully, he hasn't wandered too far into the hinterlands." What he really wanted to say was "Because if he has, good luck in finding the jerk. It serves him right for being such a hotshot."

Sloan looked at him. Either the man was schizophrenic or he was a pathological liar—she didn't believe his sudden "concern" for Norwood was genuine. Not for one minute. But she knew better than to let him know that. If he wanted to play the part, she'd damn well attend the performance.

"Well, I think everyone feels that way. Hopefully both Norwood and Lorenzo will turn up soon. It'll be getting dark soon." She muttered the last phrase as an afterthought, with her brow wrinkled and her eyes lowered. She didn't want to look Dade in the face. Couldn't stand to make eye contact with him. She also didn't think she could stand another hour of sitting here in the hotel lobby, waiting for news or word of them either. She'd be much more helpful if allowed to contribute to the search effort.

"Are they sure they have all of the manpower they need for this search party?" Her question, blurted out as she realized it might be her last chance to offer some real assistance, almost made him laugh. He smirked instead, offering a watered-down version of his view on her offer.

"Listen, sweetheart, I don't believe they see women in the same way we do back in the States. Although I might recognize that you have genuine talents to contribute, you'd have to convince the head of the group. From what I've seen of him, I'd say your chances are between nil and none," Dade advised. He wanted to add that she'd only be in the way, but knew that was "TMI," a little too much information for her to handle.

"You're probably right," Sloan said softly. Jodi, feeling as if the search party would be their best and last choice, held on to one of the journalists for dear life, offering him tidbits of personal information.

"And don't forget that they both know a lot about the terrain. Lorenzo studied ecology at the University of Southern California so he's bound to head for higher ground. And Norwood is a trained military specialist." Jodi tried to think of anything else which might make a difference.

"No problem, lady. If those guys are anywhere out there, we'll find them, and find them fast," Dade promised, wondering what the hell he had gotten himself into.

Norwood, Lorenzo, and Martin were thinking the very same thing at that very same moment. They'd given up on getting any more photographs long ago. The surf had become so rough that it threatened the first position they'd taken up. Lorenzo had to keep moving their position farther and farther back. After a while, they realized that the rising swell of the waves would soon overtake them no matter how far away they positioned themselves. It hadn't really dawned on them that waves of fifteen feet and more were cresting until they'd gotten into the vehicle and started back toward the other side of the island. Here, where the coastline was on par with the roadways and streets, it became increasingly apparent that the storm would have a major impact.

"You know, we should have thought about this more than an hour ago," Norwood said as they entered the township of St. Lawrence. Although they were still a distance from their respective hotels, the roads were becoming increasingly water sloshed. The brakes of the vehicle were continually being soaked by the high levels of water they were driving through. Visibility was diminished by the sheer force of rain, which fell in unrelenting sheets.

Lorenzo had become noticeably quiet. Norwood's mind was operating in military mode. The basic question was how much longer it would take to reach their destination. Norwood knew that the vehicle was their only hope in the equation. Without its use, they were in serious trouble. The velocity of wind, the force of the rain, and the sheer volume of water all spelled evacuate. Norwood was sure they were being faced with gale-force winds; this had to be a hurricane. His mind moved forward to survival and he made a decision.

"Listen—is there somewhere near here where we can take refuge? I don't think we're going to be able to make it all the way back to Christ Church in this deluge of water. The car's mechanisms have to be soaked. We're probably riding on a wing and a prayer as it is," he added.

As he uttered that statement, a large tree uprooted by the force of the winds and heavy with rain-filled branches came crashing down. Martin had to brake suddenly, and the car, with its waterlogged brake pads, pulled to the left as it came to a screeching halt. It was only inches from the hulking core of the giant tree, its branches splayed across the road, blocking either direction.

Shaken, shocked, and silently grateful, the three men got out. They walked around the car, then walked around the tree surveying the damage. Shaking their heads, they realized their dilemma. "Damn it, this is not good." Norwood was the first to speak. Lorenzo, choked up from seeing how close the tree had come to actually falling on the vehicle, hadn't yet found his voice. Martin, devastated by the condition of the entire front section of his car, didn't trust himself to say a word. He'd taken on a simple assignment —driving two photographers to Cherry Hill for some shots. It wasn't even supposed to take all day. Yet, look at the outcome. It was a disaster.

"Look, we can't stay here. This storm is getting worse and the sea wall in this area is even with the landscape. Are there any safety nets in place—like shelters or something?" Norwood's question rattled Martin for moment. He'd never had an occasion to need a safety net. Never thought of needing shelter. But now, at least ten miles from home, and with the roads blocked either way, it was an extremely valid question.

"Let me try and call through to the Tourism Authority again. All I got was static last time." He tried several times, but the static was constant. It seemed that the walkie-talkie would not transmit from the region he was in, or simply with the current atmosphere.

"It doesn't seem to work anymore. Maybe if we walk a little ways into the township. There has to be a house or something that can offer us shelter," he added.

Norwood and Lorenzo, each reluctant to leave his equipment behind, loaded themselves up instead. Their backpacks included cameras, tripod, flash, and the accompanying equipment necessary to capture the shots they'd flown more than two thousand miles for. The fact that a hurricane was part of the trip only made it more photogenic, up until that very moment.

The streets were deserted. Businesses had been boarded up, with windows and doors reinforced with slats of simple plywood. In some cases, proprietors had even used limbs and branches from pliable trees. Anything that would reinforce a structure's stability was utilized. As the wind tore at their faces, the rain pelting them from all sides, Norwood slipped a small point-and-shoot from his bag. The lack of people, the driving winds, the boarded-up homes and businesses, all made a statement. He captured it all in thirty-six frames of film: He concentrated on capturing the rising surf line, the downed trees with branches splayed in every direction, rain filled barrels, normally filled with fresh fruits and vegetables, and the deserted streets lined by boarded up shops and homes.

Lorenzo had had his fill of photography for the day.

He realized that if it hadn't been for his enthusiasm and lack of judgment, they would all be back at their hotels, safe and sound for the most part. As he watched Norwood capture the essence of the storm on a simple automatic camera, he wondered if they'd ever get to see the film developed.

Twenty-one

New York City

Twenty-two Kane Street overlooked the prome-
nade. For forty-seven years, the Brooklyn Heights
loft was home to hats, zippers, and belts hammered
out by industrial age equipment. Then in the early
sixties, when manufacturers found a haven of lower
taxes and cheap labor in Mexico and Southeast Asia,
the building was left vacant. The seventies brought
developers but no one wanted another factory.
There was no need, no financial advantage. With
the increase in New York's population at its peak
and housing in short supply, residential developers
turned their sights to many old, abandoned factory
sites. The high ceilings, unrestricted spaces, and
convenient locations became the new trendsetters
in residential living spaces. Facing the East River
across to Manhattan, it was home to joggers, bikers,
walkers, and those who never got tired of the beauty
of the skyline scene.

Karsten purchased the building still containing
the bones and remains of its factory self. He brought
in his own architect, instructed him as to the features he felt were necessities, and then let him do
his thing. The twenty-five-hundred-square-foot
space, with twenty-foot ceilings, now encompassed

a spiral staircase, windows which looked out onto the East River facing Manhattan, and a garage which had once been a freight elevator. The plumbing, electrical, and windows had all been replaced. Hardwood floors which had been scraped, stained, and varnished prevailed throughout the entire first floor, which contained a stainless-steel kitchen, sunken living room, full-size dining room, and a half bathroom. Stark white walls were lined with huge fourteen-by-twenty blowups of photography shots he'd done throughout the years. He even had one that had been given to him by his ex-wife. She'd captured Grover Washington Jr., horn in hand, doing what he was known to do best before his untimely death. He'd framed it and hung it, a tribute to a talent too soon gone—photographed by someone he'd always remember.

The upper level of the loft's floors were covered by thick wall-to-wall Berber carpeting the color of natural oatmeal. Exposed brick made up one wall of the master bedroom and guest room, adding to the richness and the urban feel of the loft. Adjoining the bedroom was a huge master bath which contained a dressing room and a large walk-in closet. The guest bedroom, which had been formed by putting up a ten-foot wall with a glass-block transom at the top, also had a small bathroom, complete with a shower stall. Karsten used the additional space left over as his studio. Camera equipment, unframed photographs, film, tripods, monopods as well as photography bags were all in residence.

Totally at ease with being in charge, Karsten had given specific instructions to everyone involved so that the evening's events would roll out smoothly. His direction was impeccable. The caterer would arrive at four P.M. to begin setting up. He planned to open his home to the cast members, crew, and anyone else who happened to stop by. It was all in the name of a project well done, a project completed, and some well-deserved celebration.

With events scheduled to begin at seven that evening, Karsten was amazed but pleased to see that everything seemed to be in its place when six-thirty rolled around. He greeted Alton who'd agreed to arrive early and set up the computerized CDs that would supply the evening's music. Then he made his way upstairs to shower and dress. The food was under control, the liquor stations had a good assortment of everything, and the music was being taken care of.

Less than one hour later, the two-story loft was filled with record label executives, talent from the set and recording company, two well-known New York radio personalities, a few not so well-known advertising executives and two of the members of New Deal. The other two were on their way, having to commute in from homes recently purchased in New Jersey. Sometime later in the evening, they would perform the title track from the newly released album and announce the video's release date.

The doorbell rang, the door was opened by a hired security officer dressed in a tuxedo, and Kassandra walked in. She looked around, allowing her eyes to become accustomed to both the lighting and the sheer number of people in her sight. She also waited to see if she recognized anyone. Alton spotted her, came over, gave her a big hug, and ushered her into the loft's oversize living room. Two leather sofas, their eggplant color rich and deep, usually stood face to face in the middle of the floor. For the evening's occasion, each had been pushed to opposite ends of the room. Large square pillows, covered in deep rust and pumpkin orange suede, were thrown indiscriminately into corners. People lounged on them, leaned on them, and casually made themselves at home in the space.

Alton led Kassandra to a bar station, ordered her a glass of champagne, and left her talking with one of the set design technicians. He made his way to the courtyard at the back of the loft and approached Karsten who was in conversation with a record company executive.

"Hey, man—I think you might want to make your way back inside. Someone just arrived."

"Al, this is a celebration so I expect that lots of people will arrive. Is it somebody who I have to entertain? 'Cause, man, this is a party. Everybody, every man, every woman for themselves," Karsten said, laughing.

"I don't think you understand—Kassandra just got here, man. I just thought you'd want to know." His statement said more than his words could ever convey. The look on Karsten's face showed excitement despite his efforts to appear nonchalant.

"Thanks for the heads up, man. Am I that transparent?" Karsten had to ask. He thought he'd kept his feelings well hidden—thought that whatever was happening between him and Kassandra was their own little secret.

"Well, it's not like you broadcast it, man, but don't forget I know you. Like a book. I can tell when you're into something and when you're totally turned off. Anyway, she was near the downstairs bar station when I last saw her," Alton said.

"Thanks. Look, Alton, I'll catch up to you later, man. Enjoy yourself. And thanks for everything— the assistance on the set, everything." With that, Karsten excused himself and headed for the dining room where they'd set up a bar station just beside the fireplace.

Kassandra was in conversation with the set designer, her back to Karsten as he approached. She'd worn a black spaghetti strap dress which reached her knees, black pumps, and had left her hair down, the ends curled under slightly. She looked scrumptious, elegant, and exceedingly model-like. Karsten headed toward her but was stopped several times to greet other guests. By the time he reached her, she'd turned toward him and was watching his approach. Their eyes met and they both smiled. He looked handsome and relaxed, wearing black suede jeans, a white shirt open at the neck and black suede loafers. He'd taken the time to wet his hair and slick it back, and the effect was solid. She realized that he could possibly be the undoing of her. He was that powerful, that talented, and yes, that handsome. Kassandra knew then that she was up for the challenge, no matter what the consequences. Karsten walked up and kissed her softly on the cheek.

"I see you found it. Welcome, I'm glad you came," he said, meaning it.

"Yes, it wasn't difficult—I just gave the address to the cab driver. And thank you for inviting me. It's lovely—or what I've been able to see of it. I just got here."

"Why don't I give you the fifty cent tour? Simone, you know I want to thank you for the fantastic job you did on the set design," he said, turning to the set designer. "It looks good in the editing room. I've been viewing it daily and I don't think we'll have to go back and redo anything. Thanks for everything," he added.

"Hey, when you're working with a master, it only makes you upgrade your own skill—thank you for the experience," she responded, smiling.

"Why don't you join us for the tour?" Karsten asked, taking Kassandra's arm possessively.

Simone, who was both observant and mindful of the rumors she'd overheard on the set, gracefully declined.

"No, maybe some other time. I'll probably wander around later and discover the layout. I may even have some suggestions for you. You know, the world is a set as far as I'm concerned," she laughed.

"I'm not surprised. Okay, enjoy the evening," Karsten said. Kassandra smiled, looked back at Simone, and waved.

Holding one hand possessively, he led Kassandra through the entire loft space pointing out the rooms, the artwork, his studio, all the while never once letting go.

As they entered his bedroom, Kassandra was impressed by his attention to detail. She looked around, taking in the king-size bed, the bold brown-and-black striped comforter with matching draperies, and the shutters at the windows. It was masculine, but extremely well done. He was obviously talented but had good taste, too.

Karsten closed the door quickly, turned her around, and kissed her softly. His directness caught her off guard, but she recovered quickly, kissing him back. Stepping out of her shoes, her feet sank into the tight plush carpet. She wound her arms up and around his neck, standing on tiptoe to reach up to his six-foot-two-inch height. Their lips met in a kiss that was scalding—it seemed that the video's conclusion would be the possible start to something neither had anticipated.

But, in the back of Kassandra's mind, thoughts of Norwood, Jordan, and all that had transpired between them, cautioned her. The confusion that had destroyed a promising relationship months ago, and miles away, still reigned supreme.

"I'm not sure we should be doing this with a houseful of strangers wandering around, but I don't think I can help myself," Karsten murmured against her lips.

"Mmm, neither can I," she managed to say before he kissed her again.

Karsten chuckled then. "You're terrible—and I'm even worse 'cause it's my party. Listen, let's try and get through the evening like we're two grown-ups. I promise you, when the door closes on the last one of them, you'll have my undivided attention."

Kassandra leaned down to put her foot into her shoe, leaning on Karsten's arm for support. The move gave him an unbelievable view of her breasts and his sharp intake of breath was audible. She looked up at him, realized his dilemma, and laughed.

"This should prove to be an interesting evening. I can't wait to see how long it'll take you to get rid of your guests," she laughed.

"Yeah—and you're definitely not making it any easier. Thanks a lot for the incentive shot—not that I needed it," he said, holding his hands up in feigned innocence.

They made their way, arm in arm, back downstairs then. Dinner was being served and Karsten once again circulated, making sure that his guests were having a good time and not in need of anything. It was pretty obvious that a unique relationship was in the makings between the director and the ingenue, which was not an uncommon occurrence in the industry. Karsten had already developed a reputation as a lady killer extraordinaire. The only question in the minds of those present who bothered to notice was if his latest target, Kassandra Algernon, possessed the chops to stand up to it.

It was two in the morning when the last guest departed. Despite the fact that he was an influential record company executive, Karsten was only able to get him to leave then by agreeing to audition his latest signed artist, a seventeen-year-old named Evangeline Singleton. She'd recently recorded her first single and was headed straight for the top, according to the lingering guest and vice president of RCR Records. The performance by Evangeline had been mediocre, but he recognized that with six months of grooming she'd be ready for video.

Karsten was looking forward to spending some quality time with Kassandra. He didn't really care how they spent that time; she was here in his house, and he'd wanted that for a long time. Now that he had it, he couldn't find her. He looked into the studio, he checked the bedroom. He came downstairs, checked the living room, the dining room and the kitchen, where the catering staff was just finishing up.

"Excuse me, sir, we're almost ready to leave. Was everything satisfactory?" the head maître d' asked.

"Excellent—it was excellent. By the way, tell your partner that I said to stay in touch. I may have something else for him in the not too distant future." With that, he extended a roll of hundred-dollar bills— enough to tip the staff of five that had handled the party—and said, "Thank you. Oh, by the way, has anyone seen a tall, attractive young woman in a sexy black dress anywhere?—I seem to have lost her."

They actually laughed, then one of the young women said softly, "I think if you check the outdoor patio, you may find her there. I just gave her a glass of ginger ale about five minutes ago."

Karsten mouthed "thank you" and went in search of Kassandra.

She was sitting at one of the small bistro tables he'd set up in the courtyard. Small candle votives were set in the middle of each table and provided both ambience and a small degree of light. Karsten approached, sat down, and took one of her hands in his.

Kassandra smiled and said, "You look tired. It's been a long night."

"Yeah, and it's not over yet. I've waited a long time to have you all to myself. I plan to make the best possible use of it. Come on," he said, pulling her to her feet.

"Where are we going—I was just getting used to the outdoor element of the patio, mosquitoes and all," she laughed.

They entered the house just as the final members of the catering staff were leaving. Karsten saw them out and poured a glass of champagne for himself and Kassandra before taking her hand and leading her to the living room. He lit a fire, and although it was only mid-October, the warmth of the flames quickly established primitive feelings of home and hearth.

Kassandra sat back, marveling at the set of circumstances which had brought her into his realm. She could no longer deny that she was attracted to him, no longer deny that if given the chance, she would probably do anything he asked.

Karsten continued to hold one of her hands, toying with a ring she'd worn since high school. "So, tell me just what it is that brought you here to New York. I know you told me you were almost engaged. Then something happened and you realized it wasn't the right thing for you to do. Is that why you left Chicago, or was that always something you wanted to do?"

His questions touched a nerve that left her shaking. How would she explain what had happened without sounding as if she were emotionally dysfunctional? And how far should she go? It didn't seem possible that they'd come this far so quickly. Now, all she wanted to do was avoid a discussion he was obviously more than ready for.

"Look, I know that I probably should have an explanation—especially when I already told you that I sort of broke off an engagement. But I don't know if I'm ready to discuss all of that with you right now. It's very private and, although I feel close to you, closer than anyone else I've met here in New York, I'm still not quite ready to open up to that level of intimacy. I know it sounds strange, but bear with me. If and when the time is right, you'll be the first to know all that transpired." Her eyes pleaded with him to understand, to be patient.

"So, you don't want to come clean. . . . Well, then, I guess we're not exactly where we need to be. I'd still like to spend more of the evening with you."

"I have a brilliant idea—let's have an all-nighter—a pajama party," she said, clasping his arm with excitement.

"What—you expect me to put on pajamas with a beautiful woman in my company? You've got to be kidding?" Karsten said, then looked at her, wondering if she was serious or not.

"No, I'm dead serious. You do have pajamas, don't you? Well, let's get two pairs, put them on, then we'll have a party of our own. An adult pajama party."

Karsten didn't know if he liked the sound of it or not. He had really been looking forward to getting her out of her clothes; the thought of pajamas didn't particularly turn him on. Still, it was a heck of a lot better than the clothes they were wearing, so he agreed.

They climbed the stairs to the bedrooms. He looked through his armoire, finding several sets of silk pajamas and one pair with shorts and short sleeves. Kassandra took that pair into the guest room. Fifteen minutes later, still wearing black suede pumps and white silk pajamas with black piping, she entered his bedroom. He'd donned a pair of navy blue silk pajamas and was lying across the bed, wondering what the heck he'd gotten himself into. It wasn't natural for two grown people to play pajama games. But he couldn't stop himself when he saw her in the set he'd given her. Her legs, long and well shaped, were only accentuated by the short pants which she'd rolled up several times. The top had been tied in front, high above her waist, revealing a waistline and belly button so compelling that his mouth literally watered.

"Baby, what you're doing to me is against the law. This is torture. Come here," he coaxed her.

Kassandra walked into his arms, kissed him until his hands became insistent on untying the top of her pajamas, and determined to remove the bottoms. "Now behave or I'll have to give you a two-point penalty. Slow down. We have lots of time to enjoy each other's company. Come on, let's turn on some music," she suggested.

Karsten, intent on moving things in a totally different direction, gave in and hit the CD player. The sounds of contemporary jazz filled the air, and Kassandra moved into his arms, once again, swaying to the rhythm. The feel, the touch, the smell of her was driving him to distraction. Yet, he knew it was one of the more pleasurable evenings he'd spent. Dancing, laughing, flirting—they looked through old albums, wandered throughout the house discovering new and not-so-new things, and enjoyed each other's company.

They stayed up until well past four A.M. The sky was beginning to lighten in the sky and neither of them could keep their eyes open any longer. The passion that they'd managed to keep in check for the entire evening was kept on simmer by a long kiss here, a tender caress there. As the early morning approached, Karsten actually accepted the fact that she obviously believed they should get to know one another better before becoming intimate. Throughout the night, he'd come to appreciate the process.

In Kassandra's mind, the nagging question that continued to plague her was if what had happened with Jordan Campbell was something she was programmed to repeat. Her confusion and indecision made the issue of going to bed with him a moot point. She needed clarity before that happened because Kassandra knew that making love with Karsten would be a life-changing event.

Twenty-two

Barbados

Nighttime came quickly, the darkened sky spreading across the rain-soaked island prematurely as its inhabitants braced for the worst. Gale-force winds topping 135 miles per hour tossed anything that was not nailed, fastened, or otherwise tethered, to and fro. Water filled the streets, creating free-flowing rivers as the constant downpour filled every crevice. The land was saturated—swollen with the more than twenty-five inches of torrential rain it had absorbed within the past eighteen hours.

Norwood, Lorenzo, and their driver, Martin, trudged on, headfirst into the driving winds which threatened to careen them into buildings, debris, and other items. Trees, branches, and limbs were being blown incessantly, many of which broke off and lay scattered along the ground.

"Man, how much farther is it to somewhere where we can dig in and try and wait this thing out?" Lorenzo asked. He was soaked to the skin and tired to the bone from the ordeal of walking with the wind's full-strength forces against him.

"Stop complaining—if it wasn't for your enthusiasm, none of us would be here. Just be glad that I came prepared," Norwood said, waving the flashlight that he'd carried in his gear. It had come in handy, especially as the power went out and street lights, building signs, and other electrically operated lighting mechanisms faded to black.

"I know—man, I owe you such a huge apology. If I had known this was coming, I would have definitely stayed in my room the entire day. I owe you one for this, and as soon as we get back to some normalcy, I intend to pay you back royally," he said, smiling in spite of the severity of the situation. He meant every word he said.

"Don't worry about it, dude. I am not going to hold you to any of that. Nobody could have foreseen all of this. Now, all we have to do is either walk our way back to Christ Church, or hope that we find some other form of refuge."

With many of the businesses brandishing boarded-up windows and haphazardly applied reinforcements, it looked very much like a ghost town under bad construction. The section of Holetown they walked through contained very few private homes. It was an earlier developed section of Barbados, recently left by many to forge newer, better-made homes. Chattel houses, one-story homes built on foundations to allow for easy mobility, were a part of Barbados history, a testament to the past. Most had been neglected or left years before; Norwood recognized abandonment when he saw it. He wondered if the hastily built homes would be able to withstand the constant pounding rain, the unrelenting wind, and the threat of the pounding surf. The waterline was only ten or twelve feet from where the homes began and he knew that if the storm continued, the surf would make its way across that distance by high tide.

Norwood waved the flashlight in the direction they had been walking, and realized that the area they were now in would soon end. They were approaching another undeveloped, wooded area which would then bring them into the next parish of St. Lawrence.

Martin, as familiar with the Barbados landscape as he was with the back of his hand, was becoming concerned. St. Lawrence offered even more businesses, including restaurants and hotels, but it also contained miles of oceanfront acreage. As such, with high tide approaching, it could very well put them in even more jeopardy. He'd seen the waves back at Cherry Hill as the surf pounded the shoreline, the squalls reaching ten feet and more. His throat constricted every time he thought about the effort all three of them had put into trying to get the truck out of the rain-soaked gulley the area had become. But it had been no use. The tires had sunk even more deeply into the mud with each revving of the engine. Finally they had given up. Now, as they headed to what would hopefully be some form of refuge, he couldn't shake the feeling that Mother Nature was intent on making a statement. Only time would tell what would be said. Debris and any items not nailed down were being tossed about.

Suddenly, a large piece of signage whipped across the roadway they walked on, slicing into Norwood's forehead. Blood gushed everywhere, blinding him for the moment. It also rendered him somewhat senseless. He fell to his knees, his head in his hands.

Lorenzo muttered an expletive, then quickly tried to remove the backpack from Norwood's body. "What the hell was that?" Norwood managed to ask though he wasn't at all sure he really wanted to know.

"I don't know—I think it was part of a street sign. Man, you're bleeding like a stuck pig. Let me see— is it your eye?" Lorenzo asked. He had never been any good with medical stuff, blood, or emergencies, yet he felt responsible. Martin quickly rummaged through the backpack, coming up with a miniature roll of absorbent cotton and masking tape.

"Man, this guy comes prepared for anything," Lorenzo said as he and Martin tried to administer a crude form of first aid.

"The first rule of battle is to be prepared. And don't be fooled, this storm is definitely a battle of us against nature. I always carry some first aid stuff in this backpack. See if there's some antiseptic or something in there. Damn, this hurts," Norwood said, gritting his teeth against the pain. He suddenly thought of Sloan then, wondering where she was. He hoped to God that she was somewhere safe, dry, and indoors.

Lorenzo did his best to apply the cotton, while Martin poured the small bottle of hydrogen peroxide over the wound which was right above the brow of his right eye. Thankfully, it was only a flesh wound, but the blood gushing from it was substantial. Martin quickly applied pressure with fresh cotton held in place by the masking tape and the palm of his hand. The bleeding appeared to stop and the makeshift bandage held its place.

"Listen, guys—we need to make it to St. Lawrence as quickly as possible. High tide is approaching and we want to beat it there. Any place in that town that can offer us shelter is where we should stay until this thing blows over. We won't be able to find our way in the dark," Martin offered solemnly. "With Norwood's injury, we need a doctor. Maybe we can find a phone or something in St. Lawrence."

Norwood thought for a minute, then consulted his waterproof Swiss Army watch with his one good eye. It was exactly 5:29. High tide usually came any time after six.

Lorenzo, feeling guilty, knowing it was his fault they were out in such challenging weather, spoke up. "How far is it to the next town? And are you sure we'll be able to find shelter there? These people have boarded up everything they could. I haven't even seen a church that's been left as a sanctuary. Those doors have been boarded, too," he added, frantic to do whatever was necessary to get in out of the driving rain and howling winds they'd endured for the past four hours. He was also worried about the huge bruise above Norwood's eye. It had immediately swelled, causing him to look like a prizefighter who had taken home the losing purse.

"It's probably about two and a half miles. We won't make it before high tide but we have no choice but to continue on. St. Lawrence is our only chance. There's bound to be something or somewhere there that we can use to wait this thing out," Martin offered. He wasn't 100 percent sure of the things he'd said, but as their assigned driver, he felt a serious responsibility for bringing them to safety.

The three desperate, drenched, but driven men pushed on, despite the obstacles of driving rain, forceful winds, and nonstop water everywhere they stepped. The boots and sneakers each wore were long past soaked; waterlogged would better describe their state. And with their not having had anything to eat since a hastily downed breakfast, hunger was becoming an insistent and nagging presence.

Norwood suddenly remembered he always carried energy bars in his backpack and rummaged through it. He pulled out two of the chocolate bars, quickly divided them, and laughed out loud. "It's a good thing I never throw anything away. These have been in this bag for over two months. Thank God for rations," he said, the simple prayer a testimony to his gratefulness.

Unfortunately, his water bottle had long been empty. Lorenzo's was only half full, but he offered to share it. It was ironic that water which was in existence all around them made the thirst they were experiencing even more intense. They each took a turn at the water bottle, emptying it quickly.

Norwood's headache began slowly without him even being aware of it at first. One moment he was walking alongside Lorenzo and Anthony, his sight somewhat altered by the huge bandage they'd fashioned, and the next, he realized that his head had started to pound. The pain almost matched his footsteps. And although he tried hard to ignore it, the increasing intensity only added to his frustration. There was nothing in his bag like an analgesic so he had to endure it—mile for mile, step by step, his two companions on either side of him guiding him toward a destination which would hopefully provide shelter and refuge from their daylong ordeal. He'd thought of Sloan a couple of times during the day, then quickly dismissed her. It was less stressful and more productive to think of getting through the wind, the rain, and the storm.

The rescue party discovered the abandoned truck, searched the nearby area and realized that the trio they were searching for was obviously on the move. What they were unsure of was the direction of their travel. The fact that they were on foot meant two things. One, their travel would be hampered, and most probably, slow. And two, their driver would be familiar with the area, its terrain, and quite possibly, the best route to take under storm circumstances.

"All we have to do is determine which direction they would most probably have taken—it's not rocket science," Johnson Dade advised sarcastically as the discussion progressed. Foster Hughes, one of the members of the Barbados Tourism Board, listened without comment. He knew they needed to make the right decision—three lives depended on it. If it had been him, he would have headed toward the St. Lawrence Gap area. It was slightly higher ground, it certainly was normally well populated, and it was filled with hotels and restaurants which would offer substantial refuge. That sealed it.

"Okay—we're going to head toward St. Lawrence. If we're lucky, our three wayward friends will be somewhere in that township. Come on, let's try and find these guys before we take on any more water," he said as they all climbed back into the two vehicles.

Norwood's flashlight was losing power. Lorenzo and Martin, tired of walking, hungry and thirsty, sat at the stairs of a boarded-up restaurant. They'd arrived at the outskirts of St. Lawrence and were thrilled to be out of the woods which separated the two townships. Norwood, quiet and deep in thought, tried to look for signs of life. Any movement could mean that someone, anyone, was awake and alive within the confines of a building. He recognized some of the area from the night they'd visited Time Out at the Gap, but he was bone tired, soaked to the skin, and his head felt like it weighed a ton. Suddenly, he looked up, his head tilted to one side. Squinting, he stood up, listening intently.

"What is it?" Lorenzo said, his curiosity alerted by his friend's behavior.

"Shhh, I think I hear something," Norwood answered. He tried to shine the flashlight in its direction but the batteries were long dead. No light emanated from it.

"Probably just water hitting the surface of something," Martin said, his disappointment at not having found an open space evident in his voice.

"No—listen—something is coming," Norwood answered, moving out into the middle of the roadway to get a better position. It was then that the headlights of the first Jeep became visible. And it was then that all three men stood together, waving their hands frantically, yelling all the while, smiles mixed with laughter, as they realized that their ordeal was over.

And all the while, Johnson Dade hid his disappointment. It wasn't that he wished harm to any one of the three. But he hadn't actually been rooting for an unqualified successful rescue either. He hid his disappointment, watched as the three were given blankets and water bottles and were loaded onto the Jeeps for transport. He even moved over to create more room as Lorenzo squeezed in beside him.

"Man, I want to thank you all from the bottom of my heart. I've never been so glad to see a bunch of guys pull up in a Jeep as today. How'd you know where to find us?" he asked excitedly, between long swigs of water.

"Foster up there had a hunch you guys would be in St. Lawrence. It was his call," Dade said. What he wanted to say was "If it had been up to me, we would have gone in the opposite direction." He realized, to his deep regret, that any real chance at being rid of the hick from the Midwest was now zero to nil. Women loved a hero, even without a war. He glared at the back of Norwood's head and shook his; some people were just lucky and this guy seemed to be one of them. Sloan had seemed genuinely worried when she'd asked about Norwood and the rescue effort. He'd known then that it was a lost cause. Hell, the trip was over anyway, he told himself as consolation.

The ride back was treacherous, with roads washed out at some points, and fallen trees blocking many of the paths. They arrived at their respective hotels well past midnight. By that time, the eye of the storm had moved offshore, the hurricane had been downgraded to a tropical storm, and everyone realized that real tragedy had been averted by the quick and effective thinking of a few good men.

Norwood's head injury was a priority, so they called the local physician's home. Luckily, Dr. Rice lived within walking distance of the Mango Tree Hotel and agreed to make a midnight house call.

Soaked, but too tired to walk to his room, Norwood sat in the lobby waiting for the doctor's arrival. Lorenzo took his keys, went to his room, got dry clothing for them both, and returned with it.

"Man, how are you holding up?" he asked as they changed in the lobby's bathroom. Looking into the mirror for the first time that day, Norwood winced at the dried blood on his face, the makeshift bandage, and his overall appearance.

"Okay, I guess. I'm not seeing double or anything. And the headache seems to ease up when I remain still. I think I have a pretty thick skull—it would take more than an airborne piece of metal to take me out of commission," he joked.

The hotel's management staff had prepared sandwiches, coffee, juice, and fruits, knowing that the rescue party as well as the rescued would need quick nutrition. The search party, weary and wanting to return to their own destinations, took sandwiches and coffee in plastic cups with them.

The doctor arrived, examined Norwood and immediately ordered him to be still. He didn't like the swelling or the headache, but knew he would be unable to x-ray the area until the following day. If his suspicions were correct, the patient could possibly have suffered a concussion.

Dr. Rice informed him that he wanted to re-examine him at the hospital sometime the next day.

Norwood didn't like the sound of it. He'd never liked hospitals and definitely wasn't looking forward to any medical facility off the shores of the United States. But he had no choice.

Sloan and Jodi, who'd decided to keep each other's company throughout the storm's duration, had instructed the front desk to inform them of any developments, no matter what the time. With no way to keep in contact with the rescue party which had gone out hours before, their imaginations had provided them with pictures and possibilities that were grim, to put it mildly. At forty minutes past twelve, the call came through that the missing journalists had been found, returned, and were awaiting the doctor's arrival in the hotel lobby.

They immediately rushed from the room frantic that the call to a doctor might mean some urgent or critical condition. Sloan entered the lobby first, her hair flying, wearing hastily pulled on jeans and a tube top. She hadn't bothered to pull on the hooded sweatshirt she'd worn earlier and it was quite obvious that she was not wearing a bra.

Norwood looked up, attempted a grin, then gave up. It hurt too much when he smiled, but he couldn't stop himself. She looked sexy, on edge, and worried, all at once. The complex set of emotions on her face made him want to reassure her that everything was fine. Sloan rushed over to where he was sitting, bent down and touched his face gently, noting the bandage and the dried blood. Tears formed in her eyes. No words were forthcoming. They looked into each other's eyes, acknowledging the pain, the frustration, the misunderstanding of emotions that were too fragile to describe or discuss. It wasn't necessary. Communication was now present without the use of words.

Sloan slowly put her arms around him, unable to stop herself from touching him. She'd almost lost him, almost blew the chance to tell him that she was sorry for the way she'd behaved after sharing his bed.

Norwood's surprise was evident. He'd imagined that she wouldn't care what happened to him, would only be nonchalant when they returned from a day of exposure to Mother Nature's fury. And he'd underestimated how much it would mean to him for the exact opposite to be true. He could almost feel himself gathering strength with Sloan in his arms, and he said a silent "thank you" to the universe for putting her there.

Jodi found Lorenzo in the restaurant, gathering more sandwiches and juice. She smiled when she saw him and he did, too.

"So, you made it back okay—I see you haven't changed. Still hungry," she said, laughing. She walked up to him then and they hugged for what seemed like an eternity. Finally, Jodi pulled back, wiped the back of her hand across her eyes quickly, and looked away. Lorenzo cleared his throat and picked up the tray again.

"Yeah—this is for the other guys, too. Martin is

going to stay with us until tomorrow morning. Both
he and Norwood can put away some food. Those guys
act like they haven't eaten in two weeks," he said. He
neglected to mention the four sandwiches he'd already eaten himself. Jodi then helped him bring the
tray out to the lobby, along with several bottles of
drinking water.

Meanwhile, Sloan listened as Dr. Rice described his
concerns, his prescription, and his advice. Norwood
was to remain off his feet for the next twelve hours
until he could x-ray the area. Any occurence of dizzi-
ness, nausea, or vomiting was to be made known to
him immediately. And although he wanted to issue instructions that Norwood was not to fall asleep, he
realized that would be nearly impossible to carry out.
Instead, he instructed him that his sleep would have
to be monitored. Someone would have to be in the
room with him at all times in case of seizure. With
head injuries, it was a normal doctrine. Twelve hours
of monitoring was customary. He left his telephone
number and instructions on where to meet him the
next day at one o'clock. The hospital would be
alerted.

Listening to the doctor's prescribed course of treatment, Sloan had several questions, then took charge.
"Come on, it's time you got some rest," she said, helping him to his feet. The bandage Dr. Rice had left in
place was a lot smaller in size than the makeshift one
they'd haphazardly fashioned earlier. It allowed him
to be able to use his peripheral vision to see in addition to his other eye.

"Okay—are you sure you're up to this?" he asked,
not wanting to take advantage or be seen as a charity
case. He didn't want her pity, wasn't even sure if he
wanted her love. What he did want was to be able to
be certain of what he was getting into. If this was just

her way of showing that she was sorry for him, her own little pity party, she could damn well throw it without his assistance.

"Norwood, look, you're in no condition to argue with me. Come on—you need to get some rest and I'm the assigned nurse for the night," she added, guiding him by allowing him to lean on her as she put one arm around his waist.

They entered his room as one, leaning against one another more than was actually necessary. Norwood, unsure of Sloan's real state of mind, tried to tell himself that it meant nothing, but he was fighting a losing argument. The last time they'd entered this room, passion had been the motivating factor; tonight it was compassion.

Not wanting to disturb or in any way aggravate the wound he'd sustained, she suggested he sit on the bed while she removed his boots and jeans.

"I can do that myself, I'm not helpless," he said. What he really wanted was a shower. So he headed to the bathroom, only to find himself getting woozy from moving so quickly. He leaned against the doorway, hoping she wouldn't notice. But, she did.

"Norwood, please don't make this any more difficult than it has to be. Let me help you," she added. She removed his shirt and his undershirt, then stopped. She didn't trust her reaction to his nakedness so she turned on the shower, adjusted the water, and turned her back as he continued to undress. When he was finished, she allowed him to lean on her as he stepped in, then she left the room. She was shaking.

Norwood showered quickly, not trusting the feeling he had when he stood there alone. His head had begun to throb again and he wanted to take one of the pills that Dr. Rice had left for him. He toweled himself dry and pulled on a pair of boxers.

"Are you okay in there?" she called out after only a few moments.

"Yeah—I'm coming out now." He'd handled the rudimentary elements of hygiene, then just stood under the water while it cascaded down his weary body. He hadn't been so tired in a long time.

Coming into the bedroom, he noticed that Sloan had curled up against one of the pillows. She appeared exhausted and he realized that she probably hadn't slept and maybe not eaten all day.

He watched her for a moment, studying her in profile, then turned off the lights before slipping beneath the covers. Sloan awakened startled, realized that Norwood had entered the bed, and stood up. She quickly removed her jeans, pulled the T-shirt over her head, and climbed into the bed. The warmth of his body drew her to him and although they were both worn out physically and emotionally, sleep would not be the easiest state for either of them this night.

"Are you okay?" she asked softly.

"Mmm—I'm just glad to be back. There were a couple of hours when I thought we might not make it. Thanks for agreeing to monitor me. You didn't have to do that," he added. He knew it had been a difficult decision but he was glad she had made it, glad that she was here beside him.

"You don't have to thank me. I wanted to do it. Listen, you should know some things about why I reacted the way I did after we spent the night together. It wasn't that I didn't enjoy what we shared—if anything, it was that I just didn't know how to accept that perhaps my feelings for you would grow stronger afterward. I hadn't prepared for that, didn't know how to handle it."

"Yeah, I think I understand how that could have happened. I have to tell you something though—it was probably the worst thing you could have done in terms of making me feel as if it meant little or nothing to you. When I saw you flirting with the other guys on the catamaran the next day, it reminded me of my ex. I know I never told you this, but I came home one day unexpectedly and found her in bed with Jordan Campbell—another model." His voice trailed off then and Sloan knew that the painful memory still carried a tremendous weight for him.

"I'm so sorry. My ex-husband was pretty busy too— I never actually caught him in the act though, thank God. What did the guy say when you walked in?" She couldn't imagine that situation or how one got around it.

"That's the kicker—it wasn't a guy. Jordan was another female model—they'd worked together on a shoot. I'll never forget the look on both their faces. It was really bizarre. No one said a word for what seemed like an eternity, then I just got the heck out of there," he added, one arm behind his head now as he looked up at the ceiling.

Sloan was silent for a moment still, then she curled up against him. She kissed his cheek softly and whispered, "I'm sorry—that must have awful. But, for tonight, let's try and forget the past, the present, and the future—let's just focus on now. Right now," she added, turning his face toward hers and placing tiny kisses on his lips, his brow, his cheeks. Norwood needed no further encouragement. He wound his arm around her pulling her closer to him, sealing their lips with a kiss that became scalding with passion. He'd forgotten how good she felt against him, the smoothness of her skin reminded him of a whipped chocolate parfait, light, fluffy, and excruciatingly soft.

Sloan turned into him, covering his body with one leg. She could feel Norwood's body respond to their kisses and she remembered that he'd been gentle with her when they made love before, almost as if he'd sensed her hesitancy. She wanted no holding back this night. Slowly, gently, Sloan raised herself until she was above his body. Norwood's face showed his surprise—and his excitement. She leaned down, her hair brushing his chest erotically as she moved up until her lips were level with his. Her kiss was one of surrender, passion, and most of all, temptation.

Head injury notwithstanding, Norwood's resistance was nil. Sloan quickly removed her remaining clothing. She kissed the expanse of his chest, savoring the taste and feel of his skin. He smelled like soap, like man, like wonderful, and she remembered that he had smelled the same way the last time they'd made love. Norwood groaned with pleasure. He wanted to turn the tables but didn't have the strength. She continued her bold exploration, her bare breasts blazing a trail of fiery warmth down the length of his body.

Sloan, remembering to protect them both, slowly joined with him, being careful to keep her weight on her hands which she placed on either side of them. Norwood sensed her concern, and was having none of it. He pulled her within his embrace, allowing her full body weight to ride against him as she mounted him. The exquisite pleasure which he experienced was almost unbearable. And when she moved rhythmically, controlling the pace, the depth, and the level of their coupling, he almost cried out. She covered his mouth with his own and they experienced the ultimate pleasure together, as one.

"If I had known this was waiting for me, I would have gotten back a hell of a lot sooner," he laughed when he was able to speak again. Sloan purred like a kitten, and snuggled up beside him, feeling quite a sense of accomplishment.

"All you had to do was ask—I wasn't exactly sure of where I stood. And then when I saw you flirting and swimming with the redhead from D.C., I figured you for another playa like my ex. I wasn't having any of that. It was only after Jodi told me that Lorenzo was sure you were pissed about me talking with the guys from England that I realized maybe you did have some feelings for me. I guess we were both kind of insecure," she added.

Norwood pulled her even closer, kissed her lips softly, then her forehead. "Let's be clear from this day forward. I came to this island a man in search of himself. And I found myself, my soul mate, and my destiny. Right here in Barbados, the land of my birth," he added, smiling in the darkness.

"My, my, the man is a poet, too. Do your talents know no boundaries?" she asked, laughing.

"Come here—let me show you just how talented I really am," he said, his hands already traveling over her body in a way that caused her to sharply take in her breath.

"Norwood, you have to rest—Dr. Rice said you were to take it easy for the next twelve hours. At the rate you're going, you won't get any sleep," she said, though she was already moving to position herself under him.

"I just want to be sure that you understand who's in charge here," he said as he entered her slowly. The pace he set was far different from Sloan's. And she was able to offer him a better vantage point. They'd come to know each other very well, very quickly.

"You are—you are," she cried out sometime later, turning her head back and forth as she climaxed for the second time. Norwood's mouth covered hers as he, too, found release within the hot, tight cavern that he'd come to savor.

It was a long time before the sun came up. And an even longer time before either of them slept.

Twenty-three

New York

Kassandra awakened, realized where she was, and wondered how she'd gotten there. Karsten's king-size bed felt like an ocean to her as she stretched lazily, taking up as much room as her body could encompass. She tried desperately to remember just what had taken place. Her last memory was of Karsten trying to untie her pajama top, laughing, as he kissed her neck and shoulders. He'd whispered something suggestive, then led her into his bedroom.

"So, it's taken you all evening to get me here . . . what now?" she had asked teasingly, as he backed her toward the huge bed.

"Well, the first thing I want to do is make it crystal clear that your being here is no mistake." With that statement, he had lowered her to the bed and kissed her lips gently. Kassandra returned his passion, running her hands down his back. Although it was covered by the silk pajama top he still wore, she could still feel the solid stretch of muscles beneath. Boldly, she reached under it, reveling in the feel of his skin beneath her fingertips. Karsten moaned and pressed her back into the soft, plush confines of his bed.

He reached for the knotted fabric of Kassandra's pajama top, but hesitated. Lifting his head, he looked into her eyes. Desire was plainly evident, yet something intangible held him back. "What's the matter—is something wrong?" she asked, noticing his hesitation.

"No, nothing is wrong. As a matter of fact, everything is right, really right. Hey, get some sleep. And thanks," he whispered before leaving the room.

Puzzled by his behavior, she wondered what he was thanking her for. Snuggling down into the bed felt like heaven. The only thing better would have been to be in his arms. Smiling as she tried to figure him out, she fell asleep.

The smell of freshly brewed coffee and waffles coaxed Kassandra out of bed. She finger-brushed her teeth, washed her face, and threw the dress she had been wearing the night before back on. She also twirled her hair up into a bun, securing it with the one hairpin she'd been able to find in her bag. As she passed the guest room, she noted the tousled bed and realized Karsten had slept there. Again, she wondered what would motivate him to invite her to spend the night then not even sleep in the same bed with her.

She walked into a kitchen filled with chaos. Eggs, milk, and bread were on the counter as Karsten did his best to create a breakfast of champions. The waffles he'd attempted to make were burned to a crisp in the toaster. The French toast was his second attempt.

Still wearing the pajamas she'd last seen him in, he looked as if he could use a lot more rest. Kassandra walked up behind him, put her arms around his midsection, and kissed him on the neck. She remembered the way he smelled. His cologne had long since disappeared, the natural fragrance of his body was what did it. He smelled like a cedar closet—something she associated with family, home, and relaxation.

"Okay—she's here now. I can stop pretending to be something I'm not, a chef," he said, turning into her arms. He kissed her slowly, lingering on her lips, her earlobe, her neck, her chin, finally working his way to the expanse of skin which the skimpily cut dress revealed. He kissed the top of one breast, then began to lower the strap to allow greater access. Suddenly, the smell of burning French toast reached both their nostrils.

"Oh, hell—not that again," he said, turning to reach for a spatula. He turned the burners off and looked at Kassandra with a sheepish smile on his face. "I'm afraid I'm not very good in the kitchen," he offered.

"On the contrary, you are very good in the kitchen," she said, walking into his arms. Breakfast was delayed by another fifteen minutes. By the time they sat down on the patio to consume the French toast Kassandra made, along with coffee and juice, it was past eleven in the morning.

"What happened last night? I woke up alone. I was kind of surprised. . . ." Kassandra lowered her eyes, unable to meet his. She wasn't sure she was ready for his answer.

"I think I once told you that you remind me of someone. . . . Well, you do. And I remembered that one of the things that I always wished I'd have done was to allow the relationship to grow minus the sexual aspect. I know now that it can deeply affect how the relationship ultimately develops—or not. Anyway, I've made some mistakes along the way, but I've learned a few things too. Timing is one of them," he added.

"You know, I've never heard it put that way, but you're probably right. I have to give you credit for demonstrating that kind of self-control." She wanted to thank him for not taking advantage of her vulnerability but refrained from doing so. Something told her that too much information could still work against her.

Smiling, she looked at him boldly, and said, "So, just how much time do you think we should allow to lapse before we consider ourselves 'in the know'? Let me know 'cause I don't want to miss the maturity date," she laughed. Karsten joined her. He knew then that it would be only a matter of time. A short time, to say the least.

"Listen, speaking of maturity dates and deadlines, I think I sealed a deal to shoot another video last night. There's only one problem," he added. Something in his voice alerted her.

"What—what's the problem?" she asked, a smudge of syrup on her cheek as she waited for the rest of his statement.

Karsten smiled, reached over, and wiped it off with his index finger, which he promptly put into his mouth. Laughing, he said quickly, "You—you're the problem. The shoot calls for a lovely young model, inexperienced and tender. Do you think you can deliver for me again?" he asked.

Kassandra's intake of breath was an answer unto itself. "Are you serious—you want me to be in another video? Oh, I can't even begin to tell you how great that is. It's what I've wanted from the very beginning—a new career. No longer just a session model, a runway model, a print model—acting is what I've wanted from the very first. Karsten, are you sure?" she asked then, indecision spoiling the look of pure enjoyment she'd previously had on her face.

"I wouldn't have asked you if I wasn't. By the way, if all goes according to plan, it begins shooting in about four weeks. Barbados is the location, so get your pass-

port and other things in order," he said as he began
to clear the dishes.

Kassandra jumped up, threw her arms around him,
and kissed him.

"Barbados, oh, my God, I've always wanted to go
there. Listen, Karsten, no matter how things between
us turn out, I want you to know how much this means
to me. Thank you for the chance to prove myself—
thank you for the opportunity to really have a career
in video and possibly film. And, thank you for last
night, too," she added.

He put the dishes he'd just picked up down on the
table. Turning to face her, he reached out, pulling
her into his arms. The kiss held all the promise and
passion of a man who knows what he wants, when he
wants it, and is willing to wait for it.

"You don't have to thank me, Kassandra. I think I finally realized what's important. Now, come on and
help me clean up this mess. I'll drive you home later.
Maybe we can catch a movie on the Upper West
Side—Eighty-sixth Street or something," he said.

"That sounds great."

The passion they'd put on hold would keep. She
knew it and so did he. Like fine wine, it would increase in strength, ripening and maturing, to be
savored at just the right moment.

Twenty-four

Barbados

Dr. Rice's examination, complete with X rays, was over in two short hours. Norwood did not have a concussion. The contusion over his right eye would heal without the need of stitches, although Dr. Rice did apply three butterfly clamps to hold the skin together tightly as the wound healed. The large bandage had been replaced by a surgical Band-Aid and Dr. Rice instructed him to seek follow-up care upon his return to the States.

Sloan had accompanied him, glad to be of use, happy that the final diagnosis was an uncomplicated one. When they returned to the hotel, a message from the Tourism Authority was there. They both had seats on the flight leaving the island the following day. The assignment to cover the jazz festival had, in actuality, ended two days earlier with the advent of Hurricane Grace.

"You know, I don't want to leave. Maybe it's because I've never felt like this before. I certainly didn't expect to feel like this about you," Sloan admitted as she helped Norwood pack his things.

"Yeah, you were fighting it all the way. I think I knew something would happen from the moment I saw you in that tiny dress, but I didn't want to acknowledge it either." He held his arms out and she walked into them. It felt right, it felt complete. Somehow, in the past twenty-four hours, their worlds had become one—now, he was unsure of how to separate them, how to go on, how to continue so that sometime in the very near future, they would be able to come together again.

"Sloan, are you sure about this? I mean, a couple of days ago, you didn't want to have anything to do with me. I just want you to be sure. Neither one of us can afford to make a mistake with our past histories staring us in the face. It would be like déjà vu."

"Norwood, I've never been so sure about anything in my entire life. The only puzzle to the equation is geography. You live in the middle of the country and I live some fifteen hundred miles from you. Once we work that out, we're home free."

"Okay—I have no doubt in my mind that we will. I'm not going to let you get away from me that easily. Not with those brains, this body, and the wonderful things you do to me all night long. . . ." He kissed her gently, but she could feel his desire and responded immediately, winding her arms around his neck, pressing her body against him boldly. Norwood realized that the suitcase was in the space he wanted to occupy and gently lowered Sloan to the floor. She laughed then, knowing the packing would have to wait.

"You know it's your fault that I act like a hussy whenever I'm around you. Shame, modesty, and all aspects of decorum go right out the window whenever we're alone. I can't begin to tell you how that makes me feel. Like I'm no longer in control of my own destiny. . . ." She whispered the words as he unbuttoned her blouse, kissing his way down her body. They made love slowly, luxuriating in the feel of total abandon inspired by their choice of the unconventional. Sometime later, Norwood helped her to her feet as he continued their interrupted conversation.

"Baby, I know that we're contemplating a future which we already know will be a challenge. But it'll be worth it. And let me tell you right now that I don't believe in long-distance relationships," he ended, his meaning crystal clear.

"Whatever we decide, it'll be fine. 'Cause we have the strength and power of love on our side." Sloan kissed him slowly, his arms holding her in an embrace that she could feel in the deepest recesses of her soul.

"That's right—let's go pack your stuff and then get some dinner. Didn't they say the flights leave around four tomorrow afternoon?" he asked, taking her hand.

"Yeah—Barbados direct to New York's JFK Airport. When's your connection to Chicago scheduled?" she asked as they left his room.

"I think it's for ten-thirty. Remind me to tell you how I might be coaxed into doing a little sight-seeing in New York—at least for a day or so," he suggested.

Sloan smiled, turned to him, and kissed his lips quickly. "Are you serious? I mean, I know you've already been away for a full week. Would you really be able to spend a day or so in New York? I'd love to show you around and my story will be filed by the time I get there. I've been writing it in sections all throughout the festival's scheduled concerts so I'm not on deadline or anything. Oh, Norwood, it would be perfect if you could stay awhile before going back to Chicago," she ended, her excitement evident.

"I can't promise but I already called the Tourism Authority to ask for a twenty-four-hour change in my ticket. I figured one day couldn't hurt. Avigo Publishing won't mind either. The shots I got of Hurricane

Grace probably qualify me for hazardous duty—they owe me," he added, smiling. He was happy that Sloan's reaction had been the one he'd anticipated.

"So, I'm going to have you all to myself in my home state, my native city. Wow, that's like a slice of paradise, if you ask me," she said, shaking her head in disbelief.

"Yeah, and if you play your cards right, we can also get you to Chicago sometime in the next month or so. That way, you can gauge how you react to the Midwest. You New Yorkers are supposed to be tough, but I don't know . . ." he ended, laughter shaking his entire body.

"You said that the first night you kissed me. . . . What does it take to prove myself to you?" she said then, trying to keep her face serious. The tug of war between them was a source of constant rivalry, but it was also a pleasant point of contention.

Norwood pulled her closer to him and Sloan's heart beat faster. "I'll let you know when you're getting close, but be prepared—it might just take a lifetime," he said, whispering intimately into her ear. "I'm willing to make that commitment if you are," he added, suddenly becoming serious. "Don't answer me now—take your time. I want you to be sure," he said then.

"I already am," she responded slowly, looking into his eyes, as they walked toward the elevator, hand in hand.

The next day, Worldwide Airlines flight 558 left Barbados at four P.M. bound for New York's John F. Kennedy Airport. Upon arrival, there were no lost bags, no lost souls, no lost passengers. And it landed right on time.

Dear Readers:

The Caribbean, with its exotic islands, ocean breezes and indescribable beauty, was a natural target for a romantic setting. I set out to develop characters that would enter this picture-perfect locale with all the scars, flaws and baggage that living in a fast-paced, urban environment can often create.

The passion, conflict and emotional turmoil encountered by Sloan and Norwood could only be overshadowed by something larger than themselves—Mother Nature.

I hope you enjoyed their story!

Linda Walters

ABOUT THE AUTHOR

A New York photojournalist who contributes regularly to local newspapers and national magazines, Linda Walters's coverage of Caribbean jazz festivals, culinary events and restaurant reviews are eagerly awaited by readers.

Linda attended Fordham University at Lincoln Center, is a certified access producer with Time Warner Cable and is a wholesale account manager with one of the nation's top mortgage lenders. She resides in Queens, New York. This is her second romance novel.